Uninvited Caller

"It's not so shocking a suggestion, ma'am," Kittridge barked. "I've seen you in your nightclothes before. . ."

After a moment of hesitation she let him in. "Thank you, ma'am," he said with exaggerated formality as he crossed the threshold.

She closed the door gingerly. "Would you . . . care to sit?" Cassie asked, almost whispering.

"Are you afraid someone will hear us and think we are having a tryst?" He grinned at her as he lowered himself onto her dressing table chair. "I assure you that it won't matter. We *are* married, after all."

"Yes, but . . ."

"But not quite married enough to be having trysts, is that what you're trying to say?"

She put up her chin. "I was not trying to say anything of the sort. All I intended to do was to excuse my awkwardness by explaining that I am unaccustomed to . . . to entertaining gentlemen in my bedroom."

"That much," he teased, "is obvious . . ."

The Bartered Bride

Elizabeth Mansfield

JOVE BOOKS, NEW YORK

This is a work of fiction. Names, characters, places, and incidents are either the product of the author's imagination or are used fictitiously, and any resemblance to actual persons, living or dead, business establishments, events, or locales is entirely coincidental.

THE BARTERED BRIDE

A Jove Book / published by arrangement with the author

PRINTING HISTORY
Charter edition / September 1989
Jove edition / December 1994

The Penguin Putnam Inc. World Wide Web site address is http://www.penguinputnam.com

ISBN: 0-515-11521-5

A JOVE BOOK ®
Jove books are published by The Berkley Publishing Group, a division of Penguin Putnam Inc., 375 Hudson Street, New York, New York 10014. JOVE and the "J" design are trademarks belonging to Penguin Putnam Inc.

PRINTED IN THE UNITED STATES OF AMERICA

10 9 8 7 6 5 4 3 2 1

Chapter One

The patrons of Hollings and Chast, Linendrapers, gasped audibly. One of the clerks had actually accused a young woman (who seemed the epitome of sweet-faced innocence) of trying to steal! He may not have said it in so many words, but his meaning was clear to everyone in the shop. They stared in speechless dismay as the color drained from the poor girl's face. Her lips turned so white that the onlookers feared she might swoon right then and there.

The incident would not have been quite so dreadful if the girl weren't so shy. Her shyness made everything worse, for it prevented her from speaking up for herself with any conviction. Never in her life before had Miss Cassandra Chivers been so horribly humiliated, but humiliation is the sort of emotion that makes shyness even more pronounced. The girl, who would never be described as outspoken even at the best of times, could not be expected to express herself well when things were at their worst. And what could be worse than hearing a booming-voiced clerk shatter the air of a large, busy, very fashionable shop with the accusation that one was *stealing*? It was no wonder the poor little chit became utterly tied of tongue. She could only stammer, "But I *p-paid* you!" in a small, unconvincing voice.

Mr. Dorking, the clerk behind the counter, sneered. He was the senior clerk, the most important of the fourteen clerks who handled sales for the firm of Hollings and Chast. Hollings and Chast, Linendrapers (established in 1790 and doing a thriving business at this, its original location on Wigmore

Street, London, throughout the quarter-century since its inception) was a favorite shop for members of the *ton* and ordinary citizens alike, for it was bountifully stocked with the widest possible selection of fabrics at all prices. At this very moment, for instance, all manner of patrons were making an amazing variety of purchases. At one counter a plainly dressed woman was examining a length of fine kentin for nightclothes; at another, a uniformed cavalry officer was selecting shirting. Here an overweight matron was bargaining for a remnant of muslin, and there a modish young lady was looking at a bolt of luxurious Persian silk. Every clerk was busy, and a number of customers were waiting to be served. And right before all these people, the shy Miss Chivers was being accused of thievery.

The clerk's loud accusation could be heard throughout the shop. All activity ceased. The clerks paused in their measurements or their cutting of the fabric or their rewinding of the bolts to watch Mr. Dorking "spear another sharper." Most of the patrons were too well-bred to stare, but they were not too well-bred to eavesdrop on the drama being enacted in their midst.

Dorking, the accusing clerk, was a long-nosed, thin-lipped, toplofty fellow who'd been employed by Hollings and Chast since he was a boy of fourteen. Hardened by his two decades of dealing with clutchfisted, crafty, cunning, conniving customers, mostly female, he was convinced he'd seen every kind of swindle the human mind could devise. He liked to brag to his associates that he could sniff out a deceitful canarybird at twenty paces, so he was not going to be fooled by *this* little cheat, pretty though she was. She might look as innocent as a newborn babe, but he'd learned long ago that appearances could deceive. Therefore, he looked down his nose at the trembling girl with complete disdain. "I would remember if you'd paid me, wouldn't I?" he asked loudly.

"B-but I *did* pay you," the frightened Cassie Chivers whispered tearfully. "You *m-must* remember! You said the cambric was thirteen shillings fourpence, and I gave you a whole g-guinea!"

The clerk, aware that the scene he was playing was attracting the attention of the other customers (and pleased as punch to be performing the major role), smoothed his thinning hair in a gesture of pure arrogance and sneered again. "If you gave me a guinea, miss, then where is it, eh? Is it in my hand? No. Is it lying there on the counter? No. Is it on the floor? No. Is it in the parcel? No. Then where, I ask you, can it be?"

"I d-don't know," the girl murmured, her face painfully flushed. She tried to avert her head, as if to protect herself from the curious stares of the shop's patrons, but the self-effacing movement only made her seem more guilty. "But I *gave* it to you, t-truly! That guinea was all I had with m-me, except for a few pennies. Here! S-see for yourself!" And, her hands trembling, she turned the contents of her reticule out on the counter before him.

The contents were pathetically meager: only a handkerchief, a vial of smelling salts, a comb, an envelope on the back of which was scribbled a short shopping list and three pennies. The clerk eyed them with contempt. "And what do you think *that* proves, eh?" he asked scornfully. "You could have hidden your guinea anywhere on your person, if you ever had the guinea at all. Do you take me for a flat?"

"Hidden it on my *p-person*?" Cassie stammered, appalled. "Why, I would n-never *think* of such a—!"

"What on earth," came an angry voice from the back, "is going on there, Mr. Dorking? Do you realize you are creating a scene?"

It was Mr. Chast, the only partner of the partnership of Hollings and Chast still alive. He had emerged from his office at the rear of the shop and, in a stride befitting his importance, came marching across the floor to the counter where the scene was taking place. The other clerks immediately resumed their work, and the eavesdropping customers quickly turned their attention back to their own business, all except the calvalry officer, who continued to watch the proceedings with a troubled frown.

Miss Chivers lifted her head and glanced fearfully over her shoulder at the linendraper who now loomed ominously behind her. She saw a tall, potbellied, dignified gentleman whose posture, expression and striped-satin waistcoat all contributed to his air of authority. It was plain that this gentleman was in charge of the shop. Was he going to clap her in irons, she wondered, her heart pounding in terror? "I . . . I—" she muttered helplessly.

Mr. Chast, ignoring her, frowned angrily at his clerk. "*Well*, Dorking?" he demanded in a tone that clearly revealed his dislike of public scenes.

"Sorry, Mr. Chast, but it's this ladybird," the clerk said, his demeanor suddenly becoming obsequious. "She's trying to—"

"Keep your voice down, man!" Mr. Chast chastized. "And you will *not* refer to any of our patrons as ladybirds, is that clear?"

The clerk bit his underlip in chagrin. "Yes, sir. Sorry, sir. But I do get so sick of these 'ladies' who try to filch goods. Thirteen an' four worth of cambric I cut for her, and now she says she handed me a guinea, which I swear on my mother's grave she never did."

"But I *did*!" Miss Chivers insisted, turning a pair of large, pleading eyes on the linendraper. "A whole guinea. All I had with me. I p-placed it right in his p-palm."

Mr. Chast studied the girl carefully. She was a small, pale-skinned creature with a pair of lovely, dark, expressive eyes and a wealth of curly auburn hair which she'd crammed haphazardly into a dowdy brown bonnet. *At least she's not one of the nobs*, he told himself in relief. It would not have been the first time that a member of the *ton* tried to cheat one of his clerks. Bitter experience had proved that the nobility were just as prone to dishonesty as the rest of humanity. The difficulty was in getting justice when it was a nob you were dealing with. Mr. Chast had very painful memories of trying to exact payment from an earl whose daughter had filched a bolt of figured damask. He'd been thrown out on his ear! But *this* person, thank goodness, was not an earl's daughter . . . or even a baronet's. No baronet's daughter—or any young lady of the *ton*—would appear in public in such sturdy shoes and so drab a bonnet.

But she wasn't a street urchin either, he decided, for her

dress was well-cut and her spencer was lined with a satin of excellent quality. She seemed a respectable type . . . not the sort who would perpetrate a fraud. Still, one could never be sure of a person's honesty by appearance. "Mr. Dorking has been with Hollings and Chast for twenty years, my girl," he said to the frightened creature before him. "I have never known him to lie. If he said you didn't give him the coin, then I must believe him."

"He may n-not be lying, s-sir," the girl managed, struggling to hold back her tears, "but he is s-surely m-mistaken."

"I certainly am not," the clerk insisted. "If I were, we would see the coin somewhere about, wouldn't we? And we'd see thirteen shillings fourpence entered here in my sales ledger, wouldn't we? But there's no such figure in the ledger— see for yourself, Mr. Chast!—and no such coin on the premises, either."

"Mr. Dorking does seem to be in the right of it, miss," Mr. Chast said to the girl in a voice that was firm though not unkind. "I'm sorry, but I don't see what else we can do but ask you to leave."

The beleaguered girl burst into tears. "But I *c-can't*. I live n-north of King's Cross. The ch-change from the g-guinea was to p-pay for a h-hack to t-take me *home*!"

"Enough of this," muttered the cavalry officer who'd been watching the scene with mounting disgust. "Stop torturing the young lady. Anyone can see she's telling the truth."

Only one who knows the horror of being utterly alone in a sea of antagonists can guess the emotion that swept over Cassie Chivers at the sound of those trusting words. *Someone believed in her!* It was like rain to a dying bloom, a lifeline to a drowning swimmer, a gush of air to someone gasping for breath. Her heart leaped into her throat, and her eyes turned instinctively to see who it was who'd stepped forward to offer her aid. Whatever he looked like—old, ugly, scrawny, wizened or gross—she was quite prepared to find him beautiful. But she was not prepared for what she saw: a tall magnificence in a red coat blazoned with gold braid, tight-fitting white breeches and knee-high black boots, with a sword dangling at his side and a plumed shako held under his arm.

He seemed quite literally to be a knight-in-arms. It was as if he'd ridden out of a medieval romance to enter the battle in her behalf. She could not believe her eyes. Perhaps she was not seeing clearly, she thought. After all, everything did look fuzzy through the tears that still clouded her eyes.

Meanwhile, the "knight," taking no notice of the astonishment in her face, strode past Mr. Chast and threw a guinea onto the counter. "Give the chit her goods and the change," he ordered, "and let her go."

Cassie Chivers blinked her eyes to clear her vision. But what she now saw—and with perfect clarity—made her rescuer seem even more unreal. This couldn't be happening to her, she thought. Not to Cassie Chivers. Cassie Chivers was not accustomed to miracles, yet here she was being championed by the handsomest man she'd ever in her life beheld.

Chapter Two

Mr. Chast's first instinct was to tell the interfering officer—tactfully, of course—to keep his sneezer out of shop business. But after taking a closer glance, he changed his mind. His eyebrows rose. He peered at the soldier in surprise. There was something about the fellow—an air of assurance, an ease of manner, a tone of command—that the linendraper had trained himself to recognize. He knew nobility when he saw it. The uniform of a cavalry officer might very well clothe a peer of the realm. This fellow was a nob, if he knew anything about it. Besides, there was something about the set of the officer's square chin that made one reluctant to cross him.

Mr. Chast had no intention of crossing him. Instead he bowed politely and said, "That is most gallant of you, sir. I'm sure this young lady will gratefully accept your kind assistance, won't you, miss?"

Cassie's dark eyes flicked quickly from one face to the other before she lowered them and shook her head. "I do thank you," she murmured, "but . . . no."

"*No?*" Mr. Chast's temper flared up in irritation. Why was the girl prolonging the scene that was obviously more painful for her than for anyone else? "Did I hear you aright, ma'am? Did you say *no*?"

"Good God, man, don't bark at her!" the officer ordered. "Don't you see the young lady's frightened?" He turned to the girl and smiled down at her reassuringly. "You needn't fear my assistance, ma'am," he said softly. "I mean you no harm. May I introduce myself? I am Captain Rossiter. Robert Rossiter, of the Light Dragoons."

"*Rossiter*?" Mr. Chast tensed. "That's the family name of the Viscount Kittridge, is it not? Are you, perhaps, a relation to his lordship?"

"I *am* Lord Kittridge," the gentleman replied, "although I prefer to use my military rank while I still wear the uniform." A charmingly rueful grin appeared on his face. "Unfortunately I can only call myself Captain Rossiter until tomorrow. This is my last day in service."

Mr. Chast drew in a breath. The fellow was indeed a nob, just as he'd feared. In fact, the name was well known to him. The family of Viscount Kittridge had long been patrons of his establishment. This was the scion of a fine old family. Mr. Chast winced in annoyance. It was most unfortunate that so elevated a gentleman as the viscount had to involve himself in this sordid scene.

The girl, meanwhile, dropped a little curtsey. "Honored, my lord," she murmured, barely lifting her eyes.

"Captain, please, ma'am, captain. And let me assure you, ma'am," his lordship went on to explain, "that my only purpose in interfering in this matter is a desire to help you out of this ridiculous contretemps."

"Yes, Captain, I understand," the girl said shyly, keeping her head down and hoping that no one would notice the flush deepening in her cheeks. "I . . . I'm more grateful than I can say." She tried to speak calmly, but her heart was pounding loudly in her breast. The word grateful hardly expressed what she felt. She was aware of so great a sense of relief that words could scarcely describe her feelings. This magnificent knight—never mind that he was a mere cavalry officer to the rest of the world—had come to her aid. A moment ago she'd been more miserably helpless and alone than ever in her life before, terrified of being apprehended for thievery and sentenced to prison. But now, out of nowhere, had come this rescuer, tall and handsome and strong. An *ally* had risen up from among what had seemed to her a world full of enemies! It was miraculous! She could breathe again. His coming infused her blood with courage. With an ally, she could at last face her accusers with some semblance of confidence and stand up for her rights.

"You needn't be grateful, girl," her rescuer was saying. "You need only to accept the guinea I've offered you."

"Please . . ." She hated to refuse him anything, but she had to. She lifted her hand as if to ward off a blow. "Don't ask it of me. I . . . c-can't."

"But why can't you?" he demanded.

She twisted her fingers together. "It's a matter of . . . of principle."

"Principle?" The tall officer peered down at her lowered head, bemused. "I don't understand. What principle?"

She flicked another fleeting glance over his face before she dropped her eyes again. "It's a matter of . . . of honor, Captain. If I accepted your assistance, my innocence would not be proved." The words came slowly, as if the pronouncing of each one gave her pain. But she had to make this gentleman—this beautiful red and gold knight who'd inexplicably stood up in her behalf—understand why she was rejecting him. "Taking your money would be the same as admitting that I didn't p-pay in the first place, don't you see?"

The officer stared at her for a long moment. Then he shrugged. "I suppose I do," he admitted, picking up his guinea and pocketing it reluctantly. "You want your word to be affirmed. The Truth Made Manifest, is that it?"

"Yes," she admitted in her small voice. "Just so."

"Mmm." He rubbed his chin speculatively and then shrugged. "That means we shall have to *prove* your innocence somehow." He turned to the linendraper. "How do you suggest we begin?"

Mr. Chast was disgusted. He would have to deal with a nob after all. But viscount or not, the fellow was not going to weaken his stand. The linendraper's faith in his clerk was unshakable. "I'm afraid I haven't a suggestion, my lord. Mr. Dorking has been my clerk for two decades. In all that time, I've never known him to be dishonest. It is hardly likely that he would have pocketed a guinea."

"That's sure as check," the clerk muttered under his breath.

"On the other hand," the captain pointed out, "although I've known this young woman no more than a few minutes, I feel just as sure she isn't lying either. Let's assume for a moment that they're both telling the truth. In that case, the girl's guinea would be here somewhere. How can we go about finding it?''

Mr. Chast took a deep breath in surrender. ''Oh, very well. Let's go over the incident in detail, Dorking. Tell us what happened, from the beginning.''

Mr. Dorking, who'd been basking in the glow of his employer's support, suddenly began to feel put-upon. He didn't like being made to defend himself, but he had no choice but to swallow his pride. ''Yes, sir. If you say so, sir. From the beginning. This here ladybird came up to m—''

''Dorking!'' Mr. Chast admonished.

''Sorry. The young *lady* came up to me asking for cambric. I showed her three or four bolts, and she chose the stripes here. Said she needed five yards. I measured them off and cut the piece.''

''Where did you do the cutting?'' the officer asked.

''Right there, where the yardstick is.''

Captain Rossiter carefully inspected the counter and the floor below. There was no coin. ''Very well,'' he told the clerk. ''Go on.''

Dorking smirked. ''*Told* you there's no guinea there.''

''Go *on*, I said!'' Captain Rossiter snapped.

The smirk on Dorking's face vanished at once. He'd finally perceived what Mr. Chast had noticed long before—that this gentleman was not one to cross. ''Yes, m'lord. Sorry, m'lord,'' he mumbled hurriedly and proceeded with his tale. ''After I cut the goods, I folded it like always and then I went to the table there, where we keep the wrapping paper, and I made up the parcel. Then I took it over to the lady, handed it over and asked for thirteen shillings fourpence. And that's when she said, I already gave you a guinea. But she never did.''

''No,'' the girl said, glancing from one to the other fearfully. ''It wasn't like that.''

''Then give us *your* account, ma'am,'' the officer urged. ''Go on. There's no need to be afraid.''

The girl clenched her fists bravely. ''He . . . he cut the cambric, brought it here where I was standing and folded it in front of me. It was then, you see, that I handed him the guinea. I *did, truly*! He took the coin and the fabric, turned and walked away to the wrapping table."

"Hang it," the clerk burst out, "it's a damn lie! She never—!"

"Dorking, watch your blasted tongue!" the linendraper hissed.

Captain Rossiter knit his brow in thought. "If she *had* given you the guinea, Mr. Dorking, what would you have done with it?" he asked.

"Dropped it in the cash box, of course," Dorking answered promptly. "But she didn't."

"But what if she did? Where is the cash box?"

"Right there, on the table near the wrapping things."

"Ah!" The captain's eyes lit. "Isn't it possible that you could have dropped the coin in the cash box before you wrapped the parcel? Without thinking about it?"

Mr. Dorking was not going to back down, even for a nob. Even for a nob as awesome as this one. He shook his head firmly. "No, my lord, not at all possible."

"But why not? What if you were thinking of something else? You could have dropped the coin in the cash box quite automatically, couldn't you? It *is* possible, I suspect. Dropping coins in the box must surely be a habit by this time. After all, it is something you do all day, every day."

"It isn't likely he wouldn't be aware of it," Mr. Chast put in. "You see, when he puts money in the cash box, he must note the amount on his ledger."

"But if his mind was preoccupied . . . if he wasn't thinking—"

Mr. Chast rubbed his fingers on the bridge of his nose. "Let's admit that there *is* a possibility that he dropped the coin into the box, my lord. I shall look into the matter. I give you my word that I shall personally tally up Mr. Dorking's cash box at the end of the day today, and if there is an overage of a guinea, I shall make restitution to the young lady myself."

Miss Chivers made a sound of despair in her throat. She couldn't help herself. The linendraper's words had upset her. So long a delay would spoil everything. If he didn't find her guinea until the end of the day, she would not be vindicated before the onlookers, and, what was worse, she would not be able to go home until terribly late.

Captain Rossiter fully understood her feelings. "Oh, no, Mr. Chast, that won't do," he said firmly, placing a reassuring hand on the girl's shoulder. "You shall tally up the cash box right now."

"But we can't do that, my lord. We are in the midst of a business day. Four other clerks use the same cash box. It is a complicated matter to tally the cash. We cannot disrupt our procedures for a mere guinea."

"But for a mere guinea you'd besmirch a young woman's honor, is that what you're saying?" the captain asked calmly.

"But, my *lord*—!" Mr. Chast objected.

"Captain, please, Mr. Chast. Call me captain." The officer looked the linendraper squarely in the eye. "If you have any sense at all of fair play, you have no choice," he pointed out. "If a mistake *has* been made, you owe it to the young lady to clear her name right now, in front of all these witnesses. That is only just, is it not?"

See? Mr. Chast said to himself in disgust. *There's always trouble when you deal with nobs.* Aloud he said, "Very well, your lordsh— I mean, Captain Rossiter. We'll take the cash box to my office and tally up. It will take some time, I'm afraid. I'll have Dorking bring you a chair. And a cup of tea, if you wish."

"No, Mr. Chast, I care for neither chair nor tea. However, you may have them brought for the young lady, if she wishes. But you will tally the cash *right here*, in front of all of us."

The crowd broke into spontaneous applause. For Mr. Chast, that was the last straw. His face reddened alarmingly. "Are you implying, my lord," he demanded, drawing himself up to his full height and puffing out his chest belligerently, "that *I* would not make an honest accounting?"

"I am implying nothing," the captain retorted coolly. "I think, however, that a public reckoning is the only way that would show what happened and leave no questions remaining. It would clear up the matter once and for all. Do you agree, ma'am?"

Cassie Chivers looked up at her knight-at-arms adoringly. "Oh, yes, Captain! Yes, indeed."

Mr. Chast, realizing that what the captain was suggesting was probably best for business, swallowed his ire. "Very well, Captain Rossiter. As you wish. Bring the cash box here, Mr. Dorking," he ordered. "Let's get this over with."

Mr. Chast summoned two other clerks to his side with a crook of his index finger. Then, pulling the ledger from Dorking's hand, he dismissed the fellow with an abrupt flick of his wrist. He would not involve Dorking in the tally. The two clerks he'd chosen to assist him were completely objective; thus the captain would have no possible grounds for complaint that the tally was in any way tainted.

The linendraper and his two objective clerks bent over the cash box and all five sales ledgers. Meanwhile, Dorking himself supplied Miss Chivers with a chair and a cup of tea. He could afford to be gracious; he had no doubt that the tally would vindicate him completely. As soon as the girl (whom he still thought of as a cheating "canarybird") was comfortably seated, Dorking withdrew to the rear of the store and watched the accounting with the rest of the onlookers, a group which now included all the customers, even the well-bred ones.

The captain, having taken a stand beside the young lady's chair, kept his eyes fixed on the linendraper. Miss Chivers, on the other hand, took this opportunity to study her rescuer from the corner of her eye. Never in her wildest dreams could she have imagined that so breathtaking a hero would choose to enter the fray in her behalf. He was the sort one would expect to wear the colors for a great beauty, not for an ordinary mousy creature like herself. Robert Rossiter, Viscount Kittridge, was what the *haute ton* would call "top of the trees." He was tall and sinewy, with wide shoulders and large hands. His soldierly life had browned the skin of his face, but his weathered appearance only added to his attractiveness. His dark hair, as curly as her own, was clipped short in a soldierly style that she usually didn't like, but in Captain Rossiter's case she found it quite becoming. The short, tight curls that framed his face gave him the look of a Roman centurion. But what most entranced her were his eyes, the irises a light brown edged with yellow streaks. They gleamed with a piercing intelligence that seemed able to cut through any false facade and find the truth. The directness of his glance seemed capable of withering any opponent's will. The overwhelming impression one took away after meeting him was of a controlled strength, a power that was kept in tight restraint under a calm surface. It took no more than a glance at him to tell that he would not be easily bested in a fight. What a formidable ally she had found to fight her battle!

Meanwhile, business remained at a standstill while the customers watched the linendraper and his assistants count the coins and notes and pile them up on the counter in little stacks. An abnormal silence hovered in the air as Mr. Chast and the two clerks totalled and retotalled the figures in the ledgers and counted and recounted the money. Forty-five minutes passed. Finally Mr. Chast stood erect. "Dorking!" he shouted.

Mr. Dorking came running to his side. "Yes, Mr. Chast?"

"You're a damned fool!" the linendraper snapped under his breath. "You're a guinea over! The girl *did* give you the money, just as she claimed!"

The clerk winced. "Oh, my heavens!" he muttered, clapping a hand to his brow. "What've I done?"

"Come on, you idiot," his employer ordered, picking up the wrapped package of fabric before pulling the clerk after him, "let's go and apologize to the young lady."

They approached the seated girl and the officer who stood beside her chair. "You seem to be in the right of it, Captain," Mr. Chast announced shamefacedly. "We *have* found an extra guinea in the box."

The stillness of the air was rent with a cheer from the crowd. The observers had, in agreement with the officer, long ago decided that the sweet-faced girl had to be innocent. Now they were delighted to have their judgment validated, and they showed that delight with enthusiastic applause and cries of "Hear, hear!" and "Right-o!"

Miss Chivers, who'd been too deeply occupied with the

problem of dealing with her own emotions to realize the extent of the interest she'd aroused in the crowd, leaped from her chair with a start. She stared at the cheering customers in shock. Then she turned back to find Dorking approaching her, his face ashen. "I can't tell you how sorry I am, miss," he began. "I've never done such a thing before in all my life."

"Your guinea, ma'am," the linendraper murmured, holding out the coin and the package as well. "We'd like you to have the fabric with our compliments."

The girl backed away from him, shuddering. For Miss Cassandra Chivers to find herself the center of so much attention was all too much. She could not bear to be the focus of so many eyes. She could not bear the misery on the clerk's face. She could not bear the ignominy of being offered the fabric as a gift—a sop for what they'd put her through! And she could not bear that her beautiful knight was witness to this cheap and tawdry scene. Her eyes flew from the clerk to Mr. Chast to Captain Rossiter to the crowd, and then, bursting into tears, she lowered her head and, pushing heedlessly through the crowd, ran to the door.

The humiliated clerk, not knowing what to do, gaped after her. Mr. Chast, too, seemed utterly nonplussed. The captain was the only one capable of action. Without a word, he strode through the throng after her.

He found the shaken young lady standing bewilderedly at the curb. "You'll be wanting a hackney, I imagine," he said calmly, taking her elbow and escorting her away from the store doorway where curious gapers were beginning to gather.

"Yes, C-Captain," she stammered, "but you don't have to t-trouble. I c-can—"

"No trouble at all," he said, lifting his hand to signal a passing hack.

"You are t-too k-kind!"

The hack pulled to a stop. Cassie was not so agitated that she didn't realize she had only a moment in which to thank him properly for what he'd done for her. She tried desperately to overcome her timidity, but her tongue tripped awkwardly over the words. "I don't know how . . . to thank . . . I c-can't tell you . . ." she mumbled helplessly.

"There's no need to say anything, ma'am," the captain assured her as he threw the driver a coin and handed her into the carriage. "Anyone with half an eye could see you were innocent. It was a pleasure for me to see justice done."

Before she could utter another word, his lordship tipped his plumed shako and was off, striding away down the street with a long, loping step. Cassie Chivers peeped out the carriage window to watch him go. Her eyes held an unwonted intensity. She wanted to memorize the look of him—the set of his shoulders, the swing of his arms, the manly grace of his carriage. All too soon, however, the growing distance between them misted his outline until he became just a blur on the horizon. It was only when he'd completely disappeared from view that she signalled the driver to start the carriage.

She sat back against the cushions, an inexplicable shiver passing through her body. She had just lived through the worst and best morning of her life, and her emotions were churning within her. The expected emotion was relief—relief that her honor had been vindicated. And there was a feeling of triumph, too, in that vindication. But the surge of triumph could do nothing to assuage the sudden stab of despair that clenched her chest. The cause of the despair was obvious to her; she didn't have to spend a moment analyzing it. A lifelong dream had been granted this morning: Fate had brought a magnificent knight into her life in a time of dire need. But then, after only one joyful moment, it had taken him away again. There had hardly been any time at all to enjoy the meeting. After the merest of beginnings, it was all over.

Good-bye, Captain Rossiter, she said to herself sadly. She didn't need to look into a crystal ball to know that their paths would surely never cross again. Nor did she have to be a soothsayer to foretell that, though her meeting with her red and gold knight had been the briefest of encounters, she would love him as long as she lived.

Chapter Three

It had grown quite dark and a chill wind was blowing up from the north when Mr. Oliver Chivers' phaeton pulled into the curved driveway in front of his home at King's Cross. He had just spent a long day at his office in the City and was looking forward to the warmth of his own fireside and a good dinner in the company of his daughter. Therefore, he was both surprised and annoyed when he discovered that another carriage had cut in ahead of his and was proceeding at a deucedly leisurely pace down his own driveway. He removed his spectacles (which made distant objects only a blur), rubbed his eyes and peered out the window at the other carriage. "Who the devil is that?" he asked his coachman querulously. He was tired, cold and hungry. He didn't want to have to delay his meal in order to deal with callers he hadn't invited.

"No one as I reco'nize," the coachman answered as he drew up at the door behind the unfamiliar carriage. "Per'aps Miss Cassie 'as a visitor."

"Cassie never 'as visitors," Mr. Chivers grumbled, climbing down from the phaeton. He looked over at the other carriage curiously. It was a businesslike vehicle with the words *Hollings and Chast, Linendrapers*, painted in gold leaf on its side. Was this some sort of delivery, Mr. Chivers wondered? If so, why were they making it at this time of night?

A large, potbellied fellow climbed down from the other carriage and surveyed the house. He seemed awestruck at its size and style. Oliver Chivers smirked inwardly. He loved to see strangers admire his home. He was very proud of the house he'd had built in this newly developed area of north London, and it always gave him enormous satisfaction when he caught an expression of admiration on the face of a passerby. The house, of pink brick and stone, was an architectural beauty, designed in the much-praised Adam style. It had a magnificent pedimented roof, a graceful fanlighted doorway and recessed arches for the windows. For Oliver Chivers the house was a personal triumph. No one looking at it could doubt that the owner was a person of taste and means.

The stranger who stood looking at it now was noticeably impressed. He turned at Mr. Chivers' approach and removed his hat. "Good evening, sir," he said, looking down at the smaller man curiously. "This cannot be—can it?—the residence of Miss Cassandra Chivers?"

"It is," Mr. Chivers replied. "I'm 'er father, Oliver Chivers."

The coachman, who followed closely behind Mr. Chivers, gave an I-told-ye-so snort. Mr. Chivers wheeled on him irritably. "Damnation, Measham, must ye be always eavesdroppin' on my conversations? Mind yer business and take care of the 'orses."

"Tole ye 'twas someone fer Miss Cassie," the coachman muttered as he walked away.

The stranger, meanwhile, eyed the house admiringly. "I had no *idea* the young lady's residence would be so . . . so . . . substantial," he murmured.

"Indeed?" Mr. Chivers retorted curtly. "An' who, may I ask, are you to be interested in my daughter's residence, substantial or no?"

The gentleman extended his hand. "George Chast, sir. Of Hollings and Chast, Linendrapers. You may have heard of my establishment."

"Can't say as I 'ave." Chivers shook the man's hand but peered at his face suspiciously. "Do ye 'ave some business with my daughter?"

"You could say that," the linendraper sighed. "Unfinished business. I've come to return her money, you see. And her reticule. And to give her this fabric. Gratis, of course. As a gesture of apology, you see.''

The man's words were incomprehensible to Cassandra Chivers' father, but he found them troubling nevertheless. "You keep sayin' that I see, but I don't see,'' he said testily. "What are ye doin' with 'er reticule? Why should ye be givin' fabric to 'er gratis? And what do ye need to apologize *for*?''

Mr. Chast shifted his weight uncomfortably from one foot to the other. He was unhappy enough to have to face the girl again, but to have to face the father was even worse. And what made matters even more awkward was the fact that the father was obviously wealthy. The situation was becoming more mortifying every moment. This was turning out to be almost as bad as dealing with a nob. "It seems, Mr. Chivers,'' the linendraper said carefully, "that you haven't been told about the . . . er . . . occurrence this morning.''

"Occurrence? What occurrence?'' The worry in Mr. Chivers' chest expanded alarmingly.

"Perhaps it would be best,'' Mr. Chast suggested, trying valiantly to maintain his usual air of authority, "if I spoke directly to Miss Chivers.''

"I'll decide what's best when I know what this is all about,'' Cassie's father snapped. "Let's 'ear it, man.''

The linendraper's air of authority wilted before the other man's glare. "It was all a misunderstanding,'' he explained nervously. "One of my clerks—a very foolish fellow, I assure you, whom I would certainly dismiss out of hand if it weren't for the fact that he's been in my employ for twenty years or more—well, you see, he made the inexcusable blunder of accusing her—your daughter, sir, who, of course, in all fairness I must say we had no idea that she came from so, how shall I say, so substantial a family—''

"Will ye stop yer ditherin', Mr. Chast? This fool clerk of yours accused my daughter of *what*?''

Mr. Chast dropped his eyes in shame. "Of . . . er . . . trying to steal the goods.''

"Tryin' to *steal*—? My *Cassie*?'' Mr. Chivers felt his neck grow hot. "What blasted kind of idiocy is *that*? My Cassie wouldn't steal a blade of grass from a 'aystack! Yer clerk must be touched in his upper works!''

"Yes, sir. You're quite right. We were able to exonerate her completely. That's why I'm delivering these parcels myself. She ran out of the shop, you see, before we could apologize properly, so it seemed only right, after all that happened, that I should come myself—''

"She ran out of yer shop? Are you sayin', man, that you embarrassed 'er in yer place of business? That this . . . this *accusation* was made in *public*?''

Mr. Chast lowered his head miserably. "It happened in the shop, yes,'' he admitted, taking a step backward as if trying to escape from the ferocity of the smaller man's glare.

"Good God!'' Oliver Chivers was beginning to feel quite sick. "Are you tellin' me that my little Cassie, who's so shy she can barely open 'er mouth in front of a stranger, was accused of thievery in a shop full of people?''

"Well, yes, sir, I'm afraid so. It was a dreadful misunderstanding. I myself had a suspicion—from the lining of her spencer, which was an excellent grade of satin—that she was well to pass, but my clerk is not very perceptive. And even the gentleman who aided her—a man of nobility, I assure you, although I don't believe I should take the liberty of revealing his identity—did not seem to have guessed that she was a young lady of quality. So, in a way, one can't fully blame my clerk. The girl was unescorted, after all. And all she had with her was the one guinea, you see, so—''

"Stop sayin' *you see* in that idiotic way!'' Chivers shouted. "I *do not* see! I do not see 'ow anyone can accuse my Cassie of stealing! I do not see what she was doin' in your shop without 'er companion! I do not see why she 'ad only one guinea! I do not see *anythin'*!''

"I'm sorry, Mr. Chivers, sir, but I've tried to explain—''

"Then try *again*, confound it!'' Mr. Chivers ordered, poking his index finger repeatedly into Mr. Chast's chest until the linendraper had backed up against his carriage and could escape no further. "An' tell it proper, do ye 'ear me? Step by step, from the beginning.''

Chapter Four

Oliver Chivers found his daughter in the sitting room. She was curled up in a chair near the fire, engrossed in a novel. He stormed up to her chair (ignoring the approach of Miss Penicuick, his housekeeper and his daughter's companion, who was ready, as usual, with his preprandial sherry) and dropped a parcel in her lap. "Yer cambric, ma'am. It seems ye left it in the shop this morning."

Cassie started, her eyes flying from the package on her lap to her father's face. "Papa! How—?"

Miss Penicuick gasped. "Oh, heavens! He *knows*!"

"What do I know, Miss Penicuick?" Chivers asked in a tone heavy with sarcasm, glaring at his housekeeper over the spectacles that had slipped halfway down his nose. "That ye permitted my daughter to go into town in a rented 'ack without escort? Is that what ye think I know?"

Cassie put the package aside and rose from her chair. "Hush, Papa," she said quietly. "There's no need to make accusations. Drink your sherry, and let's go in to dinner. We'll talk over the soup."

Mr. Chivers had never been one to resist his daughter's gentle handling, so he permitted himself to be led into the dining room. But even when his hunger had been assuaged, his body warmed by good wine and his temper cooled by his daughter's calm manner, he was nevertheless very annoyed with her. When he had finished his second course, he pushed away his dinner plate and swore aloud that he would never, as long as he lived, understand the girl. "I 'ope ye see, Cassie

Chivers, that the entire 'umiliatin' incident was somethin' ye brought on yerself.''

He was distressed to his core. The incident at the linendraper's was simply another example of the way in which the girl's shyness, coupled with her lack of interest in financial matters, had brought her needless difficulty and pain.

Mr. Chivers had spent his entire life studying the intricacies of finance, with the result that he'd amassed a considerable fortune from the most modest of beginnings and that his financial advice was sought even by those who were financial experts in their own right. And yet his only offspring seemed to have no interest in the subject. Money was of no concern to her. Her complete indifference to the one subject that occupied his mind above all others hurt him deeply. But what was worse, it rendered her vulnerable to just such incidents as had occurred today.

He looked across the table to where his daughter sat picking away at her beef and glazed onions that their French cook had prepared and that he'd found delicious. But Cassie was evidently not interested in the food. The poor child had quite lost her appetite, but, considering the day's event, it was not surprising. He watched her as she absently moved a tiny onion back and forth across her plate. She seemed to him to be everything that was lovely in a young woman. Her oddly shaped face, with its full cheeks that narrowed down delicately to a charmingly pointed chin, had a unique beauty; her warm brown eyes were enormous and expressive; her hair was thick and seemed more abundant because of its profusely curled texture; her neck and shoulders were graceful and revealed the most perfect skin; and her figure was both slim and womanly. In addition, she had a quiet but delightful sense of humor and a quick mind. Why, under the circumstances, was she so shy and inept in public? "It's really beyond belief," he grumbled, unable to let the matter drop, "that a girl of sense would take 'erself into town with only one guinea on 'er person."

"I'm sorry, Papa," the girl said softly. "I didn't think I would require more than that."

"Ye didn't think at all!" Her father pushed his spectacles

up on the bridge of his nose with a feeling of utter helpless-
ness. "And that's only *part* of yer thoughtlessness. Ye went
alone!" He turned his glare on Miss Penicuick, the middle-
aged, angular woman who'd been Cassie's governess in her
childhood and who now functioned not only as housekeeper
but as Cassie's companion, chaperone, dresser, confidante
and friend. "Where were *you*, Miss Penicuick, when all this
was goin' on, may I ask?"

Miss Penicuick glanced guiltily at her employer from her
place at the far end of the table and then lowered her eyes,
sighed unhappily and stared miserably down at her own untouched dinner. "Well, sir, you see, I . . . I . . ."

"Don't blame Miss Penny, Papa," Cassie said, reaching
across the table and patting her governess's hand gently. "I
ran off behind her back."

"You did *what*?"

"Well, she *did* leave me a note," Miss Penicuick murmured in defense of her charge.

Cassie's father shook his head, deeply disturbed. He was
about to utter a few nasty words about what he thought of
the girl's running off, but he was stopped by the entrance
of the butler with a tray of blancmange. Oliver Chivers
glared at the bland white pudding the butler set down in front
of him. "Not bla'mange again," he muttered angrily. "I
don't pay a French chef an enormous salary to cook a deuced
tasteless pudding! I thought I told ye to tell M'sieur Maurice I
never want to see such 'orrid stuff on this table again!"

"Come, come, Papa, you never said any such thing,"
Cassie pointed out gently. "I know you're very angry at me,
but you mustn't take it out on the rest of the household."

Her father grunted and relapsed into silence. The girl was
right. It wasn't the chef's fault that he didn't know how to
handle his daughter now that she was a grown woman. How
he wished she were still a child! She'd been nothing but a joy
to him in the early years, after her mother had passed away.
Life would have been grim indeed if he had not had Cassie on
whom to lavish his affection. And Cassie had responded to
that affection as a flower does to sunshine. She'd been a
charming, loving child. When he came home from the office

every night, she'd brighten his arrival with her glad welcome. She always followed him about the house when he was home, sat on his lap while they read nursery rhymes together, told him wonderful, imaginary stories of her day's adventures, laughed at his jokes and filled his life with gaiety. Sometimes he let her visit him at his office, where she would sit for hours and watch him with quiet adoration as he worked. How happy she had made him then.

But now that she was grown she was greatly changed. Was it her schooling that had done it? He'd wanted to give her all the advantages that the most high-born of females were given, and he'd chosen a school for her that was much favored by the *haute ton*. But perhaps he'd been wrong. Her classmates at the Marchmont Academy for Young Ladies had been, for the most part, girls of noble birth. They soon discovered she was the daughter of a "cit," and they were quick to slight her. He'd hoped that his wealth would make up for his lack of a title—after all, he was richer than most of their fathers—but he should have known that Cassie was not the sort to flaunt her wealth. Shy to begin with, she grew positively invisible among the bright flowers of the *ton*. Even the few cits among the students did not make friends with her; they were too busy toadying up to the titles. Thus it was that her experiences at the Academy increased her tendency to withdraw into herself. Her schooling had given her polish, yes, but what good was that polish, and all her other excellent qualities, if they were obscured by her overwhelming shyness?

He had to admit that her shyness, so charming in the child, was a flaw in the woman. It became a screen that separated her from other people. She could be polite and mannerly in public, but she could not open herself enough to permit the slightest intimacy to develop. She had too much reserve to reveal her deepest self. Thus, she had no young ladies whom she could call friends; no young men whom she could call suitors. The veil of shyness even separated her from her own father. She did not share her thoughts with him as she used to do. Even the dreadful scene at Hollings and Chast's might have been kept from him if he hadn't come upon Mr. Chast in the driveway. Cassie seemed to live in her own world. And he, without a wife to advise him, did not know what to do to bring her out.

Yet, shy as she was, she had dared, today, to go shopping in the heart of London all by herself. And with only one guinea in her reticule. One guinea! He would have insisted on giving her *ten*, if she'd only told him she wished to shop for fabric for a gown. What was the matter with the girl? She was shy, yes, but she had a good share of common sense. How was he ever to learn to understand her?

He pushed his dessert away and looked at her sternly. "That ye went into town unescorted is bad enough," he scolded, "but that ye ventured forth without adequate funds was completely irresponsible. What is it, Cassie, that makes ye be'ave like a wet-goose? You know that ye 'ave only to ask, and ye can 'ave all the funds yer 'eart desires. Yet ye take yerself off on a shoppin' expedition with only a guinea. One would think ye were the daughter of a pauper! No wonder the blasted clerk took ye for a thief."

Cassie, too, lowered her eyes to her plate. "Yes, Papa. I'm sorry, Papa."

"There ain't no need to apologize to *me*, Cassie. I wasn't the one who 'ad to suffer 'umiliation in a crowded shop. You should apologize to *yerself* for subjecting yerself to such shame. If you'd 'ad Miss Penicuick with you, it would have been obvious that y're a young woman of substance. And if you'd 'ad sufficient funds in yer possession, ye could've thrown a guinea into that clerk's face an' left the premises with yer 'ead 'eld 'igh."

"No, Papa, I could not. Throwing out a second guinea would not have proved I'd given him the first."

"It would've at least proved that y're plump enough in the pocket to pay for the fabric easily enough and that therefore ye'd be unlikely to try to steal it."

"But, as it turned out, sir," Miss Penicuick offered, "the overage in the cash box was a much more definitive proof than an extra guinea in her reticule would have been."

"That may be," Oliver Chivers granted, "but if Cassie 'ad not been championed by that very kind stranger, I dread to think what might've become of 'er. How could she've faced the people in the store? How would she've made 'er way 'ome? The very thought of what she might've 'ad to endure makes me shudder.''

"Yes, you're quite right there," Miss Penicuick agreed. "Thank the lord for Captain Rossiter's presence. I shall remember him tonight in my prayers."

"Rossiter?" Mr. Chivers' eyes, behind their spectacles, blinked in astonishment. "Are you speakin' of Robert Rossiter, the Viscount Kittridge? Was 'e the officer who championed ye?"

"Why, Papa?" Cassie asked, her face coloring. "Are you acquainted with him?"

"No, not personally. But Delbert Jennings, who 'andled the financial affairs for the old viscount, is a good friend of mine. 'E's often spoken of the young man. Says 'e's a very good sort.''

"He was certainly a 'good sort' to me today," Cassie murmured.

"Yes. It's too bad such a fine fellow 'ad a father as profligate as the old viscount. Now poor Rossiter'll find 'isself puntin' on tick. 'Asn't been left a feather to fly with, Jennings says.''

Cassie stiffened in sudden attention. "What do you mean, Papa? Are you saying that the captain is in a bad way financially?''

"As bad as can be. 'Is father's gamblin' debts left 'im badly dipped. All the estates are mortgaged to the 'ilt. An' the poor fellow ain't yet been told. Far away, fightin' in the war with Nappy all these years, 'e don't know anythin' of the financial maneuverings that took place be'ind 'is back. Jennings says that when 'e learns the full extent of 'is indebtedness 'e'll be knocked off 'is pins.''

Cassie stared at her father for a moment, a little cry escaping from her throat. The sound caught his attention. He peered at his daughter curiously through the thick lenses of his spectacles. "Ye seem unduly affected, Cassie. I thought financial affairs didn't 'old no interest for ye."

A blush suffused her face again. "I only . . . it's just that he was so very kind to me," she said. "I'm sorry to learn that so kind a gentleman will be so badly hurt.''

Oliver Chivers didn't miss the flush on his daughter's cheeks. "*Liked* the fellow, eh, Cass?" he asked bluntly.

Cassie dropped her eyes, unable to reply. Miss Penicuick took it upon herself to answer for the girl. "How could she help but like him after his gallantry today?"

Cassie lifted her head. "Isn't there anything you can do for him, Papa?"

"Do for 'im? What can I do? I 'ave nothing to do with the Rossiters' finances."

"But couldn't you speak to—what was the name of the viscount's man of business? Jennings?—to Mr. Jennings? Make some suggestions, perhaps?"

"Really, Cassie, ye can sometimes be a complete green'ead. Don't ye know anythin' of the proprieties of business? I couldn't make suggestions to Jennings about the finances of one of 'is clients. That would imply that I believed myself to be more competent to 'andle the affair then 'e'd be. Besides, with all the viscount's properties encumbered, there ain't nothin' I *could* suggest that would get the fellow out of 'is fix, short of—" He stopped speaking abruptly, his mouth open and his eyes staring out at nothing, as if a dazzling idea had struck him with a clunk.

Cassie leaned forward eagerly. "Short of what, papa?"

Mr. Chivers blinked, his eyes focusing slowly on his daughter's face. Perhaps he *could* make a suggestion to Jennings about the viscount's finances. It was an off chance, an endeavor with a very low probability of success, but it just might work. He'd never before known Cassie to show so great an interest in a young man. If his suggestion were taken, it could benefit not only his lordship but Cassie as well. It was certainly worth a whack. He would put out a feeler and see what he could see.

"What *is* it, Papa?" Cassie asked, bursting with curiosity. "Why are you looking at me so strangely?"

"It's nothin', my love, nothin'," her father muttered, pulling his eyes from her and looking down at the dessert. "Eat yer blasted bla'mange."

Chapter Five

Sometimes it is hard to recognize the moment when one's life falls to pieces. Robert Rossiter, Viscount Kittridge, however, could give you the date, hour and minute when it happened to him.

His lordship was no fool. Although no one in his family—not his dithery mother, his young brother Gavin, nor his recently widowed sister, Lady Yarrow—had given him the slightest clue that anything was wrong with the family finances, it took no more than two days of civilian life for him to suspect that he was in trouble. But on the third day, an encounter with a wine merchant (who'd awaited him on the doorstep of the family town house in Portman Square and who'd asked point-blank for payment of a long-overdue bill for champagne) led him to seek out his father's man of business without further delay.

What he learned from Mr. Jennings sent him reeling. The news struck him like a blow to the stomach, knocking out his breath and causing him to fall back into the chair on the edge of which he'd been nervously perched. Mr. Jennings offered him a drink of brandy, which he downed without hesitation. "As bad as that?" he asked when he'd recovered his voice.

Mr. Jennings nodded. "I'm afraid so, my lord. I had warned your father repeatedly, during the last five years of his life, that this day of reckoning would come and that it might be his son—you, my lord—who'd have to face the consequences of a situation not of your making. But the gambling fever had too tight a hold on him. He didn't seem able to stop, even at the end when the pain of his illness was almost unendurable. Every day, rain or shine, in spite of his growing weakness, he had his man carry him to his club and seat him at the gaming table.'' He shook his head in dismal recollection.

Lord Kittridge shut his eyes. ''That's not the man I remember,'' he muttered unhappily. ''You've not painted a picture of a father of whom a son can feel proud.''

''Nevertheless he loved you, my boy, as much as he could love anyone. I think one of the things that drove him on was the futile hope that he might make a killing and thus spare you some of this.''

''Yes, the prayer of every man who ever rolled dice: *One killing, dear God, one killing, and I shall give up the game forever.*''

Delbert Jennings sighed. ''Too true, my lord, unfortunately too true. A terrible disease, gaming. Your father is not the first, nor will he be the last to succumb to it.'' Sighing again, he gently pushed a folder across his desk toward the viscount. ''I've worked out a plan of divestiture, which I've been waiting to go over with you—''

Lord Kittridge held up a restraining hand. ''Not now, Jennings. I don't think I could make sense of anything right now. Let me go. I'll come back tomorrow, I promise. Tomorrow. Then we'll see what we can salvage from this fiasco.''

''Yes, of course, my lord. I quite understand,'' the man of business said as both men rose. ''But it need not be tomorrow. Take a few days to let the news sink in. Shall we say Monday?''

The day agreed on, Mr. Jennings led the viscount to the door, where they paused and shook hands. ''Try not to fall into the dismals, my lord,'' the older man counselled. ''Other men, many more than you dream, have managed to survive such blows as this.''

Lord Kittridge emerged from Jennings' offices, his head in a whirl. It was hard for him to comprehend fully the extent of the disaster his father had left behind. But one thing was devastatingly clear: The future he'd imagined for himself was shattered. He knew that he was not the only soldier to return from the wars to find things at home devastatingly changed, but the knowledge that others had been struck with similar blows was not particularly comforting. No matter how often one hears that misery loves company, there are some miseries that can't be eased by the mere awareness that others have suffered a similar catastrophe.

He began to walk down the street, the cold wind buffeting his face. He couldn't help noticing that, although it was early afternoon, the day was as dark as twilight. The sky was a stormy grey, and the air had a bite that promised snow. He raised the collar of his greatcoat, thinking that the grim weather was deucedly appropriate to his mood. He didn't quite know where he was going. He knew only that he didn't want to go home. Facing his family would require more strength than he could now summon up. He turned up one street and down another until more than an hour had passed, but he still was not able to calm his inner perturbation.

But the wind nipped at his ears and his fingers tingled with the cold, so at last he hailed a hack and gave the address of the Fenton Hotel, where his friend Sandy was putting up. Sir Philip Sanford—Sandy to his friends—had been his comrade-in-arms through all his years of military service. Lord Kittridge had never had a better friend. Sandy was too short of stature and too moon-faced to be taken seriously as a military hero, but Kittridge knew that a braver, kinder, more loyal soldier never lived. There was hardly a time that Sandy would not show a cheerful face. No matter how grave the battle situation might seem, Sandy always had an optimistic outlook. He was the most warm-hearted fellow in the world, and his broad-cheeked face was the only one Lord Kittridge wanted to see in this dark hour.

Besides, a visit with Sandy would bring back the feeling of being in military service. War was certainly as "grim-visaged" as Shakespeare said it was, but being a soldier had much to recommend it. Civilian life was messy and confusing. What Kittridge missed most at this moment was the clean, brave, unencumbered feeling he'd had as Robert Rossiter, cavalry officer. And that was something only Sandy would understand.

When Sandy's man admitted him to the sitting room of the

rented suite on the Fenton's third floor, he found his friend lounging in a wing chair near the fire, his stockinged feet propped up on the hearth. Sandy looked up from the newspaper he'd been reading, peered at his friend for one long, silent moment and jumped to his feet. "Good God, man, what's amiss? You look as if you've lost your best friend, but that can't be, for here I am, quite alive and hale."

Rossiter acknowledged the quip with a mirthless imitation of a smile. "I'm glad to hear it," he said, throwing his greatcoat over a chair. "On top of the news I learned today, losing my best friend would be more than I could bear."

"Then what is it?" Sandy asked, his usually cheerful face clouding with the realization that his friend had suffered a severe blow. "Whatever it is, Robbie, old fellow, it can't be as bad as the look on your face."

Lord Kittridge turned to the fire and held out his hands to warm them. "I've just learned that I'm rolled up, that's all."

"Rolled up? How can that be? We've been back less than a week!" He pushed his friend into a chair and went to pour a couple of brandies. "How much blunt can you possibly have run through in so few days? What have you been up to, man?"

"Not I. My father. He performed the almost unbelievable feat of squandering the entire estate. The Suffolk property, Highlands—that's the family estate in Lincolnshire, you know—the London house, everything." And, taking the drink Sandy offered him, he began to relate the whole story.

At strategic moments during the recital of the details, Sandy refilled Kittridge's glass, but even after the tale was fully told and the bottle stood empty on the floor beside their chairs, his lordship felt no effect from the drink. His spirit was so depressed that it seemed to leave no room for the brandy to do its work. "What am I to do, Sandy?" he asked miserably.

"Don't know, old fellow," Sandy admitted, taking the last swig left in his glass. "Haven't the foggiest. Finance is not a subject I've studied. But I know you, Robbie Rossiter. I've seen you lead a division across a ravine while three enemy regiments shot at us, and you, cool as ice, never hesitated or flinched. I've seen you land on your feet after your horse was shot from under you. I've seen you cut a piece of shrapnel from my thigh with the aplomb of a surgeon. I've seen you calm a brigade of terrified dragoons while a typhoon whistled round us like armageddon. If anyone can come through a crisis, it's you.''

"Those crises were easy. I'd take any or all of them in place of this one. This one has me terrified. What will my mother say when I tell her we must sell the London house? How will I keep Gavin in school? And my sister will need help, too.''

"Eunice?'' Sandy's round face reddened, and he dropped his eyes from his friend's face. "Is something wrong with her?''

Kittridge was too absorbed in his own problems to notice Sandy's blush. "Her husband—you remember him, don't you? Henry Yarrow? He was at Eton with us when we were in our first year and he was in the upper fourth. Well, he died unexpectedly a few months ago—''

"Yes, I'd heard that,'' Sandy mumbled.

"His estate went to a distant cousin, because Eunice's babies are both girls. The heir is obligated, I believe, to supply her with some sort of allowance, but I shall have to provide housing for her and her children on top of the rest.''

"That *is* too bad.'' Sandy fixed his eyes on his glass. "Is your sister still in mourning?'' he asked with studied casualness.

"Half-mourning, I believe. Why?''

Sandy hesitated. "Never mind,'' he said. "It's not important.''

Kittridge, who ordinarily would have exerted himself to draw out from Sandy what was on his mind, could not now concentrate on the matter. The thought of all his responsibilities—obligations which he had no idea how to discharge—was too overwhelming. He put his hand to his head and shut his eyes. "God! What am I to do?''

Sandy, unable to think of an optimistic answer, shook his head. Then he remembered that there *was* a bright side, a name the mere mention of which had always brought a light to Robbie's eyes. But it was a name that his friend seemed to have avoided all afternoon. "I say, old man, isn't there one person you've forgotten to speak of? Why haven't you mentioned Elinor?''

Kittridge's head came up slowly. "Oh, God! *Elinor!*" He stared at his friend, his eyes widening in horror. "I didn't even *think* of her!"

Sandy's round face took on a glow of hope. "Then think of her now, you clunch. At least you'll have Elinor to bring some light into your life.''

"No," Kittridge groaned in despair. "Even *that* will be denied me."

Sandy's face fell. "Why? Do you think all this will affect her response to your proposal?''

"Affect her response? How can it *not*? But the question's moot. I can't ask her now."

Sandy gaped. "Can't ask her? But, Robbie, you *must*! She's expecting it, isn't she? The whole of London's expecting it. You and she have been smelling of April and May since the girl came out. She's waited all through the war for you!''

Kittridge, ashen-faced, stumbled to his feet. "You don't seem to realize the extent of my indebtedness, Sandy. I have *nothing*. No income, no prospects. Only debts. I don't know how I shall manage to support my family. In these circumstances, how can I ask *anyone* to be my wife?''

"Damn it, Robbie, we're speaking of *Elinor*, not some jingle-brained goosecap. She's been loyal to you for six years. She has *character*. She will *want* to be at your side, to share in your deprivations, to help see you through.''

"She may want to, but I won't let her. What sort of man would ask a woman to make such a sacrifice? Would you?''

Sandy blinked up at his friend, trying to answer honestly. "I don't know," he admitted at last. "No woman has ever loved me in that way."

Kittridge's eyes fell. He turned and stared into the fire. "I was going up to Suffolk on Saturday to see her. It was to be our grand reunion.''

Sandy's face was a study in sympathy. "You'll still go, won't you? If she's expecting you—''

"Yes, I must, of course." Kittridge lowered his head until

his forehead rested on the mantel. When he spoke again, his voice was hoarse. "I shall have to tell her that I won't be making an offer after all."

Sandy shook his head. He didn't believe matters would turn out as badly as that. The girl was much too fine—too loyal, too loving, too strong of character—to permit him to sacrifice their happiness. She would insist on their betrothal. Why, she might even convince her father to help Robbie with his finances! All might not be as black as Robbie imagined.

But Sandy didn't say anything of this aloud. Robbie was in no mood to believe him. All Sandy permitted himself to say was that he was glad Robbie still intended to call on the girl. "Be sure you don't permit the dismals to keep you from driving up there," he insisted.

"Yes, I shall go. But it will not be in any way the reunion I've been dreaming of."

"Don't be too sure," Sandy said cheerfully, unable to keep his optimism hidden. Then he added with a kind of raucous gaiety, "Do you know what I wish, Robbie?"

"What?" Robbie responded glumly, turning to stare at his ever-optimistic friend.

"What I wish," the moon-faced fellow said, holding up the empty bottle and eyeing it in mock disgust, "is that we had another bottle of brandy."

Chapter Six

The wind had eased by the week's end, but the temperature had dropped sharply. A light snow fell quietly throughout Lord Kittridge's drive north. By the time he arrived at Langston Hall in Suffolk he was chilled through. Snow lay over everything, softening the forbidding outlines of the dark, turreted building that had housed his ladylove since birth. His lordship spent no more than a moment, however, admiring the shadowy, snow-trimmed edifice. Shivering, he loped quickly up the steps and gained admittance.

Sandy's optimism notwithstanding, the greeting he was given by Elinor's father was not very warming. "Well, Kittridge," Lord Langston said coldly as the butler helped the new arrival off with his greatcoat, "we've three inches of snow on the ground, but you're here."

"Yes, my lord," the weary traveller answered, trying to sound cheerful. "You didn't think a little snow would deter me, did you?"

"I suppose not," his host answered enigmatically. "At least Elinor didn't give up hope of your arrival, even though I tried to discourage her."

Kittridge could not fail to notice that the house was at sixes and sevens. The front hall was piled with luggage, several footmen and housemaids were busily running about carrying articles of clothing and household goods to and fro, and there were dust covers to be seen on the sofas and chairs of the drawing room to his right. "Are you going away?" he asked in some surprise.

Before his host could answer, Lady Langston came down the stairs carrying a birdcage in which a beautiful green-blue cockatoo was imprisoned. "Do you think Chickaberry will stand a sea voyage, Langston, or shall I give her away to—?" She stopped abruptly where she stood on the bottom step and stared at Kittridge with something like horror. "Good God!" she gasped. "*Robbie*!"

Kittridge, hiding his dismayed confusion, came forward and lifted her hand to his lips. "Weren't you expecting me, ma'am?"

"Well, the sn-snow, you s-see . . ." She gaped at him as if he'd risen from the dead. Then she clapped a hand to her mouth. "Oh, Robbie, my poor boy!" Bursting into tears, she turned, ran up the stairs again and disappeared from sight.

Lord Kittridge was not expecting to enjoy this visit, but these greetings were worse than anything he'd anticipated. He turned to his host with upraised brows. "Is something amiss, Lord Langston?" he asked. "Is someone ill? Good God, not . . . *Elinor*?"

"No, no, not at all," Langston assured him. "Don't pay any mind to Lady Langston's waterworks. She's easily perturbed. Any little change in routine can set her off."

"Change in routine? You *are* going away, then?"

Lord Langston's eyes wavered. "I think Elinor wants to tell you about it herself. She convinced me that you both deserve the opportunity for an interview in private, under the circumstances."

Kittridge eyed his host narrowly. "Circumstances? What circumstances?"

The other man looked uneasy. "Elinor will explain. Why don't you make yourself at home in the library, Kittridge? You know the way. I'll go upstairs and send her down to you."

Kittridge nodded and strode off down the hall. He found the library still habitable, with the furniture uncovered, the drapes drawn against the draughts and a fire burning in the grate. He stood before the fire warming himself as he wondered what his beloved had to tell him. Whatever it was, he realized, it would not be as devastating as the news *he* had for *her*.

He was so absorbed in his depressing thoughts that he didn't hear her step in the corridor. It was only when she threw open the door that he whirled around. She was flying across the room toward him. He had barely enough time to catch her up in his arms. "Elinor!" he breathed, holding her close.

Her arms clutched him tightly round the neck, and she buried her face in his shoulder. "Oh, Robbie, my darling!" she sobbed. "I want to *die*!"

He held her until the sobs subsided, kissing her hair and whispering soothing endearments into her ear. She was tall for a woman, so that she seemed to fit against him as if she'd been designed for him. Her body was lithe and supple in his arms. The feel of her made him weak in the knees. Whatever it was that she had to tell him could wait. All the news would be revealed soon enough. In the meanwhile he could close his mind to reality and permit himself the joy of this closeness. He'd dreamed for eight months—since his last leave—of holding her like this. As far as he was concerned, they could remain locked in each other's arms this way forever.

But all too soon her sobbing ceased, and she recovered herself enough to draw him to a large wing chair and settle him in it. Then she sat down on a hassock at his feet and took his hand in hers. "It is the end," she said, her voice thickened by pain and tears. "They are taking me abroad."

"I see," he said quietly, his eyes drinking in the beauty of her. Her face looking up at him was heart-wrenchingly lovely. her blue eyes still misty with ears, the skin of her oval face translucent, her lips appealingly swollen from her bout of sobs, her red-gold hair, only slightly dishevelled, caught up in a girlish bow at the nape of her neck and falling over one shoulder in a silken curl. But he couldn't let himself wallow in her loveliness; he had to concentrate on the problem at hand. "They know about my situation, is that it?"

"Yes. Papa heard rumors, and he went to London himself and made inquiries. I have been begging and pleading with him for weeks, saying that I did not care, that we would find a way to live, but he is adamant against you."

"Do you blame him? If you were my daughter, I would do the same."

"But I love you, Robbie." She lowered her head and heaved a sigh that trembled through her whole body. "There will never be another like you for me."

He lifted her chin and made her look up at him. "Nor for me, my love, nor for me. But circumstances have turned against us. I am saddled with debts that will take me a lifetime to pay. I can't allow you to join me in impoverishment, any more than your father can." He withdrew his hand and looked away from her pleading eyes. "It is . . . hopeless."

"We could elope, Robbie. Run off to Gretna . . ."

"Yes, we could. And then what?"

"I don't know. Something would occur to help us. Perhaps Papa—"

He stiffened. "You don't really think I would permit your father to support us. I am not a sponger."

"No, you're not. I knew you would say that." She looked down at his hand that she still clutched in hers. "Besides, Papa is not being generous. When he learned what your father had done to your estates, all he did about it was to insist that I disentangle myself from you. He never once offered to help you."

"How could he? It's not as if a few hundred pounds would solve the matter. We are speaking of a debt of thousands! He has your brother's expectations to think of. He cannot take so great a sum from Arthur's inheritance to throw away on me."

Elinor drew in a wavering breath and, dropping his hand, rose slowly from her seat. "I have given Papa a dozen reasons why helping you would *not* be throwing his blunt away. But he was not persuaded."

"Nor would I be in his place." Kittridge got to his feet and grasped his beloved by the shoulders as if he wanted to shake her. "Damnation, Elinor, you had no right even to ask it of him."

"No right?" She drew herself up in offense. "Because you haven't yet offered, is that what you mean? Are you implying that, not having the status of *betrothed*, I had not the right to plead your cause?"

He winced and pulled her to him with a groan. "No, my dearest, of course not. You have been my heart's betrothed since we played together as children in those fields behind this very house. You know as well as I that my offer was only a matter of form.''

She sniffed into his shoulder. ''Then, if I am truly your heart's betrothed, why had I not the right to speak to my father in your behalf?''

He held her away from him and peered at her sternly. ''Because it humiliates me to have you do so. Don't you see, my love, that I couldn't be beholden to *anyone* for so great a sum? Even if it were possible for Langston to lend it to me—which it is not—it would take too many years for me to pay it back. Don't you see how such a situation would diminish me in your father's eyes and in my own? And even, in time, in yours?''

She dropped her eyes from his face and turned away from him. ''Yes, I suppose I do see,'' she said sadly. ''That's why I've submitted to parental commands and have agreed to leave for the continent. I knew in my heart you would not marry me now.''

''Not would not,'' he corrected, his voice unsteady. ''*Could* not.''

''Could not.'' She moved to the fireplace and took up the poker. ''I understand, Robbie, I really do. I know that you have many burdens . . . your mother, your brother, and now Lady Yarrow and her children, too. I would only be another one.''

As she poked at the flames, he stared at her face. Her skin glowed amber in the brightened firelight. His throat burned in pain. ''I would never think of you as a burden, my love. But I won't be the one to deprive you of the kind of life you've known and have every right to expect to continue.''

''Yes,'' she said quietly. ''I knew you would say that, too.''

Before he could reply, there was a knock at the door. Evans, the butler, put his head in. ''Beg pardon, m'lady,'' he said, ''but her ladyship wishes to know if Lord Kittridge stays the night. And will he be wishing to have some supper?''

Elinor gave her beloved a pleading look, but he shook his head. ''Thank her ladyship for me,'' he told the butler, ''but I will be leaving at once.''

"So soon?" Elinor cried when the butler had withdrawn. "Please, Robbie, can't we have just a little more time?"

"If I stayed," he said bluntly, "we would not be prolonging being together, only prolonging the good-bye. I don't think I could bear it." He took one last look at her before crossing to the door. "Good-bye, my love. You must know that I wish you every happiness."

She gave a little cry and made as if to run to him, but he held up his hand. "No. Stay as you are, there at the fire. I want always to remember you this way, with the firelight bronzing your face."

Tears spilled down her cheeks. "Good-bye, Robbie. I shall love you always."

He opened the door, but before stepping out he looked back at her. "Elinor," he asked hesitantly, "will you . . . sometimes . . . write to me?"

"I don't suppose . . ." She seemed to choke on the words. "Papa will not let me read letters from you, you know."

"I know. But—"

"I'll write, my love. As often as I can."

"No, not often. Just sometimes. To keep me sane." And he closed the door behind him, leaving her weeping brokenly for what might have been.

Chapter Seven

The one good thing about one's life being all to pieces was that it couldn't become much worse. It was with that sense of having struck rock bottom that Lord Kittridge presented himself at Mr. Jennings' office on Monday morning. He'd dressed himself in one of his new shirts and a coat just delivered from Nugee's (all purchased in the few happy days before he'd discovered what his situation was), and he'd stiffened himself for the interview to come by taking a swig of rum, something he'd never before done in the morning. His valet, Loesby, who'd been his batman in service, came upon him while he was in the act and didn't hesitate to voice his disapproval. "Since when, Cap'n, was ye in the 'abit of tipplin' in secret? An' in the a.m., too!"

"Stubble it, Loesby," his lordship had snapped. "You'll be tippling, too, I'll be bound, when I have to give you notice."

The valet had ignored the threat and merely brushed off the lapel of his lordship's new coat. "Ye kin gi' me all the notice ye want. Do ye think I'd be lettin' ye send me off when yer swimmin' in low tide? But we was speakin' of *you*, not me. I was about t' say, Cap'n, that this is the worst time fer you t' take t' drink, if ye was t' aks me."

"I'm not asking you, you muckworm. One swallow of rum doesn't mean I'm taking to drink. And you'd better start thinking about finding yourself a new post. You can't stay with me if I can't pay you."

"I kin stay so long as ye 'ave a kitchen where I kin

scrounge a meal, so there ain't no use in threatenin' me," the valet had retorted, throwing his lordship's greatcoat on his shoulders and pushing him through the door. "Good luck with yer man of business. I'll tell 'er ladyship ye'll be back in time fer tea, so don't dawdle."

Lord Kittridge was ushered into Mr. Jennings' office by an obsequious clerk who took his greatcoat and immediately withdrew. Kittridge, in the act of placing his hat, gloves and cane on a side chair, suddenly noticed that his man of business was not alone. Sitting on a high-backed leather chair at the right of Jennings' massive desk was a small-boned, thin-faced, bespectacled little man with a mass of curly auburn hair. Kittridge started in surprise. "I beg your pardon, Jennings," he said. "I seem to have intruded. Your clerk didn't tell me you were engaged."

"No, no, my lord," Jennings said, rising, "you don't intrude. This is Mr. Oliver Chivers, whom I've taken the liberty to consult in your behalf. He is a renowned expert in investments and financial dealings. With your permission, I'd like to invite him to sit in on this meeting. I can assure you that he will be as discreet about your situation as a clergyman, and he may have some useful advice for us."

"Of course he can sit in," Lord Kittridge agreed as Mr. Chivers rose. "If Mr. Chivers is acquainted with my situation, he must know that I can use all the advice I can get."

The two men shook hands. "It's a pleasure to meet ye, my lord," Chivers said, presenting Kittridge with his card. "I've 'eard ye spoken of for many years, and always in the most admirin' of terms."

"Thank you," Lord Kittridge said as the three men took seats, "but as you'll soon discover, I deserve very little admiration in matters of finance."

"Well, a man can't be expected to be expert in everythin'," Chivers said pleasantly. "And since this muddle ain't of yer makin', my lord, there's no blamin' you."

Mr. Jennings, meanwhile, leafed through a pile of papers and folders in front of him. "I'm afraid we must begin with some additional bad news, my lord," he murmured, "for I've discovered some other debts. Your load of troubles has been augmented, I'm sorry to say, by your sister's situation. It appears that Lord Yarrow left some debts of his own. He dabbled in stocks, you see, and the timing of his death was particularly unfortunate. There was a large drop at the Exchange at just that time, and—''

"Good God!" Kittridge exclaimed, his mouth going tense. "What does that mean for Lady Yarrow, exactly?"

"It means that the new Lord Yarrow has used the fact of the debts as an excuse to cut Lady Yarrow's already meager income even further. Leaving you that much less with which to support the family."

Lord Kittridge put his hand to his forehead. Would this series of blows never end, he wondered? This last blow seemed like the back-breaking straw. The total of the family's indebtedness was more than twenty thousand pounds. And with the estates encumbered, there was no income with which he could even start to pay them. Meanwhile, current expenses were accumulating at what seemed to him a staggering rate, with only his army half-pay coming in. Kittridge had no idea what to do or where to turn. He found himself at a complete loss. Even this meeting was turning out to be a disaster. What good was it to learn that he was even deeper in a hole than he'd thought?

He dropped his hand and looked from Mr. Chivers to Mr. Jennings in bewilderment. "Under these circumstances, Jennings, I don't see why you've brought in Mr. Chivers. What good is an expert on investments when there isn't anything to invest?"

"Come, come, my lord, don't lose 'eart so soon," Mr. Chivers urged, leaning back in his chair. He propped his elbows on the arms and pressed the fingers of his two hands together. He was silent for a moment while he examined Lord Kittridge from over the tops of his spectacles. "I've gone over the figures with Mr. Jennings quite carefully, an' I 'ave some suggestions. A very few, I admit, for I'll tell ye without roundaboutation that y're in a devil of a coil."

"Yes," his lordship said dryly, "I've gathered that. So you *have* some suggestions?"

"A few. But you won't like any of 'em."

"If they can help me dig my way out of this hole, I'll like them well enough," the impoverished viscount assured him.

"Then let's see." Chivers took a pad from the desk alongside him and studied the figures jotted down on it. "If ye sell out everythin', the Suffolk property, the Lincolnshire estate an' the London 'ouse, ye'll come out with a small balance. Enough to provide ye with a modest income."

"How modest? Where could we live?"

"Not in London, I fear. A country cottage somewhere in the north, per'aps. But the family wouldn't starve."

"A country cottage, out of all society? That would be a drastic adjustment for my family to make. My mother and sister would be miserable in such straitened circumstances. It would be too radical a change for them, I fear. Have I any other options?"

"The other suggestion I 'ave is more risky, but the results could be, in time, a bit more promising. If ye sold the Suffolk lands an' the London 'ouse, ye could pay off some of the encumbrances on the Lincolnshire property. It's not as vast an estate as the Suffolk lands, from what I see 'ere, but it could begin to bring in an income if ye managed it well. Ye'd not be able to clear yerself of debt all at once, but with economical living, in a few years it could be done, and at least that one estate'd be yours once more. At first, 'owever, there'd be very little income remainin' after the existin' mortgage payments. Less, even, than the income would be if ye sold everythin'. 'Ere, these are my projections, based on Jennings' estimate of the estate's worth."

Kittridge looked them over, his brow furrowed with worry. "I would like to earn back Highlands more than anything. But I know nothing of estate management. Do you think I could learn—?"

"I don't see why not. If ye 'ired a proper land agent, studied land use and enclosure methods, worked 'ard and kept yer womenfolk from spending the profits on fripperies—"

Kittridge sighed. "Aye, there's the rub. How can one teach economy to women who've never thought about it in all their lives?"

"Necessity is a good teacher, my lord. If they 'ave to learn it, they will."

His lordship bit his lip thoughtfully. His sister and brother might learn, but his mother, never. And how would they manage during the early years, before the encumbrances were paid off? The family would be forced to live in even greater straits than in a cottage, for there would be less income available. It was a gloomy future he had to offer his family. His heart lay heavy in his breast. Neither of the two choices gave him much hope. "Thank you, Mr. Chivers, Mr. Jennings," he said glumly. "I shall think over what you've told me."

Mr. Jennings leaned across the desk toward the consultant. "Don't you think, Mr. Chivers, that you should tell his lordship about the third option you mentioned?" he asked.

Chivers shifted uncomfortably in his seat. "I don't know, Jennings. It's a bit awkward. And 'is lordship doesn't seem to be the sort who—"

Kittridge, who was already pulling on a glove, looked at the financier curiously. "How can you tell what sort I am, Mr. Chivers? I don't even know myself. What is it you're hesitating to suggest to me?"

Mr. Chivers peered at the fellow from over his spectacles. "It's not a pretty suggestion, I fear," he ventured.

"I am not in a pretty situation. Go ahead, man. Say what is on your mind."

"Very well." Mr. Chivers lowered his eyes to his fingers. "I take it ye ain't married, my lord?"

"No. Why do you ask? What has my marital status to say to anything?"

Mr. Chivers removed his spectacles and began to polish the lenses with his pocket handkerchief with great deliberation. "Because the fact that y're a bachelor gives ye one more option."

"Oh? And what is that?"

"Marriage, my lord. There's a great many wealthy men of industry who'd provide very 'andsome dowries for their daughters if those dowries brought—forgive my bluntness, my lord—a title into the family."

Kittridge stared at him. "Let me make sure I understand you, Chivers. Are you saying that any nobleman whose pockets are to let can arrange a lucrative marriage just on the basis of his *title*?''

"Exactly so. It's been done a number of times. Ye must surely 'ave 'eard of such alliances.''

"No. I've been away for years. And even before my soldiering days I didn't pay much heed to social gossip.''

"Well, ye may take my word that such marriages ain't uncommon. The cases I'm familiar with seemed to 'ave worked out well enough. The Staffords of Lancashire, for example, restored their entire estate by this very sort of an arrangement.''

"Indeed?'' Kittridge's eyebrows lifted sardonically. "What a mercenary time we seem to be living in, to be sure.'' He drew on his other glove and rose proudly from his seat. "I appreciate your advice, Mr. Chivers, but as far as this last option is concerned, I'm not interested. My title is the only thing I have left that is unencumbered. I don't think I care to put it up for sale.'' He picked up the papers from Jennings' desk and walked swiftly to the door. "Good day, gentlemen. Thank you for your time. When I make up my mind about what to do, Jennings, I'll call on you again.''

Mr. Jennings, his mouth pursed in perturbation, jumped to his feet. "No offense meant, your lordship,'' he muttered, hurrying to see his client out.

"None taken,'' his lordship replied generously, although a wrinkle of annoyance still creased his brow.

The clerk came in with his lordship's greatcoat, and an awkward silence filled the room as he helped Kittridge on with it.

"Some titles,'' Mr. Chivers remarked just as his lordship stepped over the threshold, '' 'ave brought their owners a veritable fortune.''

Lord Kittridge stopped short. "Oh?'' he asked coldly over his shoulder, his curiosity warring with his pride. "And how much do you think *my* title would be worth?''

"Enough to pay off yer debts and clear the encumbrances from yer Lincolnshire estate, at least.''

The sardonic expression on Kittridge's face changed to sincere surprise. He turned round slowly. "As much as *that*?'' he asked.

"As much as that," Chivers said firmly.

Kittridge stared at him for a long moment. Then he came in and closed the door behind him. "Good God, man," he exclaimed, "we're speaking of a dowry that would have to be in the neighborhood of *forty thousand pounds*!"

"Yes, I know." Chivers gave an indifferent shrug. "I think I can assure ye of forty thousand."

Kittridge blinked. "I can't believe that someone would pay such a sum just so that his daughter could call herself a viscountess."

"You gentlemen who're born to the purple take yer titles lightly," Mr. Chivers answered calmly. "Only those for whom a title is inaccessible know its real value. Like ice in the tropics, if ye catch my meanin'."

"Mr. Chivers is right, my lord," Jennings put in earnestly. "There's many a captain of industry who would pay handsomely to have a nobleman grace his family tree. And many a needy nobleman has made the bargain. It isn't at all a new idea. And not necessarily a bad one, either."

Kittridge slowly removed his gloves and walked back toward the desk where the little financier was still sitting. "Are you saying, Chivers, that you have a definite offer for me?" He leaned against the desk and bent toward Chivers challengingly. "That you have someone specific in mind?"

Chivers couldn't meet that level look. "I 'ave several wealthy clients who'd be interested," he equivocated, shoving his glasses up on his nose and dropping his eyes.

"But no one in particular?" Kittridge pressed, his curiosity aroused.

"Well," Chivers murmured, "I suppose I may as well be partic'lar. After all, that's the real reason I'm 'ere." He stood up, took a deep breath and looked the viscount squarely in the eye. "Y' see, yer lordship, I myself 'ave a daughter . . ."

Chapter Eight

Lord Kittridge, though he'd listened to Mr. Chivers' imperti-
nent suggestion with fascination, did not for a moment give
that suggestion serious consideration. The idea of selling
himself and his title in exchange for a dowry—no matter how
large—filled him with repugnance. Such a solution to his
problem struck him as not only too easy and too vulgar but
almost corrupt. There was something debauched, he felt,
about any man who would consider such a plan.

Thus, having rejected that idea out of hand, he was left
with only two choices for his family's future: either to sell
everything and live in unaccustomed modesty on the income
of the sale for the rest of their lives; or to sell all but the
Lincolnshire estate and try to endure near-poverty for a few
years in the hope that he could eventually coax a profit from
that encumbered and thus far unproductive property. Neither
of the two plans offered him anything pleasant to tell his
family.

He came home from his visit to the City determined to
inform them bluntly of the state of their impoverishment. It
was a necessary cruelty. He had to apprise them of the hard
facts at once so that they could learn to accept what would
soon be their much-diminished style of life. To that end, he
ordered the butler to request that the family assemble in the
drawing room in three quarters of an hour, at exactly four
P.M , when he would confer with them over tea.

In the meantime, he sat down at the desk in the room that
had been his father's study to go over the figures that Chivers

48

had given him. Attempting to calculate the exact advantages that one of the plans might have over the other, he picked up a pen. Its nib, he found, was impossibly dull, and he thrust his calculations aside to search for a knife with which to sharpen it. He opened the top drawer and discovered, to his horror, that it was stuffed full of unpaid bills.

He surveyed the crumpled, disarranged, confusing accumulation with a feeling of utter despair. Slowly, one by one, he studied them, sorting them into piles and jotting down the amounts on a tally-sheet. Every bill was overdue, and all of them—mostly household trivialities and ladies' clothing—were for amounts considerably larger than he would have expected. His mother seemed to have deliberately purchased the most expensive items she could find. Although she must have had some inkling of the state of their finances, she had evidently taken no steps to economize. There were, for example, thirty-seven bills for millinery alone! Why, he wondered distractedly, when one's finances were in disarray, would one even *consider* buying oneself *thirty-seven hats*?

He made a quick estimate of the total, but the sum sickened him. Could his addition possibly be right? Could his mother have spent almost *three thousand pounds* on these *trifles*? He recalculated the list, hoping that a more careful reckoning would yield a less horrendous total, but the second accounting was even worse. His fists clenched in bewilderment and frustration. *How could so large an amount*, he asked himself, *have been spent on useless, self-indulgent luxuries*?

As the fact of this new debt sank into his consciousness, his sense of helpless frustration gave way to a feeling of explosive fury. He seized the papers in an angry fist and strode across the hallway to the drawing room. "Mama," he demanded without a word of greeting, "what on *earth* is the meaning of this?"

The dowager Lady Kittridge, the only person in the family who'd thus far responded to his summons, was comfortably ensconced on an easy chair near the tea table, which was already laden with the tea things. She was about to nibble at a cucumber sandwich she'd taken from the tea tray when his bellow made her shudder in alarm. "Good heavens, Robbie, you startled me!'' she gasped, her hands fluttering up in alarm. She frowned at him disapprovingly and then looked down at the sandwich which his abrupt entrance had caused to fall from her fingers to her lap. "Whatever possessed you to burst in on me like that? You made me drop my—"

"Whatever *possessed* me, ma'am?" her son exploded. "*These* are what possessed me! *One hundred and seventy-four unpaid bills*!"

"Oh, those." She shrugged, picked up her sandwich and took a dainty bite. "I don't see why you should raise a dust over them. Just send them over to Mr. Jennings. He'll take care of them."

Kittridge stared at his mother in disbelief. She was not in the least discomposed by his fury, but calmly finished her little sandwich and brushed the crumbs from her lap. She was a small-boned, delicate creature, looking at this moment— with her head tilted up at him, one graceful hand draped over the arm of the chair, and one tiny, slippered foot resting on a stool—like an exquisite porcelain figurine. Her hair was so white it seemed powdered; her complexion, once so luminous that her beaux made toasts to it, was now sadly wrinkled but still translucent; her waist was still as shapely as when she was a girl; and her graceful, slim-fingered hands fluttered like birds when she spoke. It was disconcerting to Kittridge to have to scold so fragile-looking a creature, but what else was he to do? "Damnation, ma'am," he raged, "what is Mr. Jennings supposed to 'take care of them' *with*? His own pocket money?"

The birdlike hands fluttered to her breast. "What do you mean, my dearest?" she asked, blinking up at him in bewildered innocence. "Mr. Jennings *always* takes care of the bills."

"Are you trying to pretend, Mama, that you don't know that my father left us penniless?"

Her pale blue eyes widened. "Well, I knew he was profligate, of course, and that he'd run himself into Dun territory, but *penniless*—?"

"Yes, penniless! What do you think 'Dun territory' *means*?"

"I know very well what it means. But your father never asked me to stint on the household expenses. Never!"

"Household expenses, ma'am? Is that what you call these? These are nothing but bills for gowns and bonnets and nonsense like reupholstering chairs! Nothing but *fripperies!*"

Her ladyship's elegant eyebrows rose in agitated disbelief. "Are you saying I shouldn't have purchased any new gowns?"

"That's *exactly* what I'm saying!" her son snapped. "And it's not only gowns we're speaking of. How can you have bought yourself something as expensive and unnecessary as a new barouche when there were three carriages in the stables already and you *knew* Papa's finances were all to pieces? Do you realize that there are bills here, all accumulated since his death, adding up to *three thousand pounds*? I can only suppose that you've forgotten how to *add*! I cannot otherwise explain how you could indulge yourself in such knickknackery as imported laces and French champagne and silver tea services, Mama, when we can hardly afford to pay for *tea!*"

"Not pay for tea? Really, Robbie, aren't you being a bit ridicu—?"

"Goodness, Robbie," came a voice from the doorway, "why all this shouting? I could hear you all the way down the hall." And in strolled his sister Eunice, Lady Yarrow, followed by her two little girls and their governess.

"Uncle Robert, Uncle Robert!" clarioned Della, the eldest of the two children, running to embrace him. "See the portrait I've made of you!"

Kittridge, bottling up his temper, knelt down and scooped the five-year-old girl up in his arms. "Della, you minx," he said affectionately, looking at the drawing the child held up to his face, "do you really think that long-shanks looks like me? And what is that you've drawn on my head?"

"It's a picture of you in your uniform, of course," the girl explained. "That's your shako on your head—with the plume, see? And this is your horse."

"And a very good horse it is, too," her uncle laughed, placing her on his shoulders and taking the other child by the hand. "How are you, Greta, my little puss? Do you and your sister stay to tea?"

"No, they don't," Lady Yarrow said firmly. "They only came down to say hello to you. Miss Roffey will take them upstairs in a moment."

"Of course they don't stay to tea," the dowager Lady Kittridge said dryly. "We can't afford it."

Lady Yarrow turned a questioning pair of eyes to her mother. Eunice Yarrow was a tall, sturdily built woman whose strong features and dark coloring were inherited from her father. She had none of her mother's delicacy in her form or her manner. Her character could be summed up in one word—blunt. "What do you mean by that, Mama? You sound as if you've suddenly entered your dotage."

"Not I," the dowager declared. "It's your brother whose wits are addled. He says we can't afford tea!"

"Robbie!" Lady Yarrow wheeled round to her brother in alarm. "Are things as bad as *that*?"

Kittridge was, by this time, down on hands and knees giving his nieces a ride on his back. "Perhaps I exaggerated a bit," he admitted, the sight of his adored nieces having dissipated what was left of his anger. "I was making a point about buying unnecessary silver. I think we can manage to afford some tea for the girls."

"Hooray!" shouted Della, clapping her little hands together delightedly. "We're staying for tea!"

"No, you're not," Lady Yarrow said sharply, lifting the girl from her brother's back and setting her on her feet. "Our teatime conversation promises to be serious . . . much too adult for you."

Little Greta began to cry in disappointment. "I want tea wiff Uncew Wobit!" she wept, hugging her uncle tightly about the neck.

Lady Yarrow pulled her from Kittridge's back. "But you can't have tea with Uncle Robert, so stop snivelling. You mustn't behave like a baby, Greta, now that you're a big girl of three. You may have your tea in the nursery." She handed the child to the governess. "Take these crybabies upstairs, Miss Roffey. I have a feeling my brother has more important matters on his mind than playing horsey with the children."

While the governess herded the girls from the room, Lady

Yarrow studied her brother with a knit brow. "Jennings did not have good news, I take it," she said when the children were gone.

"No, Eunice, he didn't," her brother admitted, getting up and brushing the carpet dust from his knees.

"Are you badly dipped?"

"As bad as can be."

Eunice expelled a breath. "I'm sorry, Robbie. It was unforgivable of Papa to have done this to you." She walked thoughtfully to the tea table and picked up the teapot. "I suppose this means that all your dreams for the future are up in smo— Oh! Good God!" She froze in the act of pouring and glanced over at Kittridge with an expression of real pain. "What about *Elinor*! How will all this affect your plans in regard to *her*?"

"I have no such plans," Kittridge said shortly.

"No such plans?" Eunice put down the teapot, fixing a dubious eye on her tight-lipped brother. "Don't talk fustian to me, Robbie. I'm fully aware that you intended to offer for her . . . last weekend, I thought. What's happened?"

"I learned that I am *persona non grata* in their home. Her parents have taken her to the continent."

"Oh, *Robbie*!" his mother cried out, her hands reaching out to him in sympathy.

"How dreadful!" his sister gasped. "I can hardly believe the Langstons can be so . . . so mercenary."

"It is not mercenary to wish one's offspring to live in comfort," Kittridge said, picking up the teapot and pouring tea for her. "You would do the same in their place. Here's your cup. Sit down and drink your tea."

"I would *not* do the same," Eunice insisted, taking a chair beside her mother. "I am very disappointed in Elinor."

"So am I," his mother agreed, accepting a cup of tea from her son. "And as for Lady Langston, I shall give her the cut direct the very next time she crosses my path."

Kittridge was touched at his mother's foolish loyalty but would not permit himself to be distracted from his purpose by feelings of affection. "You'll do nothing of the sort," he said with what he hoped was a repressive frown. "It was I, not they, who cried off. I went up to Suffolk on Saturday for the express purpose of explaining to Elinor that I would not make her an offer after all. She and I agreed to call it quits. She has gone off to enjoy a Grand Tour, and I . . . well, I shall have all I can do to keep *us* fed and clothed. For me, a wife is out of the question.''

His sister looked up from her teacup with raised brows. ''Good God, Robbie, what nonsense is this? I still have my allowance. And, since my girls and I will be living with you, I intend to turn it over to you to add to the family income. That alone should be sufficient to keep us in necessities, shouldn't it?''

Kittridge pulled up a chair before her and gently took his sister's hand in his. ''That's one of the difficult things I must tell you, Eunice. Jennings informed me that Yarrow had incurred some debts of his own. His heir intends to cut a good deal of your income to pay them.''

Eunice paled. ''Robbie, *no*! My Henry in debt? How can that be? Henry was not like Papa. He *never* gambled!''

''He may not have gambled with dice, my dear, but he speculated on the 'change. The market was down at the time of his death. It seems he lost more than he could afford.''

''How *could* he have done something so dreadful?'' Eunice cried, snatching her hand from his hold. ''I can scarcely believe it! Had he no thought for me or his children?''

Kittridge shook his head. ''I'm dreadfully sorry, Eunice.''

''Sorry!'' She got up, put down her cup and strode angrily to the window. ''I shall never forgive him. To pauperize me is bad enough. But to leave his *daughters* in so helpless a condition—!'' She choked back the words and stared out the window with unseeing eyes.

''Try to be fair, my dear,'' her brother said softly. ''He couldn't have expected to die so young. When one is young, one doesn't think of death as imminent. One believes one has time to take risks. I'm sure that, if he'd lived longer, he would certainly, in due time, have made proper provisions for you.''

''*If* he had lived longer . . .'' Eunice shook her head, weeping silently.

"I *always* thought Yarrow was a maw-worm," came a voice from the doorway.

"Gavin! There you are at last!" Kittridge strode to the door, pulled his younger brother into the room and shut the door against any other possible eavesdroppers. "You buffle-head," he said in irritation, "do you *enjoy* seeing your sister in tears? Keep your opinions about your late brother-in-law to yourself! How long have you been standing there in the doorway?"

"Long enough to get the drift," the boy declared. "We're scorched. Isn't that what you've called us together to tell us?"

Gavin Rossiter, at seventeen, was almost as tall as his brother, but his features still had the unfinished, not-quite-in-proportion look of adolescence. His nose was pronounced, like his sister's, but his eyes were as light as his mother's. His hair was almost as curly as his brother's, but it was long and fell over his forehead and shoulders in Byronic disarray. He had come down from Eton to welcome his brother home, and Kittridge had encouraged him to postpone his return until the financial situation could be sorted out.

"Yes, we certainly are scorched," Kittridge admitted, throwing an arm over his brother's shoulders and leading him to a chair near the tea table. "I hope the news does not overset you."

"You needn't worry about me, Robbie, old fellow. I won't be a burden on you. I'll even leave school, if that will help."

"What a sacrifice!" Eunice said sarcastically. She wiped her eyes and returned to her chair. "It seems to me you'd jump at any excuse to leave school."

"We shan't talk of leaving school just yet," Kittridge said. "Let's wait until we see just what our situation will be. Your schooling is the last thing I'd wish to cut off."

"Rubbish, Robbie," the boy said, cheerfully gobbling down a cucumber sandwich. "If we're going to be paupers, who needs school?"

"Well, we won't be paupers, exactly," Kittridge said, sitting down in the family circle, "but our lives will be very different from what they've been in the past." And, leaning forward and speaking with an earnest calm, he went on to explain in detail what their options would be.

He spoke quietly for a long while. By the time he'd finished, his mother was sniffing her smelling salts, his sister was white-lipped and his brother at a loss for words. Kittridge, however, looked at their stricken faces in some relief. *At least,* he thought, *the realities are beginning to sink in.*

Chapter Nine

Kittridge stirred his tea, eyeing his family from beneath lowered lids. Their reaction to the devasting news he'd just given them was crucial. If they showed themselves to be practical and courageous, he might feel encouraged enough to choose the second option: to live a few years in dire straits so that in the end they would have Highlands, the Lincolnshire property, to call their own. But they would all have to be brave and self-sacrificing to make a success of the venture. Very brave, and *very* self-sacrificing.

The family sat in silence for several minutes, trying to digest what Kittridge had just told them. Lady Kittridge was the first to break the silence. "I suppose we shall have to sell the new barouche," she remarked in a quavering voice.

"Sell the new barouche?" Kittridge echoed, his heart sinking like lead in his chest. He'd found his mother's remark unbelievably disconcerting. Hadn't she understood *anything* of what he'd just been at such pains to explain? "Not only the barouche, Mama," he said, forcing himself to speak patiently. "The entire stable must go."

"The entire *stable*?" Gavin asked, horrified. "You must be joking!"

Kittridge winced. "*Et tu*, Gavin?" he muttered under his breath.

The boy peered at him closely. "You *are* joking, aren't you?"

"No, I'm not joking. We can't afford stables. We shall manage to keep the old phaeton and a pair—the roans, I suppose—but nothing else."

57

Gavin leaped to his feet. "You're not implying that I must give up Prado!"

"Well, yes, I am. Prado is too valuable an animal to—"

"Damnation, Robbie, you may just save your breath," the boy declared furiously, "for nothing you can say will induce me to do such a thing! You bought him in Spain for *me*, didn't you? And now you want me to give him up! Give up Prado, indeed! It's not fair! You cannot ask it of me!"

"But I must, don't you see? We can't afford—"

"This is ridiculous!" Gavin exclaimed. "I *must* have a horse to ride. And if I must have a horse, that horse may as well be Prado."

"Didn't you understand anything I said before, Gavin? We have to give up almost everything . . . this house, the London stables, the entire Suffolk property, everything. The stables are no longer ours. They belong to our creditors. We cannot pick and choose what we can keep and what we give up. And even if we could, we can no longer afford to keep racing stock or show horses to parade in Hyde Park. Besides, we won't even be here in town."

"I don't care!" the boy cried childishly. "If I can't have Prado, you may as well take me out and put a bullet in my head!" And he stormed out of the room.

Kittridge stared after him, nonplussed. He hadn't expected difficulty from that quarter. He sighed, allowing himself to hope that when his brother's tantrum had blown itself out, the boy would come to his senses.

Eunice, meanwhile, smiled ironically. "So much for sacrifice," she muttered.

His lordship sighed and turned to his mother. She was the one he expected to be the most difficult to win over. "Speaking of sacrifice, Mama," he ventured, "I hope you realize that we shall have only a very minimal staff in our new home. A cook-housekeeper, perhaps, and a—"

"You may staff your house as you see fit, Robbie," his mother interrupted. "I realize you have a difficult row to hoe. I shall not place additional problems in your path. However, my love, you must understand that for my personal service I must have my Sophy. She has been my maid since my girlhood, so to dismiss her is out of the question. And I shall also require a hairdresser, a seamstress and at least one abigail.''

Kittridge gaped at her. ''An abigail, a seamstress and a *hairdresser*?'' he asked in a strangulated voice. He didn't know whether to laugh or weep. It was as if everything he'd said had passed over her like an unnoticed gust of wind. ''We'll be in the country, ma'am, don't you understand? You won't be going to fetes and balls. Why would you need a hairdresser?''

His mother rose aristocratically from her chair. ''I have never been without a hairdresser,'' she declared, her fluttery hands patting her white curls, ''and I am too old to change now. To move me to the country, to heaven knows what sort of hovel, is quite enough of a sacrifice to ask of me. Even *suggesting* that I do without my hairdresser, Robert Rossiter, is the outside of enough. I didn't know that my eldest son, the pride of my heart and the light of my life, could be so cruel.'' And she, too, swept out of the room.

Kittridge groaned and dropped his head in his hands. He hadn't expected the interview to be easy, but *this* was beyond belief. Neither his brother nor his mother seemed capable of grasping the full ramifications of this catastrophic situation. How could he make them *see*?

He felt his sister press her hand on his shoulder. He looked up at her in gratitude; at least he could count on *her*. ''Tell me, Eunice, what must I do to get through to them?'' he asked, his voice choked and desperate.

''Gavin's only taken a pet. He'll get over it. And I'll talk to Mama. Leave her to me.'' Eunice strode purposefully to the door, but there she paused. ''When I came home to live after Henry's passing, I fully expected to pay my way,'' she said forthrightly. ''I regret, my dearest, that Yarrow's heir has forced me to become an additional burden to you. I hope you know without my saying how much I appreciate your taking responsibility for me and my girls.''

''Don't be foolish,'' Kittridge said curtly, getting up and wrapping her in a fond embrace. ''We are family. We shall swim—or sink—together.''

She hugged him tightly. ''I don't know what I'd do without

you. But I promise you, Robbie, I shan't be more of a burden than I absolutely must. I need no horses, no abigails, no hairdressers. Only Miss Roffey, of course, and a nursemaid to assist her. And I think we must have a seamstress, my love, to take care of the girls' clothing—they grow so quickly, you know. But I wouldn't keep her to myself; I could certainly share her with Mama.'' Not noticing the stunned look in his eyes, she patted his cheek fondly and whisked herself out of the room. Before he could bring himself to move, her face reappeared in the doorway. "And a tutor, of course, Robbie," she added cheerfully, "but that may not be a gross expense. He needn't live in, you know. We could employ a local clergyman for half-day wages, I expect. For a couple of years anyway."

Lord Kittridge stared at the closed door for a long time. Then, utterly discomposed, he sank into a chair in front of the fire and shut his eyes. It was as if he'd ridden into an ambush. Not expecting to be besieged, he'd found himself being shot at from all sides. And there didn't seem to be a place of safety, a rock or knoll behind which he could hide. He felt depleted, beaten, defeated. There was no escape for him, for how could he run away when he had five people dependent on him?

But what was he to do for them? How could he even begin to teach these innocents, who'd been pampered all their lives, to adjust to the drastic changes he was proposing? Even he, who had experienced the dangers and deprivations of war, would not find the new life easy, so how could he expect the others, who had no inkling of deprivation, to accept it? "Seamstresses," he moaned, resting his head on the back of the chair and covering his eyes with one trembling hand. "Abigails. Nursemaids. Hairdressers. They want a veritable *regiment*!''

"Per'aps not a regiment, but fer certain nine, minimum," came his man Loesby's voice behind him.

Kittridge sat up. "What?" he asked in confusion.

Loesby came round the chair and perched on the hearth in front of his lordship. "A staff o' nine," he explained. "Cook, houseman, Miss Sophy, the 'airdresser, the abigail, the seamstress, Miss Roffey, the nursemaid, an' the tutor. Nine.''

Kittridge groaned. "Might as well be a regiment," he muttered, "since I can't afford even a third of them." His eyes focused on his ex-batman's weathered face. "You were eavesdropping again," he accused.

Loesby shrugged. "The on'y way ye learn anythin' is to eavesdrop."

"Then, since you know so much, tell me how, on a captain's half-pay, I'm to set up a household of six with a staff of—how many did you say?"

"Nine. Not countin' me."

His lordship peered at his batman with sudden intensity. "Why not counting you? Are you going to take my advice and find yourself another post?"

"Not on yer life. I din't count me 'cause I don't 'ave to 'ave wages."

"Why should *you* sacrifice your wages, man? It's more of a sacrifice than anyone in my family is willing to make."

"Do ye need to ask, Cap'n? We been through a war t'gether. I ain't forgettin' that ye came back fer me when they left me fer dead after Talavera. Nor what ye did fer me at Badajoz, neither. It's more of a bond, per'aps, then fam'ly."

"Perhaps it is." He looked his ex-batman in the eye. "I know I'd feel in a damned hole if you left me," he admitted flatly.

"Well, I ain't leavin', so there's no more to be said about that. About the rest of the staff, as I tole ye, I count nine. Not a small staff, I'd say."

"No. Not small at all." Kittridge's shoulders sagged. "What shall I do, Loesby? I'm at the end of my tether."

"Act like a cap'n, Cap'n. Treat yer fam'ly like a cavalry division. Give 'em orders. Tell 'em flat out—no 'airdressers, no tutors, nothin'. Just a plain ol' couple to cook an' keep the place clean . . . an' me. Tell 'im wivout roundaboutation. This is how it'll be, an' that's *it*!"

Kittridge snorted. "That's it, eh? And if they don't heel, it's the firing squad?" He shook his head. "I don't think I can, Loesby. It just occurred to me that Mama may feel about her Miss Sophy as I do about you. And perhaps Miss Roffey means as much to my sister and the girls. If I keep you, how can I ask Mama to give up her Sophy? And the girls their Miss Roffey, eh? And Gavin his beautiful Prado, the Spanish stallion that I gave him as a gift? No, Loesby, it's too much to ask of them.''

"But you 'ave no choice, Cap'n, if you ain't got the wherewithal . . .''

Lord Kittridge frowned thoughtfully and got to his feet. "Perhaps I do have a choice,'' he said slowly, as if to himself, "if I'm willing to swallow my confounded pride. It's the only way out of this fix.''

"What way is that, Cap'n?'' Loesby asked, his brow knit suspiciously.

Kittridge strode to the door. "What did I do with that card?'' he muttered under his breath.

He crossed the hall in three strides, the batman at his heels. In the study, he rifled through the papers he'd taken from Jennings' office. "Here it is. Get out the curricle, Loesby, and drive down to the City at once. There's a Mr. Chivers at this address. Tell him that Lord Kittridge has changed his mind.'' His mouth tightened, and Loesby saw a telltale muscle twitch in his cheek. "Tell him the damned title is for sale after all.''

Chapter Ten

The color drained from Cassie's cheeks. "You did *what*?"

"You 'eard me well enough, my girl," her father snapped, surprised and hurt by his daughter's reaction to his exciting news. "I've arranged for ye to wed Lord Kittridge. Why ain't ye throwin' yer arms round my neck an' kissin' me in ecstatic gratitude?"

The girl began to tremble from head to foot. "Oh, *Papa*!" she gasped, wide-eyed in horror. "How *could* you?"

Mr. Chivers glared at his daughter, angry and confused. He had achieved what he considered a brilliant success, and here was his daughter—the intended beneficiary of his triumphant scheme—behaving as if he'd condemned her to a life of hard labor in the workhouse! He realized again that he would never, if he lived to be a hundred, learn to understand her. He took his sherry from the tray Miss Penicuick held out to him and downed it in a gulp. "I 'ope, Cassie Chivers," he muttered, "that y're not goin' to put on missish airs and make a to-do about this."

The girl stared at him aghast. "You've *bribed* Lord K-Kittridge to offer for me, and you don't think I should make a *to-do*?" She sank down on the sitting room sofa, the breath quite gone from her chest. "Missish airs, indeed!" she gasped. "I think I shall *s-swoon*!"

"Don't you *dare*!" Chivers commanded. "No daughter of mine'd be so cowardly as to take leave of her senses just because 'er father gives 'er a small surprise."

Cassie shut her eyes. "*Small* surprise?" she murmured,

63

taking a deep breath in an attempt to compose herself. "You don't know what you're saying, Papa. This is not a small surprise. It is a major crisis!"

Miss Penicuick hovered over her. "Shall I run for the sal volatile, my love?"

Cassie shook her head. "No, Miss Penny, I shan't let myself faint. But, Papa, I don't understand you. How can you have taken such a step without consulting me first?"

"I *did* consult ye. In fact, this only came about because you yerself asked me to do it."

"I?" She blinked up at her father in shock. "*I* asked you to *bribe his lordship to make me an offer*? I would never *dream* of suggesting something so monstrous."

"What's monstrous about it?" Chivers demanded, torn between fury and bewilderment. "Ye asked me to 'elp him out of 'is financial difficulties, did ye not?"

"Yes, but—"

"Well, what better way to 'elp him than this? 'E'll get every cent 'e needs and a wonderful wife as well."

"A wonderful wife?" The girl made a helpless gesture with two shaking hands. "How wonderful can a wife be, Papa, if she is not one of his own choosing? If he doesn't . . . l-love her."

"Love? What balderdash! A man choosin' a wife for love is romantic poppycock. The best marriages are made by interested third parties, not by a man an' a maid becomin' infatuated at a ball while executin' a quadrille. Marriages should be *arranged*, like sensible business partnerships."

"You don't understand, Papa." Cassie's lips trembled, and she put both shaking hands up to her mouth in an attempt to steady herself. "You don't remember about love anymore. For someone young, like Lord Kittridge, love is . . . everything."

"What?" The bedevilled father glowered at her in irritation. "I can't tell what y're sayin' with your mouth covered up like that!" Sighing helplessly, he sat down on the sofa beside her and took one of her hands in his. "What's the matter with you, Cassie?" he asked more quietly. "I thought ye'd be delighted by this news. I thought ye *liked* the fellow."

The girl's eyes filled with tears. "I d-do, Papa, that's just it. I l-like him too much to wish to *t-trap* him."

"But, confound it, Cassie, ye'd not be trappin' 'im! Ye'd be *'elpin'* 'im!"

The tears spilled over. Feeling quite incapable of explaining to her father the reasons for her abhorrence of his scheme, Cassie snatched her hand away, turned her back on him and said, quite firmly, "I won't do it, Papa, so please don't say any more."

"What's that? Won't *do* it?" He rose from the sofa, impotent rage washing over him again. "Cassie Chivers, 'ow *dare* ye say that to me? I'm yer *father*! I arranged this for *yer own 'appiness*! You will do as I say!"

"No, Papa, I won't." She did not look at him, and the words were muffled from behind the hands that covered her face, but there was no mistaking the determination of her voice.

Mr. Chivers' neck and ears reddened as his blood rose to his head in choleric anger. "I said you *will*!" he shouted.

There was no answer except a firm shake of her head, *no.*

Chivers turned a pair of frantic eyes to Miss Penicuick, as if seeking help from that direction, but the housekeeper could only shrug hopelessly. Then he looked back at his daughter's bent head. "Cassie," he pleaded in desperation, "ye *must* wed 'im. I *promised* the fellow. It was a *bargain*. We *shook 'ands* on it!"

"Then dash it, Papa, you must wed him yourself," his daughter sobbed, jumping up and running from the room, "for I never will. Never!"

"*Cassie*," her father shouted after her, "come back 'ere! At once, do you 'ear! Damn it, girl, don't you *want* to be a viscountess? *Cassie*!"

But the girl was gone.

He stalked to the doorway. "Kittridge is comin' 'ere *tomorrow*!" he yelled, his voice thundering down the corridor. "To dinner. I expect ye to present yerself to 'im all prim and proper, do you 'ear me, Cassie? Tomorrow at eight!"

The only response came from Eames, the butler, who came stumbling up from below stairs with an expression of alarm on his usually impassive face. "Did you want me, Mr. Chivers, sir?" he asked breathlessly.

Chivers stamped on the floor in chagrin. "No, I didn't want ye," he growled. "Go away."

The butler, surprised at this unwarranted display of temper, withdrew at once. Miss Penicuick, quite unaccustomed to such theatrics in this usually peaceful household, threw her employer a terrified glance. Wringing her hands nervously, she came to the doorway and edged round him to follow her charge. "I think I . . . I'll just go and see—" she began as she stepped into the hallway.

"Just one moment, Miss Penicuick," he ordered angrily.

She jumped. "Yes, sir?"

"You 'eard what I said just now. Lord Kittridge is comin' for dinner tomorrow. See that Cassie is dressed proper an' is ready to receive 'im."

"But, sir, you know Cassie. If she's decided that this is not a suitable match . . ."

"Not a suitable match? Are ye both *demented*? The fellow is a veritable *thoroughbred*!"

"Yes, sir, I agree. But Cassie must have her reasons. And you know as well as I that she does not change her mind once it's made up. If she says she won't come down—"

"Then ye must *convince* her, do ye understand me? That's an order! She'll be down for dinner, all beribboned an' bedecked an' with a smile on 'er face, or someone standin' not ten inches from me at this moment will find 'erself *out on the street*! Do I make myself plain?"

Miss Penicuick gulped, nodded, burst into tears and ran off down the hall. "I d-don't say I won't t-try," the poor woman stammered as she mounted the stairs, "but to g-get C-Cassie to face his lordship when she has her m-mind so set against it will t-take a m-miracle. A God-sent m-miracle."

Chapter Eleven

The next day Mr. Chivers came home from the City three hours early, having been unable to concentrate for a single moment on business matters. His hair was wild, the eyes behind his thick spectacles troubled and his knees shaky. " 'As she come down yet?" he asked Miss Penicuick as soon as he set foot in the house.

Miss Penicuick looked haggard. "No, sir," she said nervously, "not even once. She won't talk to me or open her door, nor has she eaten a bite since last night."

Mr. Chivers patted her shoulder. "It's all right, Miss Penicuick," he said, feeling contrite. "I'll take care of everythin'. Sorry I put myself in such a pucker and upset ye."

He mounted the stairs slowly, tasting the bitterness of defeat in his mouth. Tapping on his daughter's door gently, he mentally rehearsed his speech of capitulation. "Cassie, my love, open the door. I've decided that ye needn't wed Lord Kittridge after all."

The key turned in the lock and the door opened, but only an inch. "Do you mean it, Papa?" the girl asked, peeping through the narrow opening with eyes reddened from prolonged weeping.

"Yes, of course I do. I ain't a monster to force my girl to wed against 'er 'eart's wishes, although I may 'ave sounded like one last night."

Cassie opened the door and threw her arms about her father's neck. "Of course you're not a monster! Thank you, Papa, for changing your mind."

Chivers kissed her cheek. "But there's something ye must do for me in return," he said, leading her into her bedroom and seating her on the chaise near the window. "Ye must still act the 'ostess for me tonight when Kittridge calls."

She stiffened. "But, Papa, I *can't*—"

He perched on her bed. "Is it so much to ask? We shall 'ave a small, polite dinner, over in an hour, and then ye can excuse yourself while I tell 'im we've changed our minds. Givin' 'im dinner is the least I can do after renegin' on my bargain. Besides, I can't withdraw the invitation this late in the day."

"But surely you don't need *me* at the table, Papa. I'd feel dreadfully awkward, under the circumstances."

Her father eyed her irritably. "It'd be dreadfully awkward not 'aving ye there, don't ye see that?"

She clenched her hands in her lap. "Please, Papa, don't insist. You know how hard it is for me to . . . to speak to strangers."

"But the man ain't a stranger. 'E was yer rescuer at the linendraper's. Y're already very well acquainted."

"I wouldn't call that well acquainted."

"Well enough acquainted, I'd say, for a simple dinner. Dash it all, Cassie, why are ye makin' difficulties for me? Don't ye see that I need ye to act as 'ostess?"

Cassie felt miserable at having to refuse him, but she couldn't bring herself to accept. "Miss Penicuick will do very well as hostess. I can't do it, Papa. I just can't. Please don't keep on about it."

Chivers sighed, defeated again. What was he to do with the girl? He pushed his spectacles up on his nose and got heavily to his feet. "Very well, Miss, 'ave it yer way," he muttered, turning to the door.

"Papa?" she asked shyly as he was about to leave.

"Yes?"

"I'm . . . sorry."

"I know." He went gloomily to the door.

"Papa?"

He turned. "What now?"

"What will Lord Kittridge do now? About his finances, I mean."

"Ye needn't worry yer 'ead about that," he said impatiently. "I'll find 'im another heiress to wed. There are a good many girls with rich fathers who'd jump at the chance to snare a prize like Kittridge. I'll find one of 'em for 'im. I owe the fellow that."

Promptly at eight the knocker sounded. Chivers, who'd been watching for the carriage from behind the drapes of the drawing room window, arrived at the door ahead of the butler. He welcomed his guest warmly, shaking his hand with nervous enthusiasm as Eames took his lordship's hat and cane and disappeared down the hall. "I 'ope you've a good appetite, your lordship," Chivers said, clapping his guest on the shoulder. "My chef is from Paris an' makes the finest partridge *à la Pompadour* y're ever likely to taste."

Lord Kittridge was elegantly attired in evening clothes and, except for a tightness about his mouth, seemed very much at ease. "I look forward to sampling it," he said. "If your chef is half as talented as the architect who designed this house, Mr. Chivers, the meal will be splendid."

"Ah!" Chivers' eyes lit up. "Ye noticed the design of the facade, then?"

"I did indeed. The lines are superb. Impressive in scale but not in the least ostentatious. You are to be complimented."

Oliver Chivers beamed, his chest swelling with pride. Nothing Kittridge might have said could have pleased him more. He glanced at his guest with rueful admiration. It would have been very satisfying to have so presentable a son-in-law. Why, oh why, he asked himself, did his daughter have to be so damnably, stubbornly resistant?

It was time, he supposed, to make some sort of excuse for Cassie's absence. He took a deep breath. "I must apologize, my lord, for the fact that my daughter ain't—" But at that moment a sound from the stairway above them drew his eyes.

The befuddled father gasped in astonishment. Coming down toward them, her face lit by a shy smile, was Cassie herself. She was dressed modestly in a lavender gown with a ruffled neck and puffed sleeves, and she'd draped a lovely Norwich silk shawl over her shoulders. To her father's delight, she

looked very pretty. She'd even managed to subdue her unruly
hair, having pinned it back in a tight knot, so that only little
tendrils had escaped to frame her face with an auburn halo.
"Cassie!" he exclaimed, unable to disguise his surprise.
"Y've come down!"

"Yes, Papa," she said in her quiet voice, "of course I
have." She came down the last step and offered her hand to
their guest. "Good evening, my lord. We are so glad you
could d-dine with us."

Lord Kittridge, subduing a vulgar urge to satisfy his curiosity about his intended bride by gaping at her face, merely
gave her a quick glance. About to bow over her hand, he
suddenly stiffened. "But we've met, have we not?" he asked,
peering at her with a puzzled frown.

"Just last week," she said, coloring painfully. "You saved
me from d-dreadful embarrassment at Hollings and Chast."

The tightness of his lordship's mouth softened in a charming smile. "Of course. How pleasant to meet you again!"

Chivers, recognizing that Cassie's shyness had increased at
the reference to last week's fiasco, immediately urged his
guest into the drawing room. There Miss Penicuick sat waiting. Her eyes widened at the sight of Cassie in their midst,
but she managed to hide her surprise. Chivers introduced her
as Cassie's companion. The introduction was an ordeal Miss
Penicuick survived without a gaffe. Only a slight tremor of
her fingers revealed her excitement at being an observer of
this most romantic turn of events. If it came to pass that her
Cassie married this handsome nobleman after all, Miss
Penicuick's dreams for her charge would have come true!

As Eames passed among them with a tray of sherries,
Chivers sighed in relief. The evening had been launched
without the embarrassment he'd expected. Now all he had to
do was keep conversation flowing through the meal, wait
until the women excused themselves and tell his lordship that
he would find another bride for him in Cassie's place. The
evening wouldn't be nearly as bad as he'd feared.

Dinner was soon announced, and Kittridge offered Cassie
his arm with appropriate gallantry. Chivers, following with
Miss Penicuick, felt proud of the graceful polish of his daugh-

ter's acceptance of his lordship's escort. The girl knew how to conduct herself, that much was plain. Perhaps her years at the Marchmont Academy had been of some use. He noted with a sigh that Lord Kittridge and his daughter made an attractive pair. For the hundredth time that evening he regretted the girl's stubborn refusal to submit to the arrangement he'd engineered for her. *Damn the chit*, he cursed in his head, *she doesn't know what's good for her*!

Chivers found that he had to carry on the dinner conversation almost singlehandedly, for Cassie was her usual quiet self, Miss Penicuick in too dithery a state to add anything substantial, and Kittridge, though he tried to hide it, was too abstracted. But his lordship ate well and did not fail to praise the partridge, so Chivers did not consider the dinner a complete failure. But the time dragged by slowly, and when the wonderful apple soufflé the chef had concocted to give the repast a final flourish was at last consumed, he felt relieved that the meal was at an end.

All that now remained was for Chivers to inform Lord Kittridge that Cassie was unwilling to wed him. This announcement would not be as painful for Kittridge to hear as it would be for Chivers to make. Kittridge had no feeling for Cassie, after all. He barely knew her. What he wanted was a rich wife, and any candidate with a wealthy, willing father would do. All Chivers had to do was to inform Lord Kittridge that he'd locate another candidate within the week, and his lordship was bound to be satisfied.

When the ladies rose and excused themselves in order to leave the men to their port, Chivers got to his feet and crossed the room to open the door for them. "Thank ye for comin' down, my dear," he said *sotto voce* to his daughter as she was about to leave the room.

"Be sure to bring his lordship to the music room when you've finished," Cassie whispered back as she crossed the threshold.

"But . . ." Chivers gaped at his daughter stupidly. "That would mean y're invitin' 'im to make 'is offer!"

"Yes, I know," the girl answered briefly as she brushed by him.

The bewildered Chivers followed her out and grabbed her arm. "Are ye sayin' you've changed your mind?" he hissed, hardly permitting himself to hope.

"Yes." Cassie gave her father a tiny smile. "Go back to the table, Papa. His lordship will be wondering what's keeping you."

When the door of the dining room was safely shut behind him, Miss Penicuick gave an excited little scream. "Oh, my love," she cried, throwing her arms about Cassie's shoulders, "are you going to accept him after all?"

Cassie merely nodded.

"Oh, my dear, I'm so *happy*! His lordship is the handsomest, most gentlemanly, most imposing man I've ever laid eyes on! But . . ." She took a step back and, with her hands on Cassie's shoulders, peered with worried earnestness into the girl's eyes. "Cassie, you were so *adamant* before, in your refusal of him! Are you now certain of yourself? Are you *sure* you want to do this?"

The girl took her companion's hands from her shoulders and squeezed them comfortingly. "Yes, Miss Penny, I'm sure."

"I don't understand," Miss Penicuick persisted. "What made you change your mind?"

Cassie drew her shawl more closely about her shoulders and started slowly down the hall. "It was something that Papa said," she explained.

Miss Penicuick hurried after her. "And what was that, my dear?"

"He said that if *I* didn't accept his lordship, he'd have to find *another* heiress for him to wed. I decided then and there that if Lord Kittridge was determined to marry without love . . . to tie himself to *anyone*, no matter whom, so long as she could help him out of his financial fix, well, then . . ." She paused and gave her friend a wistful smile. ". . . that 'anyone' might just as well be me."

Chapter Twelve

"You did *what*?" the dowager Lady Kittridge exclaimed when her son informed her of his marital intentions. "I think, Robbie, that you've taken leave of your *senses*! How *can* you have agreed to such a thing? Didn't you give a single thought to *my* feelings? How do you suppose I shall be able to show my face in society after my son marries a *bourgeoise*?"

Her reaction was typical of all the others. Every member of the family was appalled at the news. Gavin complained that he would have "the devil of a time explaining to my friends that my own brother is marrying a cit." And Eunice burst into tears, demanding to know how Robbie could bear facing the world after the *ton* made their odious comparisons between his lovely former-betrothed, Elinor, and the drab little nobody he intended to wed.

Kittridge kept his temper. He had made a bargain for the salvation of all of them, and although the cost to him—in the pain of lost dreams and savaged hopes—was heavy, he intended to make the best of it. He turned a cold eye on his family and merely let them know that their chagrin would be easily assuaged when they balanced the benefits each of them would derive as a result of his nuptials against the petty discomfort of accepting into the family a person they considered beneath their touch. "You, Mama, will be able to remain in the London house, with a whole staff at your disposal. Eunice, you will now be able to raise your daughters in the luxurious style you yourself enjoyed as a girl. And Gavin will be able to continue to live as he always has, even

keeping his beloved Prado. None of these privileges would
have been yours, I remind you, if my 'drab little nobody' had
not come to our rescue. So, if you're not complete fools, you
will think of the advantages to yourselves in my marriage,
and you'll welcome the girl into our midst with proper
warmth.''

Within himself Kittridge was not nearly so sanguine about
his marriage as he pretended to his family. For one thing, he
couldn't put his feeling for Elinor out of his mind. He had,
that very morning, received a letter from his beloved that
reminded him too well of what he had lost. Elinor's letter,
posted in Paris, reverberated with loneliness and loss. The
magnificence of her surroundings, the adventures of travel,
the excitement of seeing famous places for the first time, only
made her miss him more. *I had hoped to see Notre Dame and
La Chapelle with your hand in mine*, she'd written. *What joy
can there be for me to see these sights without you at my
side?* His throat had tightened when he'd read those words,
and he'd struck his fist against his bedpost with such frus-
trated fury that he'd knocked it loose from its underpinnings
and caused the hangings to come tumbling down about his
head.

For another thing, he was troubled about this girl he'd
agreed to marry. He'd thought, when he'd first seen her at the
linendrapers', that she was a sweet, innocent little soul. But
now he wasn't so sure, and his ignorance of her real nature
made him uneasy. He felt strangely suspicious of her motives. The cause of those suspicions was the fact that she had
turned out to be Chivers' daughter. It was a peculiar coincidence, and it made him so uncomfortable that he mentioned
the matter to his friend Sandy.

They had met at White's and were sitting in the lounge in a
pair of wing chairs, brandies in hand, gazing out through the
club's famous bow windows at the strollers parading up and
down St. James Street in spite of a blustery wind that was
tugging at shawls and sending high tophats bowling down
the street. ''What's so peculiar about the coincidence?'' Sandy
asked.

''Don't you think it possible that this isn't mere coincidence?'' Kittridge surmised. ''Mightn't there be some cunning strategy lurking behind it?'' Strategy had been Kittridge's forte in the cavalry; he'd been almost supernaturally adept at anticipating enemy movements. His instincts in matters of strategy had earned him much admiration. Those same instincts were at work now. They set a warning bell ringing in his head. He couldn't help wondering if the girl were up to something.

''What cunning strategy?'' Sandy asked, nonplussed.

Kittridge put a hand to his forehead. ''I don't know. What if *she herself* is behind the financial arrangement Chivers made with me? Having seen me beforehand and having found me useful as a protector, might she have decided that I'm an easy mark? A mollycoddle who'll be convenient to smooth her way into society?''

Sandy stirred the brandy in his glass, his eyes troubled. ''Well, what did you expect? That's what that sort of arrangement is all about, isn't it? A cit's getting herself into society?''

''Yes, but if it were the father's idea, it'd be, somehow, more acceptable. There's something *manipulative* about a girl who arranged such matters for herself. Something almost *false*, if she disguises her managing nature behind an oh-so-shy facade.''

''So you think your shy Miss Chivers might turn out to be a manipulating *intrigante*?''

Kittridge peered glumly into his glass. ''It is a real, if repellent, possibility.''

''But only a possibility,'' Sandy pointed out. ''Look on the bright side, old fellow. She may very well be as sweet and innocent as she appears.''

But Kittridge doubted it. Sandy was eternally the optimist, but Kittridge was learning that the dice of fate rarely fell on the bright side.

Not that it mattered very much, he told himself as he got up from the easy chair and stared out the windows with unseeing eyes. If he couldn't marry Elinor, what did it matter whom he married? And if he were to be honest with himself, he'd have to admit he was as much a schemer as Miss Cassandra Chivers. Just as she was using him to win herself a title and a place in society, he was using her to get the financing he needed. Their relationship was a business matter; each expected to pay a price for value received. If the title of viscountess and the entrée into society that his name provided was the price she'd set, he had no objections to paying it. It seemed little enough to pay in exchange for forty thousand pounds.

But why had she found it necessary to be underhanded . . . to keep her identity hidden until the bargain had been made? It seemed an odd ploy. Was there something more to the business than met the eye?

Well, he told himself, time would tell. Meanwhile, he made the bargain, and he had every intention of sticking to it. He would make the girl his wife, and he would be, for all intents and purposes, an honorable husband. But there was one thing he promised himself as he stood there in the window—the little schemer would get no more from him than that.

Chapter Thirteen

Shortly before his wedding day, Kittridge asked Mr. Chivers' permission to hold a private conversation with his bride-to-be. At the appointed time, the night before their wedding day, his lordship called at the house near King's Cross. Eames admitted him, but Miss Penicuick immediately appeared behind the butler and took over his duties. Handing Eames Lord Kittridge's hat and cane, she dismissed the butler and, fluttering about nervously, began to make foolish little remarks to his lordship about her delight at the forthcoming nuptials and her concern that this visit, so close to the time of the wedding, would bring bad luck. It was not until Kittridge gave her a reassuring smile and his promise that this interview would not take long that she finally directed him to a small sitting room at the rear of the house (a room she referred to pompously as the Blue Saloon) and took herself off.

Miss Cassandra Chivers, the bride-to-be, was waiting for him. She looked quite pretty—and properly maidenly and shy—in a pale green round-gown covered with a paisley shawl. He couldn't help admiring her profusion of curly hair which the firelight tipped with glints of reddish gold. Yet the quality that one first noticed about her was her timidity, an impression that was underlined by the heightened color of her cheeks and the trembling of her fingers. It was difficult, seeing her like this, for him to sustain the belief that her shyness was a pose, a ruse that she used to mask her manipulating nature.

She offered him a glass of brandy, which he refused. But

he accepted her invitation to be seated in a chair before the fire, facing her. "Thank you for seeing me tonight, Miss Chivers," he said after a lengthy silence during which they each studied the other with surreptitious glances. "Your Miss Penicuick seems to think this interview will bring a devil's curse upon our heads."

"You mustn't mind her, my lord. She is very superstitious, especially in regard to wedding omens. If it rains tomorrow, she is bound to fall into the dismals."

"Really? Is rain a bad omen for weddings?"

"Oh, yes, my lord, it is *dire*. Have you never heard the saying 'Happy is the bride the sun shines on'?"

He shook his head. "I'm afraid I am woefully ignorant of superstitions. And of wedding omens, too. But now that you've warned me, I shall get down on my knees and pray for sunshine before I close my eyes tonight."

She gave a little gurgle of laughter. "Miss Penicuick will be delighted to hear it."

"But not *you*, ma'am?" he asked in mock alarm. "Have you no concern for the fate of our marital felicity?"

Her expression grew serious. "I must place my hopes for marital felicity on the good sense of the participants, not on the weather."

"Good for you, Miss Chivers, good for you," he said, turning serious himself. "I hope you will think it was good sense that brought me here tonight. I came because I imagine that you must find this situation of ours deucedly awkward."

"Yes," she said. "I do. Very."

"I, too," he admitted. "That's why it seems to me to be necessary that we come to some clear understanding before we make our final vows."

"Yes," she said, quietly encouraging. She sat back against the cushions, feeling a wave of relief. She had agonized all day about the nature of this interview, but now that she saw what his intentions were, her spirits lifted. He wanted to set matters straight between them. If they were to live together in any sort of harmony, they needed to agree on the rules. It was good of him, she thought, to wish to clarify matters before-hand. She peeped over at him and noted that a muscle twitched in his cheek and that his fingers gripped the arm of his chair with white-knuckled tension. She felt a stab of sympathy for him. He was as uneasy about this conversation as she was. This indication of human weakness on his part gave her more confidence in herself.

"We are strangers, after all," he went on. "And marriage is . . . is . . ."

"Intimate?" she offered shyly.

He looked at her thankfully. "Yes, exactly. I want you to know, Miss Chivers, that I have no intention of pushing those . . . er . . . intimacies on you."

Her face grew beet red. "That is . . . kind in you, my lord."

"Not at all. Intimacy, after all, is not something one can negotiate on a marriage contract. It must develop naturally, don't you agree?"

She nodded, her eyes fixed on the hands folded in her lap.

"In the meantime, Miss Chivers," he went on, "while we learn to be comfortable with each other, I'm sure that we can find ways to . . . avoid it."

There was a long, awkward pause. Then, suddenly, she lifted her head and threw him a teasing grin that was as unexpected as it was charming. "Is calling me by my given name one of those 'intimacies' you intend to avoid?"

A laugh broke out of him. "No, of course not," he said, finding himself drawn to the girl against his will. This was not a feeling he wished to encourage, having almost convinced himself that her manner was not sincere. Although he'd thus far found this conversation more pleasant than he'd dared hope and had even found the chit likable, the warning bells in his head had not stopped ringing. Her motives in this affair were not at all clear. Until he understood her nature, he would not permit himself to be an easy mark. It would take more than a small display of charm to win him over.

He sat back in his chair and crossed his arms over his chest. "You're quite right. If we're to endure a long wedded life, we can't be stiffly formal with each other. I certainly can't continue to address you as 'Miss Chivers.' Shall I call you Cassandra?"

"No, please don't," she begged. "I hate that name. Cassandra, the prophetess of doom. Would I be pushing you to too much intimacy to ask you to call me Cassie?"

"No, not at all," he said, a small smile breaking out in spite of his wish to prevent it. The girl had more spirit than he'd originally thought. He'd have to be on his guard. If he didn't keep his instincts on the alert, she might manage to manipulate him quite easily. "I'd be happy to call you Cassie if you'll agree to the equal intimacy of calling me Robbie."

"*Robbie*?" At the thought of using so familiar an appellation, her cheeks turned pink again. "Oh, no, my lord, I couldn't," she objected, her habitual shyness washing over her.

He noticed the quick reddening of her cheeks. "Robert, then," he suggested, admiring her ability to behave with such convincing diffidence. "You cannot continue to address me as 'my lord,' you know. Surely we can compromise on Robert until we grow more . . . accustomed to each other."

"Robert," she murmured, testing it on her tongue. "Yes, I think I can manage that."

"Then that's settled. Now, ma'am, if you please, I'd like to broach the matter that brought me here. It has to do with living arrangements. Have you given the subject any thought?"

She looked puzzled. "Why, no. I suppose I should have, but everything has happened so quickly."

"Yes. But I thought, in all fairness, that we should discuss the subject before the nuptials, in the event that there are some areas of disagreement to iron out."

"Disagreement? But why should—?"

"I assume, ma'am, that you anticipate taking up residence in the London house, is that not so?"

"I . . . suppose so . . . if that is your desire, my lord."

"Actually, it is not what I desire. What I'd really like to do is live in Lincolnshire. Your father has convinced me that the property there could, with proper management, become profitable. It is my most ardent wish to achieve that goal. With the estate making a profit, I could free myself of the remaining encumbrances on the Suffolk property and begin to give your father some return on his investment."

"But, my lord . . . Robert, it is my understanding that the money my father gave you was, in a manner of speaking, a dowry. A dowry is not an investment to be paid back, is it?"

"He may not have meant it to be paid back, my dear, but I shall feel more like a man when I've done it."

"Oh," Cassie murmured, feeling as if she'd been chastised. "I see. Then we must take up residence in Lincolnshire, of course."

"There is no 'of course' about it, ma'am. *Your* wishes must be considered, too. I would understand completely if you objected. All the women in my family prefer London to the country. After all, there is no society in Lincolnshire to compare to that in town. There might be, in Lincolnshire, an occasional Assembly dance or a dinner party with the local gentry, but there would be none of the routs, balls, galas, theater parties, opera evenings, and the other amusements with which town life abounds. So if the thought of quiet country evenings oppresses you, I'd quite understand."

"No, my lord, the thought does not oppress me. Although I've lived in London all my life, I've lived as quietly as any country girl. I shall feel quite at home in Lincolnshire."

"But that quiet life, my dear, was before you had the advantage of my name. I hope you'll not think me a deuced coxcomb for saying that, but surely your father must already have pointed out to you that your life will be quite different as Lady Kittridge. Why else did he arrange these nuptials but to open these doors to you? As my wife, you will be invited everywhere. As long as we remain in town, there will hardly be an evening—particularly in season—when you won't have half a dozen wonderful amusements to choose among. That is what removing to Lincolnshire will deprive you of."

"I'm aware of that, my lord. Please believe me when I say that I would prefer the quiet life. You must have noticed that I am not . . . comfortable in social situations."

He peered at her closely. This was not at all what he expected her to say. Did she truly wish to banish herself to the wilds of Lincolnshire? Was she sincere, or was this part of some deep game she was playing? "Do you mean it, my dear? Living in Lincolnshire would be very dull, I'm afraid.

You must think carefully. I want you to be aware of every option before you make a decision. I realize quite well how much you ladies enjoy town society, and I've been struggling with this problem ever since you accepted my offer. I've even considered the possibility of your remaining in the town house with my mother while I take up a separate residence in Lincolnshire—''

Her eyes flew up to his for an instant and as quickly dropped down to the fingers she was twisting together in her lap. "S-Separate residence?"

"Yes. Such arrangements are not unheard of, you know."

"Would you . . . *wish* to m-make such an arrangement?" she asked in a small voice. The suggestion had come as a blow to her. She understood that this was to be a marriage in name only, but separate residences would be no marriage at all! Why had he suggested such a thing? Was he resentful that he'd had to take her father's aid? And did that resentment include her? "Is a separate residence what you're suggesting?"

He stood up and walked to the fire. "May I speak honestly?" he asked, fixing his eyes on the flames.

"Please."

"Then, frankly, I am not. I think we should take up residence together, and for several good reasons. Firstly, I don't think your father would feel that I was living up to the spirit of our agreement if we did not. A separate residence seems to me to be an evasion of marriage rather than an entering into it, and it would surely seem so to your father. And secondly, though I know that we have agreed to . . . er . . . dispense with the connubial intimacies, I think it important that we present to the world the appearance of true wedlock. If we maintained separate residences, it would be on every tongue that we had made merely a *mariage de convenance*. That sort of gossip would be humiliating to us both, as well as a betrayal of your father's trust in me. For these and other reasons, I think we should agree on living in the same house."

She expelled a long breath. "Yes, I think so, too."

He turned his head and threw her a quizzical glance. "Do you? Then please understand, Cassie, that I intend to abide by *your* decision as to the place where we live. If you wish to live in town, I am quite ready to do so. You needn't make up your mind right now. Think it over for as long as you wish.''

"Thank you, Robert. You are both honest and fair. But I don't need any more time. If the choice is truly mine, I choose Lincolnshire.''

He turned from the fire and looked her in the eye. "Are you certain, Cassie?''

"Yes.''

He breathed a sigh of relief. "Thank you, my dear. I'm very grateful.''

She dropped her eyes from his. "There's no need for gratitude. I made the choice as much for myself as for you.''

"I'm glad of that. This decision will not only help us to avoid the speculation of the *ton* as to the nature of our relationship but will also give our union the best possible start. It goes without saying that we shall spend part of every year in London. I'll not be so selfish as to keep you hidden away forever from the pleasures of town. My plan, then, if you have no objection, is to permit my mother to remain ensconced in the town house, while you and I will remove to the country except for two months in season. I'd like my brother to be with us during those months of the year when he is not in school. My sister will, I expect, remain with her daughters in the London house.''

"I have no objection at all," Cassie assured him. "But as for your sister, doesn't she think the country is a better place than town for bringing up her daughters?''

"One would think so." He peered at her again in surprise. "Would you be *willing* to have them in the country with us? There's plenty of room, of course. The house is enormous, with, I believe, thirty bedrooms. But I've often heard that when two women rule one household, it makes for strife.''

"Oh, no, I don't think that would necessarily be true. I should very much enjoy having children about the house, I think.''

"Then I will certainly suggest it to her." He didn't notice that the words she'd just said had brought the color flooding back to her cheeks. He came away from the fire and up to her chair. Lifting her hand, he took it to his lips. "You've been more considerate than I had any reason to expect, Cassie. Your kindness has made a difficult situation more bearable. It augurs well for our future."

Cassie's hand trembled in his. "Oh, Robert, I hope so," she breathed, trying to stem the emotion that welled up in her chest so overwhelmingly that she feared it might spill over out of her eyes. "I do hope so!"

Chapter Fourteen

They were married by special license at St. Clement Danes on the Strand. The day was cloudy, with a few flurries of snow, but, as Kittridge whispered in his bride's ear, it at least wasn't rain.

It was a brief ceremony, witnessed by only a handful of people. The bride was modestly dressed in a blue walking suit and flowered bonnet and carried a nosegay of yellow roses and white baby's breath that the groom had managed to procure for her. The dowager Lady Kittridge remarked in an undervoice to her daughter that although the bride's bonnet was far from *chic*, she was willing to allow that it was not too dreadfully dowdy.

Sir Philip Sanford stood up with his friend. The rector (a distant relative of the Rossiters) beamed as the bride's father led her to the altar, but his smile was the only one in the chapel. The dowager looked impassive; Eunice looked tragic; Gavin was utterly bored; Sandy bit his lip, disappointed that his prediction that a lucky accident would occur to keep his friend from being leg-shackled to a "manipulative *intrigante*" had not come to pass; Miss Penicuick wept openly; Oliver Chivers—who'd belatedly realized this morning, with an unpleasant start, that his daughter would henceforth be missing from his domicile—was suffering from the most painful second thoughts; the groom was stricken at heart with regrets for what-might-have-been; and the bride, to whose feelings nobody seemed to paying the slightest attention, was terrified. This was the happy beginning to the couple's married life.

In a mere eighteen minutes, it was all over. With the papers signed and the vows taken, there was nothing left but to get through the wedding breakfast that Sandy was hosting at his hotel. With submissive sighs and a noticeable lack of enthusiasm, the wedding party moved out of the church and into the waiting carriages.

Kittridge's man, Loesby, dressed for the occasion with a top hat and a boutonniere in his lapel, organized the logistics of moving the wedding party from the church to the Fenton Hotel. For a man who'd moved mountains of equipment across the Peninsula, the job of herding the wedding party into the three carriages and leading them the short distance to the Fenton was child's play. Before the guests knew it, they were out of the wind, out of their outer garments and ensconced in the comfortable elegance of the hotel's dining room.

The buffet Sandy had ordered turned out to be lavish enough even for the dowager Lady Kittridge's taste. There in the Fenton's private dining salon, on a long table decorated with greens, were platters, trays and tureens loaded with delicacies: ham slices curled around soft cheddar; hot little rolls *à la Duchesse*; a whole, steamed salmon; eggs with truffles; delicately browned lobster cakes; oysters au gratin; cucumbers *béchamel*; fragrant orange peel biscuits; rum and apple pudding with grapes; chewy French nougat cake, surrounded by assorted jellies and creams; and the most delightful French champagne. The sight, smell and taste of such ambrosial viands couldn't fail to lift their spirits, and by the time their plates were loaded and their glasses filled, the wedding guests were almost cheerful. They even sounded quite sincere in their seconding of Sandy's toast to the health of the bride and groom.

After a while, Loesby came in and whispered something into Kittridge's ear. The bridegroom nodded and announced aloud that it was time for him to take his bride away; they had to start out at once for Lincolnshire if they were to reach Highlands without a night's stopover on the road. This announcement brought the festivities to an end, and the entire wedding party wrapped themselves up in their outer garments and trooped out to the street to see the pair off.

Emotions again came to the surface as good-byes were exchanged. The elder Lady Kittridge embraced her son tremblingly, whispering into his ear, "My poor boy, you shouldn't have done it! We don't deserve such a sacrifice!" in a shaken voice. Eunice kissed her brother's cheek and, glancing over at the "drab little nobody" who was now her sister-in-law, promptly dissolved in tears. Miss Penicuick (having decided, with Cassie's urging, to remain with Mr. Chivers, who would need his housekeeper now more than Cassie would) threw her arms round the bride in a kind of hysteria, as if she feared they would never see each other again. Sandy, painfully aware of the difference that Kittridge must see between the glorious Elinor and this shy, mousy creature who was now his bride, shook his friend's hand with energetic sympathy and promised, with a forced smile and an encouraging slap on the back, to come up to Highlands for a visit within the month. Mr. Chivers pressed an envelope stuffed full of bank notes into Cassie's hand, muttering in her ear that there wasn't a girl in the world who didn't need a bit of pin money, and adding, "If that damn fellow don't treat ye just right, y're to come 'ome at once, my love, do ye 'ear me? At *once*! And whatever it costs, I'll rid ye of 'im." In short, everyone seemed utterly miserable.

With the good-byes said, Loesby climbed up on the driver's box. Kittridge helped his bride up the steps of their heavily loaded carriage and jumped in after her. There was a great deal of handwaving as the bridal carriage (a magnificent new equipage in shiny blue with the Kittridge coat of arms emblazoned on the doors—a gift from his lordship's new father-in-law) rolled off down the street. The little group stood huddled together gazing glumly after it. The mood that had clouded the wedding ceremony seemed to have returned in full force.

At that moment, a thin ray of sunshine broke through an opening in the clouds and shone wanly down on them. "Oh, praise be!" Miss Penicuick exclaimed in relief, sniffing into an already wet handkerchief. "The sun! That means the bride will be happy!"

"I hope, ma'am," Eunice said coldly, "that the superstition includes the groom, also."

"Of course it does," Sandy insisted with his determined optimism. "We all wish for them both to have a happy life together."

"Yes," the dowager muttered, "but it isn't very likely."

Nobody contradicted her.

Chapter Fifteen

The newlywed couple had spent only two nights in the manor house at Highlands before winter set in, in earnest and a month too soon. The temperature dropped so sharply that no one in Lincolnshire ventured out of doors unless through dire necessity. Then, after three days of freezing cold, the temperature abated just enough to usher in a snowfall of at least a foot. Kittridge, who'd planned to traverse all the grounds of the estate with Mr. Griswold, his land agent, as soon as the weather warmed, had to postpone everything. Cassie, who'd accepted the responsibility for hiring a household staff, was unable to interview any of the village lasses, for it was impossible for them to come up to the manor house. The couple had to make do with only the Whitlocks, the elderly man and wife who'd maintained the house during the years when it had been unoccupied, and Loesby, who acted as butler, valet and general factotum.

Kittridge spent a good part of each day in a small room near the library which he designated as his study, going over estate maps, blueprints and accounts. Cassie, meanwhile, tried to make habitable the few rooms they needed for daily living. With Loesby's help, she looked into all the unused rooms and made notes of which drapes, pictures, carpets and pieces of furniture were in good condition or which she particularly liked. Then she went to Kittridge's study to ask his permission to move things about. When she got to his door, however, her usual timidity took hold of her, and she knocked so shyly that he didn't at first hear her. When she was finally admitted, she told him what she'd been doing and hesitantly made her request, fully expecting a reprimand.

He looked at her in surprise. "You don't have to ask, my dear," he pointed out. "This is your house as much as mine. More, if you remember that it was your 'dowry' that made it possible for us to live here."

"That's not how I feel about it," she responded, forgetting her shyness in her determination to make him understand fully the liberties she intended to take with the furnishings. "These are things that have been in your family for generations. There is a tradition about these things, you know. In some families, the placement of a portrait or the arrangement of the Chinese vases on a mantelpiece is sacrosanct. So you see, Robert, I'd certainly understand if you'd prefer not making changes. I wouldn't wish to upset tradition."

He smiled up at her, noting that this was the first speech she'd made to him that didn't seem painfully shy. "I'm not sentimental about furnishings, Cassie. To be honest, I don't think I ever notice them. Please do as you like, and don't give tradition another thought."

Thus, happily free to rearrange the household as she wished, Cassie promptly set to work to make their rooms comfortable. With the help of Loesby and the Whitlocks, she removed and replaced the drapes in the smallest sitting room, brought in a pair of wing chairs from the drawing room, and rearranged the furniture so that all the seating would be close to the fireplace. The arrangement was especially designed so that it would be a room in which they could be cozy in the cold evenings.

That completed, they cleaned the two bedrooms from top to bottom, replaced worn carpets and hangings with better ones from other rooms, and hung various paintings—still life studies and florals, mostly, that Cassie discovered in unused rooms—on walls that had been unadorned or hung with drab, dismal portraits. Soon the bedrooms were comfortable and cheery. And although no guests were expected in this dreadful weather, they readied a guest bedroom, too, just as a precaution against the unexpected.

It was dusty, strenuous, tiring work, but Cassie enjoyed it.

Not only did the work keep her feeling useful, but the resulting improvement in the appearance of their surroundings pleased her. When Robert remarked, one evening after dinner, about the cheeriness of the sitting room, she was quite overcome. The kind word from him was the reward she'd wished for.

Thus encouraged, Cassie started redecorating the Great Hall, a high, vaulted entryway large enough to accommodate the stairway which bifurcated at the second floor and descended in two sweeping arches to the first. She and her willing assistants polished the marble floors, scrubbed and whitewashed the smoke-blackened walls, replaced the shabby carpet with a gold and blue gem of a rug she discovered in a third-floor bedroom, installed a claw-footed chaise against the south wall opposite the doorway beneath the curve made by the two stairways and removed the large, forbidding portrait of the first viscount that hung over it. Cassie confided to Loesby that she found the man's face frightening and felt the portrait gave a gloomy greeting to anyone coming in the door for the first time. She replaced the portrait with a wonderful landscape she'd found in an unused sitting room in the building's west wing. It was an early work of John Constable, the landscape painter who was creating a great stir in London these days. Cassie believed the painting to be a real treasure—a country scene with a pond and a haywagon that was a joy to look at. She and Loesby agreed that it was a great improvement over the gloomy portrait as the first thing to greet the eye of new arrivals. "Makes the 'ole 'ouse look 'appy an' new," Mrs. Whitlock exclaimed when she saw the transformed hall. "Y're a wonder, m'lady, an' that's a fact!"

"She *is* a wonder," Loesby said to his captain that night, relating the day's events as he helped Kittridge remove his boots. "Seems t' me y're luckier in yer bride than ye 'ad any right t' expect."

But Kittridge, still unsure of Cassie's true nature, only grunted.

His lordship went to bed feeling irritable. The wind had shifted to the west and was whistling ominously outside his windows. The sound, so cold and barren, exacerbated his

feeling of loneliness. It seemed to him that the already prolonged cold snap that had kept him housebound since his
arrival would continue on forever. The weather, like his life,
showed no promise or hope of change. Very sorry for himself, his last thought before he drifted off was to wonder
disconsolately if there would ever be a spring for him.

Later that night, his lordship was awakened from a fitful
sleep by a high-pitched, trilling sound that seemed like an
inhuman, eerie shriek. *It's only the wind*, he told himself as
he tried to burrow deeper in his bedclothes and catch at the
skirt of sleep before it flitted away from him altogether. But
he soon realized that the sound was not the wind. A whiny
sound accompanied the blowing but was more intermittent,
and its pitch was much higher. What on earth was it? It was
just such sounds, he thought, that made people believe in
ghosts.

Knowing that he would get no more sleep as long as that
eerie wail continued, he threw off his comforter and, after
lighting his bedside candle, put on a robe and slippers. With
the candle held out before him, he opened his door and came
face-to-face with another candle. It took a moment before he
could make out that it was being carried by his wife. "Good
God, Cassie," he exclaimed, "you startled me. Did that
unearthly shrieking rouse you, too?"

"Yes. Isn't it awful? Mrs. Whitlock tells me it's the Rossiter
ghost. She sounded rather proud of him, actually. Says he
makes Highlands a real castle. She warned me that he comes
calling when the wind blows from the west."

"Then, if it's a ghost, why aren't you hiding under your
bedclothes, as any properly frightened female would do?"

She grinned at him over the smoky flame of the candle. "I
suppose I would, if I really thought it *was* a ghost. But I don't
believe in such things, I'm afraid."

"Don't believe in them?" he mocked. "What sort of
unnatural female are you?"

"Unnatural enough to have grave doubts about the existence of supernatural phenomena. I suppose you must think
me dreadfully prosy."

"On the contrary, ma'am. I begin to think you are unusually sensible. But if you don't believe it's a ghost, why didn't you simply turn over, cover your ears and go back to sleep?''

"Well, you see, the noise is so loud, I feared it would disturb you and everyone else in the household. So I decided to try to track it down.''

"All by yourself?'' He lifted his candle higher and looked closely at her face. Her eyes glowed with the flame's reflection, and he was struck by the charm of her nighttime appearance. Her unruly hair had been crammed into a large, ruffled nightcap that was tied tightly under her pointed chin, but little rebellious tendrils had escaped from the sides and back and made her look like an adorably blowsy, if elfin, scrubwoman. "Is this the shy Cassie speaking?'' he demanded. "How can you pretend to be so timid and self-effacing in society and still be brave enough to go searching all alone through a large, dark house for a nonexistent ghost?''

Flustered by the sudden turn of the conversation to her own personality, Cassie colored to her ears. But she managed to answer without stammering. "People and society make me timid, my lord, not empty houses.''

"Nevertheless, ma'am, it was a foolhardy intention. You are not yet familiar with the byways and passages of this enormous, cavernous edifice. What if you'd fallen down a stair or tripped on a carpet and fainted? We might not have found you for days!''

"Are you saying, my lord, that I may not go?'' she asked, her voice plainly revealing her disappointment.

The wind rose at that moment, and the eerie scream so intensified in volume that it became decidedly unpleasant. "Well, we can't let that horrid wail go on forever, I suppose. Come. We'll *both* search out this ghostly shrieker.''

He took her hand in his and, with a long, purposeful stride, led her down the hall. She had to scurry on her tiny, slippered feet to keep up with him, her full-skirted nightgown flapping behind her in the draughty corridor. The wail grew louder as they turned the corner to the west wing. "It seems to be coming from the corner room at the end of the corridor,'' he said.

He was right. When they came up to the door, they could

tell at once that the sound was emanating from within the closed room. "You wait here," he ordered. "Don't move from this doorway until I come back."

"Oh, no, Robert," she cried, unwilling to be prevented from partaking in the solution of this mystery and even more unwilling to let go of his hand. "I want to go with you!"

"Very well, ma'am," he said with mock foreboding, "but if you're snatched away by evil spirits, never to be seen again, don't blame me."

The wind and the wail rose again, so loudly that she shivered. "If I'm snatched away," she rejoined, laughing nervously, "I shall return, most appropriately, in spectral form, and then you and Mrs. Whitlock can boast that Highlands has *two* shrieking ghosts in residence."

He laughed, too, but he opened the door with gingerly care and held his candle aloft for a good look within before setting foot in the room. It was one of the unused bedrooms, a large, square, corner room with windows on two walls. It was icy cold. They both drew their robes closer about them as they stepped over the threshold. Robert looked round in distaste. The room was full of cobwebs, and the air of ghostliness was emphatically underlined by the pale dustcovers that were draped over the furniture. "Ugh!" Robert grunted. "One has to admit this is the perfect place for the Rossiter ghost to haunt. Are you sure, my dear, that you still believe the ghost to be nonexistent?"

A shriek echoed shrilly through the room. "Yes," Cassie retorted bravely, "but I'll l-leave it to you to look under the b-bed."

"Thank you," he said dryly. "I suppose you wish me to look under all the Holland covers, too."

"No," she said, suddenly alert. "I think the sound is coming from here. This window . . . on the west wall."

He listened. "I think you're right. Stand back, girl, for I'm about to throw open the drapes. If a transparent figure with black eyeholes is standing behind them, flee for your life, for that's exactly what I intend to do."

He flung the drapes open, releasing a cloud of dust into the air that caused them both to cough. But there was nothing behind the drapes but a large, multipaned window with a white, moon-washed landscape beyond. "Dash it all," Robert muttered, "the damnable fellow's eluded us again."

As if in response, the wail came up loud and clear. It seemed to mock them for a moment, and then it died down again. There was no doubt that the sound came from the window. Robert lifted his candle and peered at one pane after another. Suddenly the candleflame flickered and went out. "A draught," he said triumphantly. "Right—" He leaned toward the pane he was examining and ran his fingers round the frame. "—here!"

"I don't understand," Cassie said, puzzled. "What has a draught to do with it? Surely a little draught can't make such a sound."

"Wait until it shrieks again. I'll show you."

Of course, because they were waiting for it, the sound did not come for several minutes. But as soon as it rose up again, Robert put a hand flat against the pane, as if to hold it steady. The shriek stopped at once.

"It was a slight rattle in the pane," Robert explained. "The putty holding this pane in place has dried and fallen off, so there's a small space between the frame and the glass. When the wind blows strongly enough, it sets the pane vibrating so quickly that it makes a whine."

Cassie could scarcely believe it. "But . . . so loudly?"

"Yes. It's like rubbing your finger round the edge of a crystal goblet. Didn't you ever do that as a child? The action of your finger sets the crystal vibrating, and the glass 'sings.' The faster you run your finger on the rim, the shriller the sound. Eunice and I used to do it in the nursery. It made the governess frantic. Here. Try it for yourself. As soon as the wind comes up, put your hand on the windowpane."

Cassie did so. When the wind came up and the wail began to shrill, she could feel the glass vibrate.

"There," he said triumphantly. "Feel it tremble? That's what's making the whine. Now press hard to keep the glass steady."

She pressed, and the noise ceased at once. "That's marvelous," she said in amazement. "I wonder if all ghosts can be so rationally explained."

"Probably," he said, relighting his candle with the flame of hers. He took her hand and led her out of the room. "They used to talk about a ghost at the Langstons' when I was a boy . . ." He entertained her with the tale of the "chimney ghost" at the Langston estate as they strolled back down the corridor to their own rooms, relating how he'd become convinced that there was something loose in the chimney that made the ghostly rattles. He'd begged the Langstons to let him climb the chimney, but they'd refused. "I think they, like Mrs. Whitlock, liked believing that the manor house was haunted," he remarked as they came up to Cassie's door.

"Yes," she sighed as she turned to bid him good night, "I think it will be a real disappointment to Mrs. Whitlock when she learns there's no Rossiter ghost. Do you think we ought to keep our knowledge to ourselves and let the ghost wail at will whenever the wind is in the west?"

"Not on your life. I want to be able to sleep soundly at night. I shall tell Loesby to putty away the ghost first thing in the morning." He squeezed Cassie's hand. "Good night, my dear. I was glad to have had you at my side through this frightening ordeal. You've been a most intrepid adventurer tonight."

She gave an embarrassed little nod and whisked herself off into her room before he could see the blush of pleasure that suffused her cheeks. He, on his part, found himself smiling as he returned to his bed. It was the first time in weeks he'd smiled like that. Perhaps Loesby was right, he thought, as his eyes closed. Perhaps he *was* luckier in his bride than he had a right to expect.

Chapter Sixteen

Everything seemed cheerier the next morning. The wind had died, the sun shone and the temperature rose. Kittridge lingered over breakfast with his wife for almost an hour before taking himself off to his study. Cassie hummed to herself as she worked in her sitting room, mending a pair of gold velvet drapes for the drawing room. The future seemed to have promise after all.

But the end of the day changed everything. A carriage drove up to the door through the snowbanks just at sunset, and out jumped Sir Philip Sanford, their first visitor. He had started out for Lincolnshire just before the snowstorm and had been forced to put up at a nondescript hostelry for three boring days. "As soon as I heard that the roads were open, I came posthaste the rest of the way," he told his host as Loesby relieved him of his greatcoat. "Can't tell you how glad I am to be here at last."

"You started out before the snow?" Kittridge asked incredulously. "We'd been here less than a week. Didn't anyone ever tell you, you gudgeon, that newlyweds should be given some time alone before seeing guests? Have you never heard of a honeymoon?"

"Of course I have. But it's not as if you made a lovematch. I thought, under the circumstances, that you'd be glad to see me."

"I am glad to see you. I was only twitting you. And here's Cassie come down to greet you. I'll wager she's just as happy to see you as I am. It's been almost a fortnight since she's had any face to look at but mine and the servants'."

Cassie greeted their guest with shy warmth, but in truth she was not as glad to see him as she pretended. She had met Kittridge's friend only briefly, at the wedding, and felt him to be a stranger. Since strangers always made her uncomfortable, she had to strain to appear at ease. Sandy, however, was not the sort to put a hostess on edge. His moon-shaped face was cheerful, and conversation flowed easily from his tongue. It wasn't long before he won Cassie's liking, and within an hour from the time of his arrival, they were all three joking comfortably together in the sitting room like old friends.

It wasn't until dinner time that the mood changed. They had just finished the first course, a modest offering of cabbage soup, filet of sole and buttered carrots that Mrs. Whitlock had concocted at the last minute, when Sandy remembered that Eunice had sent a packet of letters that had been delivered to her brother at the London address. He withdrew the packet from his coat pocket and tossed it across the table to his friend. While they waited for Loesby to serve the second course, Kittridge flipped through the envelopes. When he spied two large, square buff-colored envelopes, his expression changed. Without a word of explanation, he excused himself, picked up the envelopes and left the table. He did not return to the dining room. Cassie and Sandy were forced to conclude the meal without him.

By the time he did return, more than an hour had passed. Cassie and their guest had repaired to the sitting room and were making desultory conversation while Sandy sipped at a glass of port. Kittridge seemed not the same fellow that he'd been earlier. While his remarks to Sandy were friendly enough, his attitude toward his wife was formal and distant. Cassie couldn't understand it. What had happened to make him angry with her? She could only surmise that she'd committed some blunder that had earned his disapproval, but what that blunder was she couldn't imagine.

She lowered her head and sat in silent misery as Kittridge and Sandy conversed. They spoke of political events, discussed the illness of one of their mutual friends and reminisced at length about life in the Dragoons. Occasionally Sandy directed a remark in Cassie's direction, which she answered with a monosyllable, but her husband never turned his head in her direction. She endured his unkindness as long as she could, and then she excused herself and went to bed. She cried for several hours before she fell asleep.

Kittridge appeared in the breakfast room the next morning before Sandy came down. Cassie, heavy-eyed and miserable, was poking desultorily at a coddled egg. "Good morning, my dear," her husband said in an ordinary voice as he helped himself to the eggs and hot muffins that Loesby had set out on the sideboard. "I hope that Sandy's unexpected arrival did not discompose you."

"No, not at all," she murmured. "He is an easygoing guest. I . . . enjoyed his company."

"Yes, so did I." He took his place opposite her and began to eat. "I only asked because I thought you were unduly reticent last evening."

"Was I?" She looked across the table at him and took a deep breath. "If I was," she ventured bravely, "it was because I had the feeling that . . . that I had angered you."

His eyebrows rose in genuine surprise. "Angered me? You? Why on earth would you think so?"

She fixed her eyes on her egg. "Because you seemed . . . short with me."

"You're imagining things, Cassie. I don't remember being short with you, ever."

"It seemed so to me. You left the table before finishing your dinner, if you remember, and when you returned, you . . . you . . ." Here her courage failed her.

"Yes?" he prodded, studying her with a frown.

"Never mind," she muttered, reaching for the teapot. "It's not important."

"But it must be important. If my behavior offended you, you must say so. It won't do to keep silent on such matters."

"Well, Robert, if you insist on it, the truth is that you scarcely said a word to me all evening," she burst out bluntly.

"Oh. I see." He put down his fork, his brow furrowed. "I'm sorry, Cassie. I'd had some letters that . . . well, that spoiled my mood. But they had nothing to do with you, I assure you."

"Was that it?" she asked, shamed. "Now *I'm* sorry." She'd made a fuss for no reason. His letters had brought him bad news, and she'd thought about nothing but her own feelings. Now her sympathy was all for him. "I should not have taken offense. Forgive me, Robert. Was your news very troublesome?"

"No, nothing worth speaking of. Will you pass the teapot, my dear? I wonder if Sandy intends to sleep the morning away."

Recognizing that he had purposely turned the subject, she had no choice but to let the matter drop.

For the rest of the day, Kittridge went out of his way to be kind to her. Her company was requested for every activity the gentlemen engaged in; they even invited her to watch them play billiards. By evening they were so cozy together that Cassie could hardly believe her own ease of mind.

After dinner, the two friends insisted on teaching Cassie to play Ombre, a perfect card game for their circumstances, because it was three-handed. Her innocent enthusiasm for the game delighted the gentlemen, and when, at the end, she so far forgot her shyness as to give a loud curse when she lost, crying out, "Blast it, I should have played the six!" they all had a hearty laugh.

In the days that followed, Kittridge, busy making plans to renovate the farm buildings, expand the sheep herds and build new housing for tenants, found it necessary to go out with his land agent, Mr. Griswold, for several hours at a time, leaving Cassie to entertain their visitor. This task proved to be more pleasant than she expected. Sandy was always boyishly open and cheerful. And when he discovered that she'd been spending her days exploring the unopened rooms, looking for whatever small treasures of art or furnishings she could find, he eagerly requested permission to join her on her rambles.

They spent many agreeable hours exploring the house together. They dusted old paintings, peeped under Holland covers, and studied old vases for identifying marks. When they found many of their discoveries to be in an alarming state of disrepair, they decided to make a workshop of one of the third-floor rooms, where they could touch up the gilt on shabby picture frames, glue broken bits of porcelain together and refinish old pieces of furniture. The *ton* of London might have found such activities eccentric for a viscountess and a peer of the realm to indulge in, but, as Sandy pointed out, there were many among the *ton* whose eccentricities were much more reprehensible. "Besides," he added, "who in London would ever know?"

The indispensible Loesby installed a large wooden slab on two sawhorses as a worktable for them and supplied them with paints, brushes, sandpaper and tools. The two spent many hours contentedly laboring at restoring the many treasures the household contained.

During these explorations and restoration activities, Cassie found Sandy so easygoing and companionable that she forgot to be shy. On his part, Sandy discovered that the girl he'd thought too mousy and colorless for his friend was, instead, intelligent, witty and charming. Very soon, he completely forgot that he had ever thought otherwise.

One evening, after he'd spent a week in their company, Sandy announced to his friend Robbie that he'd decided to extent his stay another fortnight. "Might just as well," he explained. "I have no pressing engagements in town this month, and I'd as soon spend my evenings here quietly as dash about town escorting insipid females to operas and balls and such."

Kittridge nodded in acquiescence. Cassie had already retired, but the two men had remained in their easy chairs at the sitting room fire. Their feet were propped up on the hearth, and they were contentedly drinking brandies from large snifters. "Stay as long as you like, old man," Kittridge said. "As far as I'm concerned, you're welcome for as long as you can endure this dull, bucolic life."

"I don't find it dull. Surprising, isn't it, that after the excitement of those long years of army life and then months of living in town, I can still enjoy the utter peace of the country?"

"No, not surprising. It's your nature, Sandy. You always see the best in everything."

"Are you saying that you don't?" Sandy studied his friend

with sudden concern. "I thought you were beginning to find contentment, Robbie. Am I wrong?"

Kittridge shrugged. "I'm not discontent. I enjoy the challenge of estate management, at least so far. The days are not dull."

"But . . . ?" Sandy prodded.

His friend lowered his head. "But this is not the life I'd dreamed of."

"I know that. But, Robbie, you should consider yourself lucky. Cassie has turned out to be a gem, don't you agree?"

"Yes, I suppose so." Kittridge took a melancholy sip of his drink. "At least you and Loesby are agreed on it."

"But not you?"

"I said yes, didn't I? My wife is a pearl beyond price." He gave a short, bitter laugh. "And with a forty thousand pound dowry, I must consider myself fortunate indeed."

Sandy's genial face contorted into an unaccustomed glare. "She don't deserve that tone, Robbie. I think she *is* a pearl beyond price."

A shadow of pain darkened Kittridge's eyes. "Yes, I suppose she is. But you see, Sandy, I thought, once, that I would wed a diamond."

Chapter Seventeen

The weather warmed, the snow melted, and the inhabitants of Lincolnshire emerged from hibernation. Wagons again rolled on the roadways, and tradesmen appeared at the kitchen door with foodstuffs and supplies. Cassie began to interview candidates for staff positions in the household, and, with Loesby's help and Sandy's good-natured meddling, hired two housemaids, a scullery maid, an assistant cook to help Mrs. Whitlock in the kitchen, and a laundress. She left it to Loesby to engage footmen and stable help.

With the staff thus amplified, Cassie set about enlarging their living area. In addition to arranging for pleasant housing for the staff, she brightened up the dining room, readied a second guest room, ordered the new maids to clean and refresh the library and had the breakfast room repainted a sunny yellow. The only room she left untouched was the drawing room, explaining to Sandy that, since she'd taken out the best pieces for their sitting room, she was waiting for the opportunity to buy new furniture for the drawing room with the "pin money" her father had given her on her wedding day.

Sandy was still comfortably in residence when another carriage bearing guests arrived at their door. It was Eunice and her daughters. Kittridge, just returning from an outing with his land agent, was the first to greet them. "What a delightful surprise," he welcomed, picking up both his nieces in his arms.

"The girls insisted on seeing their Uncle Robbie before

winter would make the trip north quite impossible," Eunice babbled, kissing her brother with warm affection. "Besides," she added, whispering with naughty malice in his ear, "I thought you would be dying of boredom by this time, stuck away here with no one to talk to but your mousy wife, so I came to save you."

But Kittridge was too engrossed in the children's happy chatter to pay her any heed.

The hallway was in veritable chaos by the time Cassie and Sandy came down from the third floor (where they'd been happily engaged in refinishing a fine old Henry Holland pier table) to see what was causing the commotion. The scene they came upon made them blink in astonishment. Mr. Whitlock and the two new footmen were running in and out, bringing in a mountain of boxes; the little girls were squealing with delight as their uncle tossed them, one after the other, in the air; the maids were scurrying about trying to help the new arrivals remove their outer garments; Miss Roffey, the governess, was attempting to calm the children's excitement; and Mrs. Whitlock was following Loesby (who himself was directing the footmen's placement of the luggage) about the hallway, attempting to discover how many mouths she would be expected to feed and when she would be expected to feed them.

Cassie hastily removed the soiled smock she was wearing and, acutely embarrassed by her stained fingers and general dishabille (especially in comparison to Eunice, who was resplendent in purple half-mourning), came slowly forward to welcome her guests. "Lady Yarrow," she said, flushing, "what a lovely surprise!"

"Ah, there you are, my dear," Eunice said, touching her sister-in-law's cheek with her own. "I was wondering where you were hiding. And *Sandy*! I had no idea you were still—" At that moment, her eye fell on the Constable painting on the south wall. "Good God, Robbie, what have you *done*?" she shrieked. "You've taken away the *portrait*!"

Cassie whitened. "The . . . portrait?" she gasped.

Kittridge set little Greta on her feet. "I don't know what you're talking about, Eunice. What portrait?"

"I think she means the p-painting that used to hang there . . . on the south w-wall," Cassie stammered, trembling in guilt and shame.

"Of course that's what I mean. The portrait of our great-grandfather, Algernon Arthur Rossiter!"

"Oh, that," Kittridge said carelessly. "It must be somewhere about. Why all the fuss?"

Eunice stamped her foot petulantly. "But he belongs *here*! He's *always* been here. Really, Robbie, how *can* you have been so heedless of family tradition as to have taken him down?"

"*I* t-took him down, your ladyship," Cassie admitted miserably. "I didn't think . . . I'm sorry. I'll restore him to his rightful place this v-very day, I promise."

"There, you see? Nothing to fly into alt over," Kittridge said calmly, picking Greta up again and taking Della by the hand. "Cassie will set things to rights. Meanwhile, come upstairs, everyone, and let's sort out where you will all stay."

Eunice, satisfied by Cassie's promise, dropped the subject and followed her brother and the children up the stairs. Miss Roffey, Loesby and the servants trooped up after them. Cassie, shaken, just stood and watched. Sandy came up behind her and put a hand on her shoulder. "Don't take it so hard, Cassie," he said consolingly. "Eunice can be overbearing sometimes, but she's a good sort, really."

Cassie, who'd been hurt at school by just such "good sorts," was not consoled. "Is she?" she muttered dejectedly.

"Yes, she really is. I've known her for years, and I swear she can be the sweetest, most generous—"

Cassie, who'd been snubbed by her sister-in-law at their first meeting at the wedding, was not convinced. "I'm afraid you're blinded, Sandy—either by your natural optimism or by infatuation."

"*Infatuation?*" He drew himself up in real offense. "That's a jingle-brained thing to say."

Cassie was startled by the vehemence of his reaction. She turned to him in astonishment. "Heavens, Sandy, have I hit on something?"

Sandy began to utter a loud protest, but, too honest to maintain a pretense, stopped himself and shrugged. "I've always had a secret fancy for her," he admitted, his moon face reddening. "But that doesn't mean I condone her behavior when she acts so deucedly high-handed. She had no right to order you about. Robbie should have put her in her place. I'll have a word with him."

"No, please, Sandy," Cassie begged, a look of alarm leaping into her eyes. "Don't say anything to him. Robert is right. It is nothing to make a fuss over. You must promise not to devil Robert with this matter."

Sandy, not one who liked to indulge in arguments, promised. "But you must make me a promise, too," he bargained. "You must stop looking so Friday-faced. One would think, looking at you, that you've been bested in battle."

"I *have* been bested," she pointed out.

"Not on your life," Sandy declared. "The battle's not over yet."

Cassie smiled at him wanly. "I hope you're right. Meanwhile, for your sake, I'm glad we have Lady Yarrow's company."

He eyed her suspiciously. "If you're getting matchmaking ideas, Cassie, put them out of your mind. Eunice doesn't give me a passing thought. I'm not particularly delighted that she's here. But the children will be an entertaining addition to our circle."

"Yes, they will." She gave him a real smile at last and took his arm. "Come upstairs with me, Sandy, and let's see if we can find a suitable place for a nursery."

Sandy's promise prevented him from giving his friend Robbie a good scold. Loesby, however, was under no such constraints. "Yer sister likes t' rule the roost, don't she, Cap'n?" he remarked while laying out Lord Kittridge's evening clothes. "If I was yer wife, me nose'd be out o' joint."

"Would it indeed?" Kittridge asked absently as he buttoned his shirtsleeve. "And why is that?"

" 'Cause yer sister 'ad no right to order 'er t' replace the damn portrait, that's why. Me an' yer missus, 'er ladyship I mean, took real pains t' fix up the entryway. Lady Yarrow 'ad no right t' spoil it.''

Kittridge made a dismissive gesture. ''Confound it, Loesby, it's only a portrait. It doesn't spoil anything. Come, man, help me with this damnable neckerchief instead of moping about over female foolishness.''

By dinner time the forbidding portrait of the first viscount had been restored to its original place. Unfortunately for Cassie, however, Eunice's desire for restoration did not stop there. No sooner had her bags been unpacked than Eunice ordered that her bedroom be returned to its original solemnity (requiring Cassie to search for hours to find where she had stored the dismal paintings she'd taken from the room). Eunice also rejected Cassie's suggestion to locate the nursery in a bright suite of rooms with south-facing windows. She preferred instead to use the old nursery where she'd spent summers as a child. Ignoring Cassie's shyly offered observation that the north-facing nursery might have been pleasant in the summer but might be hard to keep warm in this season, Eunice insisted not only on using those rooms, but on keeping everything in them just as they were when she was a child. Cassie, not able to bring herself to argue, felt as if she'd lost another skirmish.

During the days that followed, Eunice steadily usurped Cassie's place as mistress of the house. Having long been accustomed to running a household (her own with Yarrow and her mother's as well) without opposition, she took over the reins of household management at Highlands without giving a second thought to Cassie's superior claim to the position. Cassie, on the other hand, gave over those reins without a struggle. She had suffered humiliation at the hands of just such strong personalities at school and hadn't learned any means of survival except complete withdrawal. She thought about what Sandy had said about a battle, but she was no soldier. She didn't know the first thing about fighting. So, reverting to her earlier habits, she retired into her shell and became just what Eunice expected her to be—a mouse.

Chapter Eighteen

Within a week, Eunice had enlarged the staff by six: she'd hired a seamstress, a children's nurse, a butler, an abigail and dresser for her own use, and a drawing master for little Della. She also had taken over the selection of the daily menus, the arranging of the household staff's work schedule, and the choice of activities for the day for everyone in the household but her brother. Although there was an undercurrent of discontent in the household with this new arrangement, little was said aloud. Everyone felt that, since Lady Yarrow was only visiting for a few weeks, things would soon return to normal.

But, as Kittridge had long ago suggested, two women heading one household leads to strife. And strife was about to burst forth.

It came about when Eunice decided that the drawing room had to be made immediately habitable. She didn't see how they could exist without it. Using the little sitting room as a drawing room, as the family had been doing before she arrived, was, she declared, vulgar and gauche. She therefore ordered the footmen to take the chairs and furnishings that Cassie had removed from the drawing room for furnishing the sitting room and restore them to their original positions in the drawing room.

Cassie endured the denuding of her sitting room without a word. Sandy, appalled at Eunice's arrogance, asked Cassie why on earth she'd permitted it, but Cassie only said it didn't matter.

The work was completed in midafternoon of the very day

Eunice instigated it, and she promptly put the room to use. She informed everyone that tea would be served, today and every day hence, in the drawing room.

Kittridge, engrossed in studying the intricacies of sheep breeding, was not aware of any of this. But on the day of the opening of the drawing room, he ceased his labors early and decided to go up to the nursery to spend an hour playing with his nieces. He found Miss Roffey there all alone. "Sir Philip came up and invited the children down to tea," she informed him.

He quickly ran down the stairs again. At the bottom he was accosted by a rotund stranger, who bowed with pompous formality and said, "Lady Yarrow is awaiting you in the drawing room, my lord."

"And who might you be?" his lordship demanded.

"I'm Dickle, my lord. The new butler."

"Oh? Lady Kittridge didn't tell me she'd engaged a butler," Kittridge muttered, puzzled.

"It was Lady Yarrow who engaged me," Dickle said.

"She did, did she? Seems to me I heard that she engaged a nursemaid and an abigail, too." His brows drew together in annoyance. "I think I'll have a word with Lady Yarrow," he said ominously.

"Yes, my lord," said the butler, who, though he guessed that his lordship seemed not to approve of his being hired, did not show a sign of distress in his impassive face. "You'll find her in the drawing room."

Kittridge wondered why his sister wanted him in the unused, overly large and draughty drawing room, but he set off down the hall. Before reaching his destination, however, he heard the sound of a child's laughter from the little sitting room and looked inside. He gaped in dismay at the sight that met his eyes. The room was empty of all furniture except a small table near the window. The large carpet that Cassie had installed was gone, and only a small four-by-six rug had been placed near the fire to replace it. Sandy was sitting on the rug, a teacup and saucer on the floor beside him, playing spillikins with Della, while Cassie was seated on the hearth with little Greta in her lap. She was feeding the child some hot tea with a spoon. "Good God!" Kittridge gasped. "What's *happened* here?"

"Uncew Wobit! Uncew Wobit!" Greta cried, trying to leap from Cassie's lap.

"Ah, Robbie," Sandy greeted, grinning up at him, "here you are at last! If you hadn't buried yourself away in your study all day, you'd have discovered that the drawing room's been restored. Your tea awaits you there."

"I'm winning, Uncle Robert," Della bragged, indicating the pieces scattered on the rug.

But her uncle scarcely heard her. "I don't understand," he said in confusion. "I thought, Cassie, that you prefer using this room."

Cassie threw him a nervous glance. "Eunice feels strongly that a small sitting room like this is a poor substitute for a proper drawing room."

"*Eunice* feels so? And you *agree* with her?" He ran a bewildered hand through his hair. "Then why aren't you there, taking your tea?"

"The room was too cold for the children," Sandy said, "so we took our cups and came here."

"Little Greta was shivering," Cassie added apologetically.

"I was shivewing, Uncew Wobit," Greta grinned, proud of being talked about.

Kittridge stepped over the threshold, still confused and dismayed. "Knowing that the drawing room is a draughty barn, why on earth, Cassie, did you permit Eunice to do this? I thought we were all agreed that we were more comfortable here."

Cassie didn't know what to say. "Well, you see, I . . . I . . ."

Sandy came to her aid. "When does your sister Eunice ever ask permission?" he asked sardonically.

As the situation began to become clear to him, his lordship's expression hardened. "Are you suggesting, Sandy, that Eunice took it upon herself, without asking Cassie, to re-arrange this house?"

"So it seems," Sandy responded carelessly, turning back to his game.

"Is this true, Cassie?"

Cassie's eyes met his, wavered and dropped. "I don't blame her for wishing to keep the house as it was, Robert. I understand the feeling one has about the places of one's childhood. There is a tradition in houses, you know. Tradition is not something to be despised. It is, after all, one of the few links that we have to the past."

"Nonsense," Sandy said in what was for him a tone of strong disapproval. "A tradition that insists that every chair must remain where one's ancesters placed it is . . . is . . ."

"Sheer sentimentality," Kittridge finished for him. "Didn't I say before, Cassie, that I don't give a hang for such nonsensical traditions? Confound it, ma'am, this is *your* house, not Eunice's."

"But if your sister—" Cassie began.

"Good lord, Cassie," Sandy cut in, "don't make excuses for Eunice! It's time Robbie learned the truth about his sister." He paused for a moment, looking down at where the happy Della was making the winning throw in their game, and then, while the child chortled gleefully, he got to his feet and faced his friend. "I yield to no one in my admiration for your sister, Robbie, old fellow, but she does sometimes have a high-handed way about her."

"Now, Sandy—" Cassie said in disapproval, hoping to stop him.

But Kittridge cut her off. "Am I right in assuming, Cassie, that you didn't give Eunice permission to engage that stiff-rumped butler either? Or all the other maids?"

"Well, I . . ."

Sandy glared at her. "Speak up, Cassie, dash it! Of course you didn't!"

Kittridge stared at his wife for a long, silent moment. Then, without a word, he strode over to where she sat, pulled the teacup from her hand, set it down on the hearth, plucked Greta from her arms and carried the child to Sandy. "Take the girls up to Miss Roffey, will you please, Sandy?" he asked, his mouth tight.

"But Uncle Robert, we want to play horsey with you," Della whined.

"Yeth, Uncew Wobit," Greta chimed in, "*hawthy!*"

"Later, my loves, later," Kittridge said shortly, crossing back to where Cassie still sat. He took her by one hand and pulled her to her feet. "As for you, ma'am," he said between clenched teeth, "you will come with me!"

Pulling her ruthlessly behind him, he strode out of the sitting room and down the hall to the drawing room. He burst into the room, banging the doors open with so great a crash that his sister, who'd been sitting near the tea table sipping her tea in solitary splendor, shuddered with fright, causing most of the tea to slosh over into her lap. "*Robbie!* What on earth—?"

He yanked Cassie across the room until the two of them stood in front of his flabbergasted sister. "Tell me, Eunice, do you know who this is?" he snapped.

"What?" She looked up at her brother in utter bafflement.

"Do you know who this is?" he repeated even more angrily.

"Have you lost your *wits*? Of *course* I—"

"Then *what is her name*?"

"Her *name*?" Her eyes were popping in stupefaction. "Cassie, of course. But what—?"

"Her *full* name!"

"Cassandra Rossiter *née* Chivers."

"Never mind the Chivers. Her *present* name, with title and address, if you please."

"Robbie, what is this all about? I don't understand—"

"There's nothing to understand. I want you to tell me this woman's *full name*!"

"Oh, very well! But I think, Robbie, that you've gone berserk!"

"Her *name*, please!" Kittridge thundered.

Eunice threw up her hands. "Cassandra Rossiter, Viscountess Kittridge, of Highlands, Lincolnshire."

"Ah, then you *do* know," he said, his voice dripping with sarcasm.

His sister gaped at her brother in confused frustration. "Of course I know. What nonsense *is* this?" Leaning forward, she turned to Cassie in appeal. "*Tell* me, Cassie, *please*! What is this all about?"

But Cassie seemed not to hear. She was staring up at her husband with eyes so wide she seemed mesmerized. What Eunice could not know was that Cassie was gazing at a golden knight, the same one who had done battle for her once before and was now doing it again. The look she'd fixed on her husband was one of sheer adoration.

"What this is about, sister mine," Kittridge was saying, "is your apparent ignorance of the fact this this lady, whom you evidently *do* recognize as the Viscountess Kittridge, is *my wife* and the *mistress of this house*."

"What is the *matter* with you, Robbie?" Eunice asked in bewildered chagrin. "I am not ignorant of that fact."

"You must be. Why else would you take it upon yourself to move her furniture about and hire her servants and run her household?"

His meaning began to dawn on Eunice. She fell back against the chair. "But, Robbie, I didn't mean to—"

"Not meaning to is a very lame excuse."

"I know this is her household to run," Eunice said shakily. "Surely, Robbie, you don't believe I *intended* to . . . to . . ."

"To slight my wife?" Kittridge supplied icily. "Your intentions were good, is that what you mean? Have you perhaps heard, Eunice, of the destination of the road paved with good intentions? Frankly, I don't believe your intentions *were* good, but even if you meant well, the result was both arrogant and harmful."

Eunice had never been spoken to in such a tone by her brother. "Oh, Robbie!" she cried, quite overset. "I'm so . . . sorry!"

"You should be. But sorries are not enough. You will make up for the damage you've wreaked, and at once. Firstly, Eunice, you will restore everything to the way it was when you arrived. Secondly, you will offer my wife a sincere apology. And, furthermore—"

Cassie placed a light hand on his arm. "That's enough,

Robert," she said, low-voiced. "Eunice has already apologized. Twice."

The softness of her voice halted the outpouring of his anger. He looked down at his wife, blinking her face into focus. "Did she?" he asked. "I did not hear—"

"Perhaps you were only listening to yourself," Cassie suggested gently.

Eunice stared at her sister-in-law as if she'd never seen her before. "I *am* sorry, Cassie," she said, her eyes filling. "I never meant to . . ." But, realizing she was making the same lame excuse again, she burst into tears, rose from her chair and ran from the room.

Cassie looked after her with a troubled frown. "Go after her, Robert."

"No," his lordship snapped. "Let her weep. She deserves a little suffering."

"Then so do I, because this whole muddle is my fault, too."

Kittridge, surprised, took his wife by the shoulders and turned her to him. "How, my dear," he asked, finding himself suddenly calmed by his wife's gentle self-possession, "can this possibly be your fault?"

"Because I *permitted* her to have her way. I should have held out against her."

"Yes, you should have," he agreed, taking his wife's chin in his hand and tilting up her face, trying to force her to meet his eye. "You are my wife, Cassie. Why are you so afraid to act the role?"

She lifted her eyes to his at last and gave him a long, level look. "Perhaps because it *is* a role," she said.

His comprehension of what she'd said dawned slowly. "Of course," he muttered, feeling stunned. "How *can* you feel like a wife if our bond is largely a pretense? We are two strangers under one roof."

She lowered her head in painful agreement. "That's why it was hard for me to act your wife before a sister who is more your . . . your intimate than I am."

Sadly, he pulled her to him and rested his cheek on her hair. "My sweet Cassie! What you mean to say, in that quiet way of yours, is that, in truth, all this is more my fault than anyone's.''

She stayed in his arms for a moment, savoring the tenderness of his affectionate gesture. Then, lifting her hand and brushing it ruefully on his cheek, she withdrew from his embrace. ''It's not your fault that I don't feel like a wife,'' she said, turning and moving slowly to the door. ''It's the fault of our unnatural situation. Perhaps it was all a dreadful mistake. Perhaps we . . .'' She threw him a last, sorrowful look before departing. ''Perhaps *I* never should have done it.''

Chapter Nineteen

Dinner that night was a silent affair. Everyone looked gloomy, even the butler, who surmised that his days in this house were numbered. Sandy tried to keep up a flow of cheerful conversation, but since a monologue is difficult to maintain for very long, even he admitted defeat by the end of the first course and lapsed into silence. Finally, over dessert, Eunice spoke up. "I shall be leaving tomorrow," she announced in a tearful voice.

Kittridge put down his fork. "That," he said bluntly, "is a coward's revenge."

"Be still, Robert," his wife scolded gently. "You've said enough unkind things to your sister today. Lady Yarrow, you surely are not serious about leaving. You promised to stay for at least another week."

Eunice put up her chin. "Yes, but under the circumstances, I think I am justified in breaking that promise. You needn't worry, Robert. I will see that everything is put back as it was before I go."

"I've seen to that already," her brother retorted.

"Then you can have no objections to my departure," Eunice said sullenly.

"Only that taking your leave now sounds very much like the sulks to me."

"I wish, Lady Yarrow, you'd reconsider," Cassie urged. "We should all be very sorry to see you leave so abruptly."

"You needn't be polite to me, my dear," Eunice said proudly. "After my arrogant and insensitive behavior, you cannot pretend to wish to endure my presence among you any longer.''

"But I do wish it," Cassie insisted. "No pretense."

Eunice knit her brows, puzzled. "Why would you want me to stay, after what I've done, if not for mere politeness?"

"Because I believe we will do better now," Cassie responded with a small smile. "Don't you agree? Now that the barriers between us have been somewhat breached, might we not become better acquainted at last?"

Eunice gave her sister-in-law a long, considering look. "Yes, my dear, I begin to think we might. I'm suddenly realizing, Cassie, that I have more to learn about you than I had at first believed." Wavering, she fiddled with her wine glass. "But surely Robbie has had his fill of my company," she mumbled with uncharacteristic uncertainty.

"You know better than that, my dear," her brother assured her. "And even if it were true, I would still hate to lose the company of your daughters."

"Besides," Sandy added, "you can't take the children away now. Greta seems to have a cough."

From across the table Eunice gaped at him in amazement. "You, of all people, Sandy, cannot pretend you wish me to stay."

"I?" Sandy asked, reddening. "What do you mean?"

"You haven't said a kind word to me since I arrived. You've done nothing but criticize my every move."

Sandy gave her a teasing grin. "But that was only because every move you made was misguided."

"Don't mind him, Lady Yarrow," Cassie put in. "I promise you that he wants your company as much as any of us."

"Very well, Cassie, I'll reconsider," her sister-in-law said, "but only on the condition that you stop calling me Lady Yarrow."

The awkwardness thus put behind them, they were able to spend the rest of the evening pleasantly enough. However, Eunice made it an early evening, explaining that she wanted to look in on Greta before going to bed. Sandy soon followed, leaving Kittridge and Cassie alone. In unspoken agreement, they made their way up the stairs together and headed toward their bedrooms, Kittridge so lost in contemplation that Cassie refrained from making a sound. Only when she paused at her door did he shake himself into awareness. "I've been poor company, I'm afraid," he apologized. "I haven't been able to put out of my head the things you said this afternoon."

"I wish we would all put the events of this afternoon out of our minds," she said, coloring.

"I don't. You gave us some moments of rare honesty. It was good both for Eunice and me to hear the truth for once." He took his wife's hand in his and added thoughtfully, "I thank you, too, for your gentle handling of Eunice this evening. It would have made a harmful family rift if she'd gone back to town in a sulk. Are you sure you won't mind enduring her presence for what remains of her fortnight's visit?"

"Not at all. I think she and I will get on famously together now. Thanks to you."

His eyebrows rose. "To me?"

"Of course." She smiled shyly up at him. "She won't dare to oppose me in anything more, not after you stood up to her so . . . so nobly in my behalf."

"Nobly? Do you now call my explosion of temper noble?"

"It *was* noble, Robert. You were like a . . . a knight of old, championing your lady in distress."

"Good God! Is *that* how you saw me?"

"Oh, yes!" A flush suffused her cheeks, but she admitted it anyway. "That is *exactly* how I saw you."

He peered down at her, trying to make out her expression in the dim light of the hallway that was illuminated by only a few candles set in widely spaced sconces on the walls. "Even though you used that so-noble scene as an opportunity to point out to me how far we are from being a truly wedded couple?" he asked in disbelief.

"That has nothing to do with it. The knights of old often championed ladies who were not their wives."

He grinned ruefully. "So, though I'm a failure as a husband, I make a passable knight?"

"Oh, much more than passable, my lord," she insisted, a dimple he'd never before noticed appearing in her cheek. "Quite glorious, in fact."

"Glorious!" A laugh burst out of him, but his smile immediately faded. "Cassie, my lady," he muttered, pulling her to him, "you *are* a pearl. I don't deserve you."

Startled at finding herself in his arms for the second time that day, Cassie blinked up at him open-mouthed. He, on his part, was startled too. He hadn't expected to embrace her but, having done so, found himself reluctant to let her go. There was something both touching and enticing about the adoring way she was gazing up at him. The color in her cheeks fascinated him, too, with its tendency to pale or redden with the changes in her emotions. And her hair, bursting wildly, as always, from the restraining ribbon with which she'd tied it back, seemed so alive with glints of reddish light that he felt a powerful urge to bury his fingers in its curls. But in the end it was her mouth, which until this moment he'd found too full-lipped for his taste, that suddenly seemed more irresistibly desirable than anything else, and to that urge he succumbed. Forgetting for the moment all the doubts and qualms that had kept him distant from her all these weeks, he kissed her with hungry abandon.

But before either of them had a chance to realize fully what was happening, a cough from down the hall caused them to jump apart. It was Dickle, the new butler. "I beg pardon, my lord," he said impassively. "I was on my way to turn down your bed."

"Thank you, but that won't be necessary," his lordship said irritably. "My man will have taken care of that."

"Then I will say good night, my lord. Good night, my lady." With that he turned about stiffly and disappeared down the stairs.

Kittridge glared after him. "Damned jobbernowl!" he cursed. "I hope, Cassie, that you intend to sack that fellow."

"Only if Loesby is willing to continue to play the double role of butler and valet," Cassie said, feeling a joyful, if budding, confidence in herself as head of the household. "And if he is," she added with a giggle, "then I shall let Eunice do the sacking."

"Very well," Kittridge grunted, glumly aware that a special moment had been spoiled beyond repair. He turned and started toward his bedroom. ''Then I'll say good night, my dear.''

Cassie watched him open his door, her eyes shining. The moment had not been spoiled for her. ''Good night, Robert,'' she whispered, her soft voice revealing no sign that her heart was singing inside her. But sing it did. If a real marriage depended on intimacy, it said to her, tonight had been a beginning.

Chapter Twenty

When Cassie asked him, Loesby admitted that he cared little for butlering. He'd never considered himself a proper butler and had no aspirations in that direction. He therefore encouraged Cassie to keep Dickle on. "I know 'e's a toplofty sprag," the valet said with cocky assurance, "but don't ye fret about 'im, me lady. I'll take the fellow down if 'e gets too 'igh in the instep."

Kittridge made a face when Cassie told him what had been decided, but since he'd left the staffing of the house in her hands, he accepted her decision. Eunice, however, was delighted. She considered a "proper butler" *de rigueur* in a well-run household, and Dickle was just the style she liked. To show her appreciation for Cassie's concession to her wishes, she had the portrait of the first viscount removed from the Great Hall and the Constable landscape rehung, a detail that Kittridge, when he'd ordered the sitting room restored, had forgotten.

A few contented days passed, marred only by the fact that little Greta's cough persisted. But since the child was not feverish, no one was particularly alarmed. The days were busy, and in the evenings the four adults found many ways to amuse themselves. They played hearts and silver-loo until cards began to pall; they spent a few delightful hours in the music room when Cassie was discovered to be quite adept at the piano and was able to accompany Eunice, who sang the most enjoyable ditties in a praiseworthy contralto; they repaired once or twice to the billiard room where the ladies

121

watched the gentlemen compete; and they made companionable conversation in front of the sitting room fire. It soon became apparent that Sandy had more than a friendly interest in Eunice, and when, one morning, she put aside her half-mourning and came downstairs in a dress of grey-green muslin, he took it as a most encouraging sign. With Kittridge treating Cassie with what seemed a growing affection, and Eunice and Sandy smelling of April and May, the house was a happy place indeed.

The atmosphere took an abrupt turn, however, when a messenger arrived from town. He'd been sent by the dowager Lady Kittridge to deliver a package of letters that had been posted to the viscount's London address. Kittridge rifled through the pile while all four were seated at the dinner table. Cassie noticed with concern that his mouth suddenly tightened at the sight of two of the same distinctive, square, buff-colored envelopes that had disturbed him the last time he'd received letters from London. As soon as his eyes lit on them, he excused himself from the table and, taking the letters away with him, disappeared into his study for the rest of the evening. He didn't emerge even to say good night to his guests.

The next morning, when he appeared at breakfast, it was apparent to Cassie, if not to anyone else, that his smiles and polite demeanor were forced. And the morning greeting he gave his wife was much cooler and more remote than it had been all week. It was as if the fondness that had been growing between them had suddenly died. But before she could inquire into the reason for the withdrawing of his affection and the change in his mood, Miss Roffey came down to tell Eunice that Greta's cough had worsened considerably and that her forehead was very hot to the touch. The four ran upstairs to look at the child, hoping they would discover that the governess had exaggerated. But Miss Roffey had, rather, understated the problem. It was immediately obvious that little Greta was seriously ill.

Lord Kittridge, inquiring of Mr. Whitlock the direction of the nearest doctor, was horrified to discover that there was none closer than twelve miles to the south, in the town of

Withern. And even there, the physician, Dr. Horace Sweeney, was elderly and, in Whitlock's view, not particularly praiseworthy. On the other hand, he said, there was an apothecary right down the road—a Mr. Phineas Church—who was much admired by the locals for his ability to diagnose ailments and his skill in prescribing curative nostrums. In order to leave no stone unturned, Kittridge decided to send for both. He dispatched Loesby southward to fetch the distant doctor, while he himself went for the apothecary.

He came back in half an hour with Mr. Church, a half-bald, excruciatingly thin fellow with a black-ribboned pince-nez perched on his very long nose. The apothecary examined Greta carefully. He listened to her cough with his ear against her chest, he tapped his fingers on her back, and he looked down her throat. "A putrid infection of the bronchia," he pronounced when he was done.

Kittridge and Cassie exchanged worried glances, while Eunice burst into frightened tears.

"It'll do ye no good to weep, ma'am," the apothecary said disparagingly. "It'll do ye better to set to work an' get the child's fever down. We don't want to see the infection deepen to pneumonia."

"Pneumonia!" Eunice paled at the dreaded word and tottered backward.

Sandy put a supporting arm about her. "He didn't say she had pneumonia yet," he pointed out.

Mr. Church reached for the large, black bag he'd carried in. "I'll cup 'er now," he explained, "since bleeding is a prescribed remedy for coughs. An' again tomorrow, if the fever is still high. But no more, for I don't want to weaken the child. What *you* must do, my lady, is to make the child perspire. Keep 'er warm, an' watch to see she don't throw off 'er blankets. Diaphoretic drinks will help. A hot tisane of barley water and lemon every few hours—that's the thing."

Greta moaned and tossed about in her bed, causing all eyes to turn to her. "Shouldn't she be given some mercury water?" Eunice asked fearfully, not at all sure that Mr. Church's advice was sound. "And perhaps James' powders?"

"Quackery, ma'am, sheer quackery," the apothecary snapped. "Now stand aside an' hand me my cupping glass."

After the child was bled and Mr. Church had taken his leave, Eunice and Cassie remained in the sickroom. They covered the pale, shivering child with several warm comforters and watched as she fell into a fitful sleep. Cassie suggested that Miss Roffey be kept out of the sickroom so that she would not carry any infection to her other charge. Eunice nodded, grateful for the suggestion. Next to getting Greta well, it was imperative to keep Della from falling victim to the same complaint. And since Eunice didn't intend to leave her baby's side, Miss Roffey's assistance in the sickroom would not be needed.

The doctor from Withern arrived four hours later. Dr. Sweeney was the apothecary's opposite. He was short, potbellied and had a full head of white hair topping his apple-cheeked face. His manner, too, was the opposite of Phineas Church's, being obsequious and optimistic where the apothecary had been dour and curt. "Oh, not pneumonia," he assured them cheerfully. "She won't develop pneumonia, my word on it. With a little bleeding and a little medication, she's bound to recover."

"What medication?" Eunice asked, eager to believe him.

"Leave that to me, my lady," the doctor chuckled, patting her shoulder. "A little of this and a little of that."

"Mercury water?" Sandy probed. "James' Powders?"

"Mercury water, of course. But I prefer a powder of my own concoction, made up of ground eggshells, raw turnips, sugar candy and a few secret things."

"Quackery, ma'am, sheer quackery," Kittridge whispered into Eunice's ear.

Eunice, shaken by her brother's disparagement of the doctor, pulled Cassie aside. "Robbie thinks Dr. Sweeney's a quack," she said worriedly. "Now I don't know whom to believe."

"Neither do I," Cassie said, "but my instincts lean toward Mr. Church."

Sandy, when questioned, indicated a preference for Dr. Sweeney, an optimist like himself. Eunice, unable to reject the practitioner who offered the cheerier prognosis, elected to believe the doctor. She let him bleed Greta again, and she accepted a supply of his powder. But when he was about to force a dose of mercury water down the groggy child's throat, her confidence failed her. Mercury water was strong medicine for a child. She gave a little outcry as she stood frozen with indecision.

It was her brother who stopped the doctor's hand. Kittridge had long objected to the use of mercury as a curative. A medical man he'd met in the Dragoons had remarked to him that he'd never known mercury to deliver a proven cure. And the apothecary had not wanted to use it, either. His sister's frightened outcry was enough to push him to action. "We'll give it to her later," his lordship said, wrenching the spoon from Dr. Sweeney's hold. "Thank you, doctor, for coming all this way. My man will see you home."

Eunice didn't scold Kittridge for preventing Dr. Sweeney from further medicating her daughter, for her confidence in the elderly doctor was not strong. And it soon became obvious that even permitting him to bleed Greta had been a mistake; the cupping had weakened the child. Greta lay limply on the pillows, too sapped even to toss. Only when a cough racked her did she move. "Perhaps Mr. Church was right after all," Eunice murmured, bending over her stricken child helplessly.

Cassie, who'd believed in the apothecary from the first, remembered his advice and ran for another tisane. Happily, the hot drink seemed to soothe the invalid, and she soon fell asleep again. Eunice, now convinced that her faith in Dr. Sweeney had been misplaced, handed Cassie the envelope of powders that the good-natured doctor had given her. "You may take this concoction of eggshells and turnips and secrets," she muttered, "and toss it to the winds."

Eunice sat beside the child half the night. In the wee hours, Cassie tiptoed into the sickroom and prevailed upon Eunice to go to her room and get some sleep. She took over the vigil until daylight.

When the apothecary called the next morning, he scolded them all for permitting the child to be bled again. "I warned ye it would weaken her," he muttered, feeling Greta's forehead. "I'll not bleed the poor little tyke again. Nothing to do now but keep 'er warm. Don't let 'er kick the covers off. A mustard pediluvia, mayhap, when she's better, but the barley-lemon tisane'll do more than any quackish medicine, that I promise ye, but I can't promise any more. I'll be back to look at 'er tomorrow, for all the good that'll do. The fever'll break if it's God's will." And with that meager hope, he left them.

For three terrifying days, they watched at Greta's bedside, taking turns. Eunice and Cassie shared the nights, Kittridge and Sandy the days. Sometimes the child slept fitfully, but mostly she tossed about in a kind of stupor, her hair matted on her forehead and her cheeks ruddy with her internal burning. It broke all their hearts to see the little girl suffer and to be so powerless to do anything about it.

Sometime during the third night, Kittridge, who couldn't sleep, came in to the sickroom to see his niece. He found Cassie struggling with Greta on the bed, trying to hold the comforters over the shuddering child. "Thank God you've come," Cassie flung over her shoulder at him. "She's having convulsions."

Lord Kittridge tensed in alarm. "What can we do?"

"I'm not sure, but I think she's entirely too hot. Perhaps . . . do you think a cool cloth on her forehead—? Here, hold her while I get one."

They struggled for almost an hour against the terrifying tremors that racked Greta's little body, but after a time it became apparent that, slowly, the convulsions were subsiding. When at last Greta ceased to shake, Cassie and Kittridge expelled long sighs, as if they'd both held their breaths until they were sure Greta was safe. Then Cassie, with Kittridge's help, washed the child down and changed her nightgown, and they tucked her in between clean, dry sheets. As Kittridge spread a comforter over her, Greta's lashes fluttered. "Uncew Wobit!" she managed to croak before her eyelids drooped and she fell promptly to sleep.

"Uncew Wobit," Cassie mimicked in joyful relief, eyes glowing, "I think she's *better*!"

"Thanks to you," Kittridge said in a choked voice.

He held out his arms to her, his eyes warm with admiration and tenderness. Cassie's heart leaped up to her throat as she took a step toward him. Perhaps this would be the moment for another step toward the intimacy she so dearly craved. But at that very moment, as abruptly as the dousing of a candleflame, something in his face changed. It was as if a light within him had been instantly extinguished. Some thought or memory had crossed his mind, and, whatever it was, it effectively blocked any intention he might have had of making an advance in her direction. His arms dropped, and he actually took a step back from her.

Cassie's heart clenched painfully, and one hand, of its own volition, came up in appeal. "Robert?" she asked, bewildered.

He took her hand in his, but the gesture was awkward and stiff. "You were remarkable this night," he said, a rigid politeness diluting the effect of his admiration. "Eunice and I will always be grateful. Always." Then he kissed her hand with distant formality and was gone.

When Eunice came in the next morning, she found Greta sleeping comfortably, the ruddy color of her cheeks much less fiery and her forehead actually cool. The worn-out mother stood for a long moment at the foot of the bed, gazing lovingly at the child for whom, the past few nights, she'd prayed with fervent desperation. Then she turned her eyes to Cassie, whose very appearance had changed for her. The woman she'd considered a "mousy nobody" now seemed—after all the hours they'd spent in shared tension and fear—a wise, devoted, supportive friend. "Oh, Cassie," she sighed, embracing her sister-in-law with tremulous gratitude, tears of relief running down her cheeks, "this is the happiest morning of my life."

"I know," Cassie said, fondly mopping her sister-in-law's cheeks with a handkerchief. "Mine too." That was not a lie, Cassie realized. She was truly overjoyed at Greta's recovery. And since the possibility of happiness from another quarter was becoming more and more remote, this might very well be as much happiness as she was ever likely to find.

Chapter Twenty-One

It was not clear to Cassie, during the critical days of Greta's illness, how much Robert's gloomy mood was affected by his concern for his niece's health and how much by some other cause. But when the child began a steady, even cheerful, convalescence, and the signs of strain still showed about his lordship's mouth, Cassie knew beyond a doubt that his below-the-surface misery had another source. She tried to probe for the cause, asking him outright one morning, when they were alone at breakfast, if his letters had brought him bad news again. He again turned the subject, thus effectively cutting off any possibility of pursuing the matter.

It was a rainy morning, only a few days after Greta's fever had broken. Cassie sat staring at her husband across the breakfast table, wondering in despair if there was anything she could do to break the stalemate that her relationship with Robert had become. It was only a week since the day, so special in her memory, when, by an act of breathtaking intimacy, he'd revealed a sincere desire to transform the peculiar bond that tied them to each other into a real marriage. What was it, she kept asking herself, that had happened to cause him to back away? She knew, this time, that it was no act of hers that had deterred him. The change in him was directly traceable to the letters. But if he didn't wish to share his secret troubles with her, there didn't seem to be anything she could do about it. No matter how many ways she turned the problem over in her mind, she could discover no way to coax him to open up to her. She was at an impasse.

She reached for the teapot. "Della will be devasted by the rain," she remarked, hoping to reach him by some other route. "She was expecting to take a riding lesson this morning, but after what happened to Greta, Eunice is too frightened of the possibility of chills to permit her to go outdoors in the rain. Would you like to go up to the nursery with me, Robert? I'm sure that only a visit from her Uncle Robert will put a smile on Della's face."

Kittridge shook his head, not looking up from the paper he was studying. "I'm expecting Griswold in ten minutes. Tell Della I'll see her at teatime."

"That will be small consolation," Cassie remonstrated mildly. "In the morning, teatime can seem a year away to a child her age."

Kittridge gathered up his papers and got to his feet. "That may be, but even children must be made to realize that business must come before pleasure. First things first, Cassie," he muttered defensively as he headed out the door, "first things first."

"First things first, indeed," she mocked sarcastically under her breath when he'd gone. "And will you use that excuse, my lord, when you have children of your own?" But of course it was a silly question. The way things were going, he was not likely to have children of his own at all.

She spent the morning in the nursery, helping Eunice to keep the children busy with rainy-day activities. Playing with the girls was so entertaining she almost forgot her troubles. But after luncheon, when not only the children but Eunice, too, took to their beds for a nap, her problems returned to her consciousness in full force. Sore at heart, she headed for the third-floor workshop, hoping that some purposeful physical activity would distract her from this dreadful self-pity. Refinishing the old Henry Holland table had given her pleasure in the days before Eunice came. Perhaps it would again.

It was there in the workshop that Sandy found her an hour later. But she was not working. She'd evidently prepared for work by pushing up the sleeves of her gown and covering herself with an apron, but she was absolutely immobile. She'd seated herself on a stool at the worktable with a pot of varnish in front of her and a brush in her hand, but her eyes were fixed on the raindrops making rivulets on the window-panes. "You won't make much progress just sitting there, Cassie," he greeted with genial raillery, but he stopped himself as soon as he saw the unhappy expression in her eyes. "I'm sorry, my dear," he apologized at once. "I didn't know— Have I barged in at the wrong time?"

She shook herself out of the doldrums with an effort of will and smiled up at him wanly. "Of course not, Sandy. I was only . . . thinking."

"They were not very happy thoughts, I fear." His voice was warm with sympathy.

"The rain depressed me," she mumbled, putting down her brush and picking up a little stick with which to stir the varnish.

"Don't lie to me, my girl. It wasn't the rain." He perched on a stool opposite her. "You needn't tell me your thoughts, of course, if you don't wish to, but I'm quite willing to give you a penny for them."

She looked at the stirring stick as if she didn't know what to do with it. "I was only thinking that . . . that I may g-go home to my father for a while."

"What?" Sandy peered at her, troubled. "Do you mean it, Cassie? Soon?"

"I don't know. In a day or two, I suppose."

"But why? Have you had a message from him? Is he ill?"

She shook her head. "No, nothing like that. It's only a . . . a whim."

"Oh, don't leave us just for a whim, Cassie. That would be cruel to your guests, you know. What would we do without you? What would *Robbie* do without you?"

Abruptly she started to stir the varnish with unwonted vigor. "Robbie would do very well without me. He probably wouldn't even notice I'd gone."

"*Cassie!*" Sandy exclaimed in surprise. "You don't mean that!"

The hand stirring the thick liquid slowed. "No, of course I don't," she said in a small voice. "I shouldn't have said that."

He reached across the table and took her hand. "You can say anything you like to me, Cassie," he said seriously, "you know that. You needn't guard your tongue with me. I hope you know that I am, and always will be, your friend."

"I know," she said quietly.

"Then tell me what's wrong. Have you and Robbie quarreled?"

"We never quarrel," she sighed. "I sometimes wish we would."

"Why would you wish anything so silly? What good is quarreling?"

"It has its purpose in a marriage, I think. It brings things out in the open. It shows feeling. It clears the air."

"Yes, I suppose you're right. But you can't run home to your father because you and Robbie *don't* quarrel. That makes no sense."

She looked up at him earnestly. "Does it make sense if my reason is that I'm tired of living with a stranger?"

"Robbie? A stranger?" He frowned at her disapprovingly. "How can you say such a thing?"

"Robert said it himself. And it's quite true. He shares nothing of his deeper thoughts with me. He tells me nothing of his feelings, or his cares . . ."

Sandy was surprised. "Doesn't he?"

"No. Never."

"Then perhaps he doesn't feel there's anything significant to tell you."

"But there is, Sandy. That's just it. There is."

"There is? What makes you think so?

"He seems so . . . troubled."

"It's the estate, I suppose," Sandy speculated. "I know the responsibility of making the estate show a profit weighs heavily on him, but that's not something he would care to burden his wife with. You can't blame him for wishing to put those problems aside when he joins the family for amusement and relaxation at the end of the day."

"No, it's not the estate," she insisted glumly. "It's something else."

"What makes you so certain?"

She hesitated before replying. Then, as if driven by a need to unburden her heart, she went on. "Did you notice, Sandy, the night the messenger brought the letters from London, that Robert left the table and never returned?"

"Yes, but that was only—" He stopped himself abruptly.

"Only what?"

Sandy didn't answer. His eyes dropped from her face in sudden awkwardness.

Cassie's heart began to pound. "*Sandy*! Do *you know* why he left the table that night?"

"Well, yes," he said, studying her with a puzzled frown. "Don't you?"

"Would I be asking if I knew? Please tell me, Sandy. Was it something in those envelopes? The square, buff-colored ones?"

Sandy shrugged. "I would have thought you'd have guessed. Those letters were from Elinor."

"Elinor? Who's Elinor?"

Sandy gasped. "Weren't you ever told about her?"

"Evidently not. Who is she?"

"Damnation!" he cursed, getting up from the table in perturbation. "I've been too free with my tongue! I thought you *knew*. I thought everyone in *London* knew."

"Well, I don't, so I wish you'd stop talking in riddles and tell me."

He blinked down at her, his moon face tensing with anxiety. "I don't know if I should, under the circumstances. Perhaps Robbie doesn't want you to know. I could bite out my blasted tongue!"

"Oh, my heavens!" Cassie exclaimed, her eyes widening in sudden, painful understanding. "This Elinor is someone special to him, is that it?"

"Cassie, I . . . Must I say?"

"Please, Sandy, yes! I feel as if I've been blundering about all this time in darkness." Her large eyes looked up to his beseechingly. "Did he . . . does he . . . *love* her?"

His instinctive good nature could not resist the appeal in her eyes. "Dash it all, Cassie," he swore, sitting down and reaching for her hand again, "*someone* should have told you!

They were going to be married, you see. They'd intended to announce their betrothal as soon as he was out of uniform. He had no idea, at that time, that his father had impoverished him. But when her family learned of the state of his finances, they broke it off and whisked her away to the continent."

"And that's when my father, with his forty thousand pound offer, came on the scene?" Cassie asked quietly.

"Yes."

"I see." She put down the stirring stick, slipped from the stool and walked to the window. "And, despite his . . . his marriage, they still correspond?"

"No. You misjudge him, Cassie. He does not answer her letters. Her family would not let her accept any communication from him in any case, I expect. But she writes to him on occasion. They broke it off quite amicably, I understand, so I suspect she only writes to assure him there's no bitterness. But the letters probably don't mean anything, Cassie. Robbie is no deceiver. You do believe me, don't you?"

Cassie stared numbly out the window. Outside, beyond the rain-smeared glass, a wet, winter-grim lawn, as misty as the clouds, stretched away to the distant horizon, so colorlessly grey that the line separating earth from sky was almost invisible. "Yes, I believe you," she answered in a voice as colorless as the view. "The letters probably don't mean anything."

Chapter Twenty-Two

It was utterly foolish, Cassie told herself as she lay awake that night and listened to the rain, to make too much of what Sandy had told her. Nothing really had changed. She'd known when she married Robert that he didn't love her. So the new knowledge that he loved another made very little difference.

But there *was* a difference, and before the night was over she was able to admit it. Before she'd learned about Elinor, she'd been able to hope. She'd let herself believe that he would grow to love her . . . that in a month, or at most a year, he would see in her those qualities which make a man love a woman. But today she'd learned he'd already found those qualities in someone else. So now all hope was gone.

Throughout her life, Cassie's hopes of happiness had never been very high. She had dreams, of course, but the circumstances of her life had not encouraged unrealistic expectations. From her earliest years she'd been deprived of a basic source of joy: intimacy. She had not had a mother to console her childhood tears, nor loving friends to share her thoughts and feelings when she was at school. Although her father had always been adoring and indulgent, he had had to spend his days doing men's business, giving over the responsibility of her daily care to hired employees. Miss Penicuick had sincerely loved her, but the governess was too simple to fully understand how to draw out the complex thoughts of her inhibited charge. Thus, Cassie had never known true intimacy, the happiness that comes from sharing one's secret heart with another. Her life had not been joyful, nor had anything occurred before her marriage to make her believe that the circumstances would change. She'd long ago accepted the limitations of her life. She'd long ago decided to make the best of things.

It was only when Lord Kittridge had materialized so miraculously on her horizon that she'd permitted herself to dream that life might offer her more. Not at first, of course, when he'd defended her at the linendraper's. Nor when her father had first offered her the opportunity to wed him. It was only afterward, when she'd been made to understand that he was willing to marry *anyone* who could help him out of his difficulties, that she'd let herself go. She was, after all, better than just anyone. She loved him! She'd agreed to wed him in the belief (because of her feelings for him) that she could, in time, make him happy. That in time they would learn to share their deepest feelings. That in time they would become close.

With that hope she'd married him. And now she knew with certainty that it had been her life's worst mistake. Before she met him she'd at least had peace. Now she had only pain.

As the rain continued unrelentingly to beat on the windowpanes, she sat up in the dark bedroom, piled the pillows behind her and pulled the covers up to her neck. She'd made a mistake, and she had to think about what could be done about it. Certainly it could not be undone. Once a marriage was made, it was forever. Grants of divorcement were so rare that they were, in effect, unheard of. Unhappy couples could live separately, but divorce and remarriage were out of the question. Separation was, in fact, the first thing she thought of. Should she leave this house and take up a separate abode? she asked herself. Should she run home to her father? If she did, would her pain be less?

No, she reasoned after considering the possibility for a long while, running away was not the answer. It would not ease her wounded spirit to return to her childhood surroundings, and it would only pain her father to learn that she was unhappy in the life he'd so proudly purchased for her. And it would pain Robert, too. Before their marriage he'd expressed real revulsion toward the idea of separate abodes because of the gossip it would generate. He'd been glad she'd agreed to live in the country with him. If she wanted more from their "arrangement" than he could give, it was not his fault. He hadn't promised her anything more than he'd given. He hadn't promised her intimacy.

She shivered as the wind sent a flurry of raindrops battering against the windows. Was the rain keeping Robert awake, too? she wondered. Poor Robert. He, too, was suffering in silence. But he knew nothing of this internal struggle of hers. How would he feel if she left him now? He didn't love her, but he would certainly be perturbed at her defection. She was, after all, making a home for him.

Now that she thought about it, she realized that separation would not in any way be a benefit to Robert. Her departure would not bring his Elinor back to him. He would not be able to have Elinor under any circumstances. He had to live with that pain, just as she, Cassie, had to live with hers. Therefore, she realized with a start, the best thing for both of them would be for her to continue to play her role. She would be no worse off remaining here than going back to London. In fact, there were some benefits to her in remaining where she was. She could continue to make a home for Robert, to be the lady of the house, to entertain their guests and do all the little things that a woman can to help a man achieve his goals. There was much to enjoy in this country life. All she had to do was to give up her dreams of love and intimacy

"Just give up my dreams," she repeated aloud as she slipped down under her comforters and curled into a sleeping position. Giving up those dreams would be a painful adjustment but not unendurable. She'd accepted life's limitations before. She could do it again.

Chapter Twenty-Three

Not many days later, Sandy announced his intention to depart. He had neglected some business matters for too long; his conscience could no longer permit him to postpone his return to London. Besides, he confided to Cassie, he wanted to be in town when Eunice returned. He intended, at that time, to press his suit in earnest.

On the morning he took his leave, everyone in the household stood on the steps waving farewell. As soon as his carriage rolled away down the drive, a wave of gloom swept over the household. The absence of his cheery face was deeply felt by all of them, even the children. It was as if a holiday had ended, and the serious business of life would now have to be resumed.

Later that day, while Cassie worked over her embroidery in the sitting room, Eunice prowled about the room aimlessly, crossing from the sofa to the window and back again and sighing so dejectedly that Cassie felt impelled to console her. "You needn't fall into the dismals, Eunice," she said with all the good spirits she could muster. "You'll be back in town soon and will undoubtedly find Sandy waiting on your doorstep with flowers in one hand and his heart in the other."

Eunice perched on the sofa beside her. "Do you think so, Cassie? That his heart is really engaged?"

Cassie smiled over her needlework. "I think you've held his heartstrings for years. He just couldn't reveal his feelings before now. You were happily wed to Yarrow, after all. It is only since you've put aside your mourning that he's been free to reveal himself."

"But how can you be sure? His nature is so sweet and open that he showers affection on everyone. Why do you think I'm in any way special to him?"

"I am not at liberty to reveal confidences," Cassie said primly. But she followed the statement with a giggle that clearly indicated what the content of those confidences had been.

"Oh, Cassie," Eunice breathed "*really*?" This was followed by a long pause, and then, "Oh, dear!"

The second exclamation was not a joyful one. It sounded so troubled, in fact, that Cassie stopped stitching. "Goodness, Eunice, what is the meaning of that 'Oh, dear'? You're not going to tell me that *your* heart is not engaged."

"I wish I knew," Eunice said, leaning back against the sofa and tucking her legs under her. "I certainly enjoyed his company these past few weeks. And the girls have grown fond of him, too. But as for my heart . . . well, how can one be sure?"

Cassie's eyebrows rose. "Are you saying you don't know how to recognize the feeling of love? But, Eunice, you've been married! Don't you remember your feeling for Yarrow?"

"Yes, I do," Eunice said thoughtfully. "And it was equally bewildering at first."

"Then it must have been later, *after* you were wed, that you knew you loved him, is that it?"

Eunice shook her head. "It was later, after I was wed, that I knew I *didn't*."

"Eunice!" Cassie gasped in astonishment.

Eunice gazed at Cassie with an arrested look, as if she were surprised at what had slipped from her tongue. "Good God, Cassie! I've never said that to another living soul! You, my dear, are astoundingly easy to confide in."

"Am I, Eunice?" Cassie felt a little twinge of pleasure at the compliment, for she'd never before been told such a thing. "That is very nice to know," she said, blushing as she knotted her thread and bit it off. She stuck the needle into her pincushion and pushed the embroidery frame away, her brow wrinkling in confusion. "But, my dear, I'm not sure I understand just what it was you confided to me. Did you mean that you *never* loved Yarrow? Never in all your years together?"

"Not for a moment. The truth is, Cassie, that Yarrow was a fool. Oh, he was beautifully educated and quite handsome, and he said all the right things when he went about in society, so it took me some time to see through the shiny surface to the silliness underneath. Perhaps I didn't want to see through the shiny surface. But the nature of marriage is such that one can't keep one's illusions about one's spouse for very long."

"I suppose not," Cassie murmured, mulling it over. "Marriage is so . . . intimate."

"Exactly."

Now it was Cassie's turn to sigh. "Were you very miserable?" she asked in quiet sympathy.

"Oh, no. You mustn't feel sorry for me, Cassie. I grew used to my husband after a while. I even became fond of him, in a motherly way. And then I had the children, and they quite filled my life. Mother love is a very strong emotion, you know. And when it strikes one, there's no doubt about what one feels. No doubt at all."

"Doubt such as you feel about Sandy?"

"Yes." Eunice frowned worriedly. "I feel a sincere affection for Sir Philip Sanford, really I do. But I keep wondering if this feeling will last. Good heavens, Cassie, what if I decide to wed him, and then discover, later, that I don't care for him any more than I did for Yarrow?"

"I don't know how to answer that," Cassie admitted. "The love feelings *I've* experienced have had no doubts, you see. In love matters I've felt only certainty. I may not have experienced the happiness one expects from love feelings, but I haven't experienced the doubts."

"What are you saying, Cassie?" Eunice turned herself about on the sofa to stare at the girl beside her with a sudden intensity. "These love feelings you're describing— Do you mean . . . toward my *brother*?" she asked in her blunt way.

Cassie lowered her eyes and nodded. "I've never told *that* to another living soul," she said.

"Oh, *Cassie*," Eunice cried with a heartfelt agony, "you poor dear! Tell me you don't mean it!"

"I wish it were a lie," Cassie admitted. "Or a joke. Or even a schoolgirl infatuation. But it's not."

"Not even the tiniest doubt?" Eunice pleaded.

"Not the tiniest."

"Dash it all," Eunice muttered, "I'm so *sorry*!"

Cassie met her sister-in-law's eye with a level look. "Because he doesn't reciprocate?"

Eunice bit her lip. "You know about Elinor, then?"

"I've heard." Cassie gave her a small smile. "Perhaps I'll grow used to it, as you did with Yarrow."

"Perhaps. But loving him . . . with no doubts at all . . ." She threw her arms about Cassie in a tearful embrace. "Oh, my sweet little sister-in-law, I think it will be very hard."

But Cassie didn't feel tearful. She'd known from the first that loving Robert would be hard on her. But having a sympathetic friend to whom she could reveal her feelings would make things easier. She could not be tearful when she'd just engaged in the very first intimate conversation of her life. In fact, she was startled at how pleasant it had been, in spite of the painful subjects they'd discussed. The exchange had been soothing, somehow, and full of unexpected, deep affection. *How strange!* she thought. How could she suddenly feel so fond of Eunice when only a week ago she'd utterly disliked her? Moreover, she had an inner certainty that they would never go back to being strangers. No matter what happened in her marriage or in Eunice's relationship with Sandy, she and Eunice had forged a bond. A strong, durable, wonderful bond.

Eunice felt it, too. This shy little creature, her sister-in-law, had in a few short weeks become a treasured friend, while Elinor, whom she had known and admired for years, had never come nearly as close to her heart. The truth was that she was delighted that Cassie was her sister-in-law. *How strange!* she thought. She'd been wishing so hard, these past months, that Robbie could have married his Elinor and been happy. Now, suddenly, she found herself wishing that Elinor had never been born!

Chapter Twenty-Four

Winter weather reappeared soon after Sandy departed, keeping all Eunice's travel plans in abeyance. Since she would not subject the children to long hours in a draughty carriage, she explained, a return to London could not be considered while the weather was so cold. The postponement of their departure pleased everyone, even the servants, for Eunice had long since given up running the household. "An' now that yer sister an' 'er ladyship 'ave become thick as thieves," Loesby reported to Kittridge, "the 'ole place 's as peaceful as Talavera after the battle."

Robert was delighted with the developing friendship between his sister and his wife. For one thing, there was no more struggle for authority between the two. For another, the strain at the dinner table to make comfortable conversation was considerably lessened by the easy flow of banter exchanged between the two women. Kittridge was especially thankful for the way Eunice's friendship had brought Cassie out of her shell, for he was well aware that his own relationship with his wife had deteriorated badly.

As far as that deterioration was concerned, he knew that he had only himself to blame. He had unwittingly encouraged Cassie, by his impetuous kiss, to believe their marriage could grow into something more than it was. But the letters from Elinor had reminded him where his heart really belonged. He had been forced to marry elsewhere, but his love for Elinor remained constant. He would not sully the memory of that love by giving even a small piece of his affections to another woman, even his wife. Elinor, who had given him her unwavering devotion all during their long wartime separation, deserved nothing less from him.

Sometimes, when he felt particularly lonely and despairing, he locked himself in his study and reread the handful of letters she'd written. He knew it was self-indulgence of the most foolish, sentimental kind, but he couldn't help himself. Perhaps if he'd been able to respond, to let out his feelings in messages to her, he could have treated her letters more casually, but the frustration of this cruel, one-way correspondence skewed his emotions. He kept imagining what Elinor was feeling, enduring waves of guilt for what she must be suffering at not having even the small solace of a word from him. When those feelings of guilt and frustration rose up in him, he found himself resenting not only the circumstances of the trap in which he now found himself but the wife who, in some mysterious connivance with her father, had entrapped him. Illogical as he knew the feeling was, he sometimes blamed Cassie for keeping him from Elinor.

There were other times, however, when he felt quite affectionate toward Cassie. There was no doubt that she sometimes charmed him. She had an unaffected innocence, an irrepressible blush that revealed every feeling and an odd-shaped but endearing little face. And when she looked up at him, adoration shining in those soft brown eyes, he had to admit that he found her hard to resist. But his conscience forced him to resist her; those few times he'd forgotten himself with Cassie made him feel almost adulterous, as if his prior commitment to Elinor had a stronger claim on his honor than his commitment to his wife.

Thus he, like the other members of the household, found many advantages in the developing closeness between Cassie and Eunice. The two women were such good company for each other that Robert was able to pursue his own interests without feeling guilty that he was neglecting them. And, best of all, their closeness made it easier for him to keep his distance from his wife.

The women, meanwhile, were busily occupied with common pursuits: They played with the children together, took

companionable walks together, sat at the fire reading novels
together, and even spent hours in the workshop together,
Cassie having convinced Eunice that furniture restoration made
a very enjoyable pastime. The friendship progressed so well,
in fact, that the two women could even engage in sharp
disagreements. Robert overheard them one afternoon arguing
over a painting Eunice wanted to place at the top of the
stairway. "That, my dear," Cassie declared firmly, "is the
ugliest still life I've ever seen."

"Ugly!" Eunice drew herself up in offense. "It's by a
student of *Kneller*!"

"I don't care if it was by Kneller himself. The colors are
muddy and the vase is all out of proportion."

"Really, Cassie, you are quite unfair. I love the blue iris
lying there beside the vase. And the drapery, here, has a very
nice line."

Cassie studied the painting, head cocked, for another moment. "The drapery may be nicely done, Eunice, I grant you
that. But the rest is deucedly awkward."

"Well, *I* like it," Eunice insisted mulishly, "and I think it
ought to be hung."

"You may hang it if you wish, my love," Cassie said as
she marched off up the stairs, "but only in your room. I will
not have it on the top of the stair where our eyes would have
to suffer it ten times a day."

As Eunice followed Cassie up the stairs, still arguing the
merits of the painting tucked under her arm, Robert closed the
door of his study, grinning. His shy little wife, he thought
with some satisfaction, had come a long way. And for that
matter, so had his sister. Their friendship was fertile soil that
gave them both a healthy growth.

It came as no surprise, therefore, that Eunice decided not to
return to London at all. She announced one night at dinner
that she and her daughters had talked it over and had agreed
that they would—with Cassie's and Robert's permission—
remain for the rest of the winter right here in Lincolnshire.
Robert immediately acquiesced. "We're delighted to have
you for as long as you wish," he assured her. "Let me
remind you, my dear, that before Cassie and I left London, I

told you that you and the girls were welcome to make your home with us permanently, should you desire it."   .

"That was a kind gesture," Eunice responded, "but I didn't believe, then, that I could bear being away from town. I don't know, even now, how permanent our stay will be, but I'd certainly like to remain until spring."

"Have you lost your mind, Eunice?" Cassie asked later, when she and Eunice had left Robert at the table with his port and were alone in the sitting room. "You *can't* stay until spring!"

"No? Why not?" She grinned at her sister-in-law archly. "Are you tired of us already?"

"Don't be silly. But have you forgotten *Sandy*? He probably knocks at your mother's door daily to ask if you've arrived."

Eunice's smile faded. "Oh, yes, Sandy. With flowers in one hand and his heart in the other, isn't that how you described him?"

Cassie peered at her friend worriedly. "Have you decided you don't care for him? Is that why you don't want to go home?"

"I don't want to go home, my dear Cassie, because the girls and I are so happy here. And as for Sandy, I've decided that I don't want to decide. When one is a girl of eighteen, one feels pushed toward marriage for fear of finding herself, at twenty, left on the shelf. But when one is a twenty-eight-year-old widow, she can't ever be called an old maid. And being left on the shelf seems much less dreadful. So the push to wedlock is less urgent. I shall, therefore, take my own good time before giving in to a second marriage."

"Is that the reason girls get married?" Cassie couldn't help asking. "To avoid being left on the shelf?"

"Of course it is. What other reason is there to tie oneself up at eighteen? Isn't that why *you* married? You can't pretend it was for love, Cassie, for you didn't know Robbie then."

"Ah, but I did."

Eunice gaped at her sister-in-law. "You did? How? When? Why did you never tell me?"

"It's a long and silly story, which I won't tell you now,

with Robert about to join us at any moment, but which you'll undoubtedly pull out of me in all its embarrassing details before the week passes. In the end, however, the tale will only prove that love is not a much better reason for 'giving in to marriage' than fear of being left on the shelf. Although in your case, Eunice," she added, patting her sister-in-law's shoulder, "if you decide you love Sandy, I think you'll have a very happy marriage indeed."

"Do you?" Eunice asked earnestly.

"Yes, I do," Cassie answered as Robert strolled in to join them, "but by all means take your own good time. Take all the time you need."

Chapter Twenty-Five

With matters in his household in a state of relative contentment, Kittridge felt free to absent himself from it for a few days. The Duke of Bedford (a progressive landowner whose estates were both productive and profitable, and whose annual "sheep shearing" was an event that drew farmers and landowners from all over the midlands to his estate in Bedfordshire) had heard that Lord Kittridge was interested in developing his own herds and had generously invited him to Woburn Abbey to exchange ideas. With the assurance from his wife and his sister that they would do very well without him, Kittridge accepted the invitation and, early on a cold February morning, set out for Bedfordshire.

Cassie had risen at dawn to see him off. Eunice, however, being neither wife nor lover, had not felt any need to deviate from her usual habit of sleeping until midmorning. Thus, as soon as Robert left, Cassie found herself alone at the breakfast table and utterly miserable. She did not know why her husband's departure left her feeling so bereft, for he was hardly an affectionate companion when they were together, but the feeling persisted anyway. In order to shake off her depression, she searched about in her mind for some engrossing activity to distract herself from her gloomy self-pity.

It took but a moment for the perfect solution to burst upon her brain: This was her best opportunity to make her husband's study more habitable. She had wanted to remake the room from the first, but Robert, being in almost constant occupancy, had not permitted it. Today, however, with Robert absent, was the perfect time to start. She jumped up from the table at once and ran eagerly down the hall to the study to give it a complete examination.

Her first impression, on looking round, was that the room was much too small for its purpose. Just the few pieces of furniture it held—a one-piece secretary-and-bookcase, a chair, and a pier table under the single window—were enough to crowd the room. She would have liked to move him to a larger room, where she could fit him with a library table to sit behind, with plenty of room underneath for his long legs. But she knew he would not hear of it. He had many times insisted that this room suited him perfectly. So, with a sigh of resignation, she studied the place to see what could be done.

The fireplace took one entire wall and the window, with the pier table beneath it, another. With the bookcase-desk against the third wall and the door in the fourth, there was little she could do to rearrange the furniture. The only things that could be done were to find some way to store the maps and blueprints that were piled in untidy rolls on the pier table, cover the window with new draperies, find an interesting, masculine painting to hang over the mantel and, perhaps, to replace the secretary-bookcase with some sort of table with a larger work surface.

She looked at the high desk speculatively. It was actually a beautiful piece, the bookshelves enclosed with delicate glass doors and the whole frame topped with an inlaid arch and carved finials. It might, she thought, be the work of Daniel Langlois, a cabinetmaker of the last century whose designs she'd always admired. She would quite understand if Robert objected to its being replaced. But he must surely find the work space too cramped, and there was no possible way, underneath, for a man to stretch his legs. He would be bound to appreciate a more spacious desk, once he tried it.

To prove to herself that this desk was inadequate, she lowered the lid. As she suspected, the opened lid comprised the entire writing surface, for the area within was completely taken up with cubbyholes, all overstuffed with record books and papers. How, she wondered, could he do his work amid such a profusion of—?

Suddenly she turned quite pale. Her heart seemed to cease beating, and her blood froze in her veins. For right there, in the center cubbyhole, was a packet of square, buff-colored envelopes tied with string. *Elinor's letters!*

She shut the lid hurriedly, with the awkward nervousness of a spinster who'd opened a door and come upon a gentleman in his smalls. She had trespassed on Robert's privacy! It was in this room that he hid when he wanted to be alone. It was in this tiny place where he stored his secrets. It was here, and here alone, that he could truly be himself. She realized, with belated shame, that she should not have come in at all without asking his permission. It was his *sanctuary*, and she had no right to invade it.

She could do nothing to alter this room now, for he must never know she'd entered! She looked quickly round once more to make sure nothing had been disturbed. And then, quite ridiculously, as if she'd accidentally invaded the chapel of an alien religious sect, she tiptoed to the door.

But with her hand on the knob, she paused. Elinor's letters—the words and thoughts of the one woman whose character aroused her fascination more than any other in the world—lay right there within reach. She could, right at this moment, take them out and read them. No one need ever know.

But that was a *hideous* thought, she told herself. Cheap and vulgar and dishonest. And quite beneath her character. She could never permit herself to perform so dastardly an act! If coming into this *room* had seemed a dreadful invasion of her husband's privacy, what would reading his *most private letters* be? The very *thought* was sinful . . . sinful to the point of sacrilege! She had to leave this room, and at once!

But she didn't move. She knew, with a sickening certainty, that she was going to go back to the desk and read the letters She simply *had* to. As ugly, as dishonest, as *immoral* as the act was, she was going to do it. It was as if some force beyond herself was compelling her. Trembling convulsively, she moved like a sleepwalker back to the desk. As she lowered the lid with shaking fingers, a horrid picture flashed into her mind . . . Bluebeard's forbidden room, where the mutilated bodies of the six wives who'd disobeyed his stricture lay strewn about in bloody heaps. Would she, too, come to the end of this misadventure to find herself, like those other too-curious wives, a dismembered corpse?

But even that repulsive image did not stay her hand. She sat down at the desk, carefully removed the letters from their niche and undid the string. Then she gingerly removed the first letter from its envelope and, bracing herself as though expecting a blow, read it through.

It was worse than she expected. Elinor Langston, she discovered, was not the sort to exercise restraint. Every pang of loss the girl experienced was expressed in detail in the lengthy document, every tear and sigh duly noted and placed in its time and setting so that the reader—Robert—might suffer too. It was as if Elinor were trying to keep him tied to her by a rope of guilt, woven strand by strand with the threads of her pain.

The next letter contained more of the same . . . and the next . . . and the next. At a dance at the Belvedere Palace in Vienna, Elinor ached to feel his arms about her. At a concert in Salzburg, the Mozart *"was a meaningless jumble of discord"* without Robert's presence at her side. At the Louvre in Paris, the mere viewing of a painting upset her. *"It was,"* she wrote, *"a portrait by Titian, called 'Man with a Glove.' It so disconcerted me because of its likeness to you, my love, particularly about the eyes and mouth, that I burst into sobs and had to be led from the exhibit—to the consternation of Mama and Papa and the amused curiosity of everyone else— and laid on a chaise in the ladies' retiring room until I could come to myself."* And after witnessing a performance of *Fidelio* at La Scala in Milan, she wrote, *"Oh, my most beloved, when I saw the lovers rewarded for their faithfulness and sent out to pursue a life of happiness, how I wished that you and I could be rewarded too. But I know it is beyond hope, and that our opera, if such were ever composed, must have a tragic end. If I were writing it, I would arrange it so that we'd be chained together somewhere in a dungeon where we would die in each other's arms. I think I prefer that ending to this terrible, interminable, boring separation we are being made to endure!"*

Cassie stared at the letters spread out before her, a wave of fury flooding over her. How could this contemptible girl dare to torture her Robert this way? she asked herself. Did she have to flaunt her self-pity in his face and make him suffer agonies of guilt?

But a second reading altered her thinking, especially the letter in which Elinor tried to face the fact of Robert's marriage. *"Mama told me yesterday that you are wed,"* she wrote on pathetically tear-stained paper. *"I cried all night. I almost hated you, but now, after some calmer thought, I do understand. You did what you had to do. I know you cannot love the despicable creature who married you for your title and whom you married for her wealth. I know, too, that your love for me remains untarnished. I admit that the tiny flame of hope I kept in my heart, the hope that we might, somehow, find a way into each other's arms, has flickered out, but the knowledge that our love will not die still burns brightly for me. It is that knowledge that keeps me alive."*

This last letter made it achingly clear that Elinor and Robert truly loved each other, and that they had been cruelly wrenched apart. Those were facts that Cassie had to face. In those circumstances, she asked herself, weren't the lovers justified in feeling pain? In being sorry for themselves? Wasn't their suffering just as pitiable as her own?

And it was *she,* Cassie, who stood between them! She was the "despicable creature" who was to blame for their unhappiness. Elinor's words jumped out from the page and struck at her soul. *I know you cannot love the despicable creature.* The very appearance of those words on the page made her cringe. But it was a final reading of the words, *the knowledge that our love will never die still burns brightly for me,* that utterly undid her, and she dropped her head on her arms and wept as if her heart would break.

The sound of the doorknob being turned froze her in midsob. With her breath caught in her throat, she lifted a terror-stricken face to the opening door. Whoever it was—Loesby or Dickle or any other of the servants—she would not be able to face him ever again. But if it were *Robert* at the door, returning by some ironically hideous quirk of fate to pick up a forgotten item on his desk, she would simply die! She would die on the spot!

But it was Eunice. "I've been looking for you all over," Eunice began cheerfully, but the sight of Cassie's reddened eyes and terrified expression startled her into alarm. "Good God, Cassie, what—?"

"Eunice, *p-please*," Cassie begged, stammering in embarrassed misery, "pretend you haven't f-found m-me, and g-go away!"

But Eunice saw and thought she recognized the letters. *"Cassie!"* she exclaimed in shock. "Are those *Elinor's*? What've you *done*?"

"Just what you th-think," Cassie admitted, dropping her head down on her arms and beginning to sob again. "I'm the m-most d-despicable c-creature in the world!"

"Of course you're not," Eunice declared loyally, striding into the room and kneeling beside Cassie's chair. "Despicable, indeed!"

"I read all his l-letters!" Cassie wept. *"Twice!"*

"Well, it might not have been an admirable thing to do, my love, but it's not an offense that warrants a hanging."

"Yes it is. It was a low, m-mean-spirited, ugly, d-despicable thing to do!"

"Yes, it was." She stroked Cassie's bent head. "And very human. I know I'd have done it, too, in your place."

"No you wouldn't. You have too much ch-character."

"Not nearly as much as you, Cassie, and that's the truth. It was love that weakened you, that's all. Now, stop that weeping, take this handkerchief and blow your nose. And let's get these letters back in place before someone else comes in and discovers us."

Cassie nodded and tried to comply. She sat up and blew her nose, but when she replaced that last, cruel letter in its envelope, the tears began to flow again. "Robert must think I'm d-despicable, even if you don't," she wept, dabbing hopelessly at her eyes. "I'm the one who stands between him and the wonderful g-girl of his dreams. Me! The pathetic c-creature who had to p-purchase a husband for f-forty thousand p-pounds!"

For that Eunice had no answer. "My poor Cassie," she murmured, taking her sister-in-law in her arms and rocking her like a baby, "my poor, poor Cassie." There was nothing else she could think of to say that would be soothing, for the truth was that even at a thousand times forty thousand pounds, Robert's love could not be bought. And that one unpurchasable commodity was the only thing in the world the weeping girl wanted.

Chapter Twenty-Six

It did not take Lord Kittridge very long after his return from Woburn Abbey to notice a change in his wife. It was not that she was cooler to him, exactly, but that she was somehow *withdrawn*. She did not meet his eye when he spoke to her, nor did she smile up at him with that tremulous little smile she used to give when he said something kind or amusing. And when he came down to breakfast—the only time of day they were alone together—she quickly finished her tea and scurried out of the room, as if she were purposely trying to avoid any private conversation with him.

He didn't notice any change in the way she behaved toward anyone else, but to make sure his impression was accurate, he asked Loesby about it. The valet raised his brows at the question. " 'Er ladyship, changed?" he repeated, peering at Kittridge as if he'd dipped too deeply in the brandy. "Not as far as I kin see. It's just like I been tellin' ye, Cap'n. She wuz a wonder from the start, an' she's a wonder still."

Unsatisfied, Kittridge applied to Eunice. He caught her on the stairs, on her way up to the nursery. "Have you a minute, Eunice?" he asked. "There's something I want to ask you."

"Of course, my dear," she said, pausing in her climb. "What about?"

"About Cassie. Do you notice any change in her? Does she seem, in the last few days, to be . . . well, different?"

"How different?"

"I can't put my finger on it. Distant, somehow."

"Distant? Not to me."

"Then you two are still as good friends as when I left for Woburn?"

"Better, I'd say."

"I don't understand." Kittridge's brow knit in puzzlement. "Then it's only toward *me* she's changed. I wonder if I've offended her. Did she say anything about it to you?"

"If she did, you wouldn't expect me to repeat it, would you, Robbie?" She turned away with a toss of her head and proceeded up the stairs. "If you want to know anything concerning your wife, my dear," she threw over her shoulder, "you'll have to talk to *her*. Don't expect *me* to be your intermediary."

Kittridge glared up at her as she disappeared round the turning of the stairs. "Women!" he muttered in annoyance and took himself off to his study.

As the days passed, his feeling that Cassie had changed toward him persisted. He told himself that it didn't matter . . . that, indeed, her coolness suited him perfectly well, under the circumstances. He'd pledged himself to remain faithful to Elinor, and this distance between himself and his wife made it easier for him to keep his pledge. When he found himself becoming snappish and short-tempered, he blamed the mood on the absence of letters from Elinor. Why, he asked himself several times a day, wasn't his mother forwarding his letters more frequently?

But as many couples learn, the Gods of Love have decreed a terrible irony in the playing out of the games between men and women: when one of the pair draws away, the other almost inevitably wishes to draw close. Thus, the more Cassie seemed to avoid Kittridge's company, the more he desired hers. He began to miss her little smiles, her cheerful morning conversation, the adoring glances he used to catch her casting at him when she thought he wasn't looking. For the first time in the months of his marriage he worked at trying to please her. He told her his plans for the day at breakfast in an attempt to keep her at the table; he brought her a pair of Wedgwood candlesticks that he'd purchased from one of his tenants; and he tried, by all sorts of ruses, to prevail upon her to remain in the sitting room at night after Eunice had gone up to bed. But no matter what he did, Cassie remained politely, unshakably distant.

At last he decided to take the bull by the horns. He tapped on her bedroom door one night after they'd all retired. She opened the door an inch and held a candle aloft to see who it was. "Robert?" she asked in surprise. "Is anything wrong?"

"No, but I'd like to talk to you, Cassie. May I come in for a moment?"

She hesitated. "Well, I . . . you see I've already undressed . . ."

"Then put on a robe. It's not so shocking a suggestion, ma'am. I've seen you in nightclothes before, if you remember."

After another moment of hesitation she let him in. In the candlelight it seemed to him she looked as delicious as she did the night they went hunting for the Rossiter ghost, with her ruffled nightgown peeping out at the bottom of her robe and her unruly hair bursting out in rebellion from the control of her spinsterish nightcap. "Thank you, ma'am," he said with exaggerated formality as he crossed the threshold.

She closed the door gingerly. "Would you . . . care to sit?" she asked, almost whispering.

"Are you afraid someone will hear us and think we are having a tryst?" He grinned at her as he lowered himself onto her dressing table chair. "I assure you that no one is near enough to hear us. And even if someone were, it wouldn't matter. We *are* married, after all."

"Yes, but . . ."

"But not quite married enough to be having trysts, is that what you're trying to say?"

She put up her chin. "I was not trying to say anything of the sort. All I intended to do was to excuse my awkwardness by explaining that I am unaccustomed to . . . to entertaining gentlemen in my bedroom."

"That much is obvious," he teased.

She sat down on the edge of her bed and folded her hands primly in her lap. "You said you wished to *talk* to me, my lord, not to twit me about my . . . er . . . inexperience."

"So I did. It's something that's been on my mind since I returned from Woburn. I wish to ask you, Cassie, quite bluntly, if I've done something to offend or anger you."

"No, of course not. What makes you think you have?"

"Something in your manner. You've changed, you know."

"I am not aware—"

"You must be aware of it," he insisted, getting to his feet impatiently. "You've been doing all you can to avoid me."

"That's silly. Why would I—?"

"I don't know." He confronted her boldly, lifting her chin and forcing her to look up at him. "That's just what I'm trying to determine."

"You are imagining things, my lord," she said stiffly.

"There! You see? It's that stiffening. You did not, before, stiffen up whenever I approached."

She turned her face away, wresting her chin from his hold. "You did not, before, approach me in my bedroom, my lord."

"And that's another thing. For months you've been calling me Robert with perfect ease, but tonight you've 'my lorded' me at least twice."

"If that's the source of your discontent, my lor—Robert, I shall try to remember not to do so again."

"Damnation, ma'am, that's *not* the source!" he burst out, pulling her to her feet. "Please, Cassie, don't be afraid to be open with me. I'd hoped that by this time we'd be dealing better with each other. What's happened to our intention to bring about some intimacy into this marriage?"

"I am n-not aware that we had such an intention," she murmured, lowering her head to avoid his eyes.

"Not aware? How can you say that? Didn't we discuss it from the first?"

"You only said, then, that you wouldn't f-force intimacy upon me."

He groaned in frustration. "Come now, Cassie, I was speaking of a later conversation, as well you know! It was when we admitted to each other that we were still behaving as strangers." He pulled her into his arms, determined to have an honest confrontation that would, he hoped, bring them to a more comfortable closeness. With one arm holding her tightly to him, he tilted her face up to his, as if to force her to remember their former embrace. "I had the distinct impression, that day, that you were *encouraging* the development of that intimacy.''

"Let me go, Robert," she said, quietly firm. "That impression was false."

Her words enraged him. He was not such a coxcomb that he could have mistaken her response to his kiss. Why was she denying it now? "It was *not* false!" he declared furiously. And to prove it, he lifted her up against his chest so that he could kiss her again and evoke the remembered response.

"Robert!" she gasped, startled. *"No!"*

His eyes glittered with angry but unmistakable desire, a desire fanned by her stiff resistance. "Let me remind you of how it was," he said roughly, pushing away his awareness that the situation and the sensations he felt now were very different from the last time. Heedless of his own internal warnings and the look of utter fear in her eyes, he crushed her against him and kissed her in a way that was too urgent and too angry to be husbandly.

She struggled to free herself in spite of the sudden surging of the blood through her veins and the astonishing waves of warmth that flowed all through her. Even though she pushed with all her might against his shoulders, she could feel her body, free of the constrictions of stays and undergarments, bend back under his pressure like a slim, green tree in a storm. Her body seemed to be pursuing desires of its own, trying to mold itself to him as if it wanted nothing more than to cling to him forever. But her mind, pinpricking her with reminders that the man holding her in this most intimate of embraces did not love her, kept some inner kernel of her spirit stiff, cold and unyielding.

At first, Robert responded only to the signals of her body. Soft and pliant in her unrestricting nightclothes, she was at this moment more desirable than any woman he'd ever held. He could feel the racing beat of her heart, the heat of her skin, the sweet taste of her lips. He could have her now, he told himself, oh so easily. It was his husbandly right. He could lower her gently on the bed that stood waiting right there at his side and teach her the secrets of marital bliss. Every lovely, lissome, warmly shivering inch of her seemed ripe for it. But his mind, too, kept nagging at him to hold back. It warned him to recognize the firm core of resistance that was keeping her, despite the passion that enveloped them both, from surrendering. He couldn't force himself on her. So after an inner struggle of what he considered herculean dimensions, he let her wrench her mouth from his. Then he set her on her feet and, feeling like a fool, released his hold on her.

Breathless and confused, they stared at each other until he could no longer bear to see the look of shocked accusation in her eyes. He turned away and leaned weakly on the bedpost. "So you see," he muttered in a lame attempt at irony, "the impression was not false."

She sank down upon the bed. "I think, my lord," she said, her voice trembling, "that you'd better go."

He turned to look at her. "Now I *have* offended you," he said, shamefaced.

She would not meet his eyes. "Yes," she said.

Her stubborn intransigence, one of her qualities with which he had no previous familiarity, brought his earlier anger sweeping over him again. "When one considers the usual husbandly privileges," he said in cold, tight-jawed self-defense, "what happened just now was a mere trifle."

"I thought we'd agreed from the first that the 'usual husbandly privileges' do not apply in our case," she pointed out quietly.

"Damnation, woman, I never intended to forgo them *forever*! I thought it was understood that we only meant to postpone them until we became comfortable with each other."

She got slowly to her feet and faced him with chin high. "And was it understood, my lord," she asked proudly, "that *you* were to decide when the time was right, or that I was?"

He was taken aback by the question. "Why, *you*, of course."

"Then my decision is that we should accept our marriage as it is, with the limitations and restrictions we placed on it from the beginning."

He stared at her in agonized disbelief. "But . . . good God, Cassie, *why*?"

She turned away. "I can't . . . I'd rather not explain."

He came up behind her and took her gently by the shoulders. "Can you give me some hope that the right time will be soon?"

"N-no," she said, her head lowered. "None."

She could feel him stiffen. "Cassie! Do you mean you wish to keep to those limitations *permanently*?"

She nodded. "We made a bargain. An exchange. My fortune for your title. We, neither of us, have a right to demand more from each other."

His hands dropped from her shoulders. "Very well, ma'am," he said, suddenly cold as ice. "If that is the way you see the terms of our 'bargain,' I shall certainly honor them. I shall not invade your room again. Good night, ma'am."

She shuddered at the slam of the door behind him. *Oh, Robbie*, she wanted to cry, *come back! I didn't mean it. I didn't mean any of it!*

But of course she had meant it, every word. She had to keep him at arm's length, or she'd not be able to endure the life she'd chosen. And she'd not be able to endure it if she gave her heart to him while he withheld his from her. What she'd just done was battle for her survival.

The scene just ended *had* been a battle, and she'd won it. Any impartial observer would surely have named her the victor. Then why did she have this empty, frightened, lonely, miserable feeling that indicated quite distinctly that she'd lost?

Chapter Twenty-Seven

As the temperature between the lord and lady of Highlands turned chill, the temperature outside warmed. Any icy February turned into a muddy March. The trees in the orchards began to show tinges of color, the lawns began to green, the air was crisp and resonated with the sound of saws and hammers as the renovation of the farm buildings began, the ewes gave birth to a number of little lambs, some new pieces of furniture for the still unfinished drawing room arrived from London, and Della's riding lessons, long postponed because of the cold, were resumed. Spring had arrived at last.

The last week in March brought not only the official beginning of the new season but a visit from Oliver Chivers. Cassie's father thoughtfully brought Miss Penicuick along with him, and the reunion was a truly joyful one. Both her father and her old governess were delighted beyond words by the apparent change in Cassie from a painfully shy schoolgirl to the confident mistress of a grand manor house. Her father almost chortled in glee at the success of his "investment."

While Miss Penicuick joined the ladies in their daytime activities, Kittridge took his father-in-law round the property and showed him the plans for its reconstruction. The grandeur of the manor house impressed Chivers mightily, as did the size of the property and the potential for income of the farms and new tenant houses. While he pooh-poohed Kittridge's claim to be able to pay him back in ten years for the "dowry" —insisting that he would not accept a penny of it—he was nevertheless proud of his son-in-law for wishing to make the attempt. "My daughter," he confided to Miss Penicuick, " 'as got 'erself as fine a fellow as ever was."

But neither Mr. Chivers nor the fluttery governess had ever developed the sensitivity to discern the subtle undercurrents in human relations. Although they extended what was to be a two-day visit to a full week, they never noticed the coolness and tension between Cassie and her husband. Mr. Chivers was even impelled, one evening at dinner, to drop a broad and vulgar hint that he expected to hear any day that his Cassie was "breedin'." Although Kittridge's jaw tightened and Cassie turned alternately rose-red and ashen white, it never occurred to her father that he'd made a gross *faux pas*. He and Miss Penicuick departed from Highlands as happy as grigs, complacently convinced that their Cassie had been granted every blessing that a beneficent God, and a rich father, could bestow.

To Eunice and Cassie, the subtle undercurrents governing Kittridge's moods were abundantly clear. As the days passed and no letters were forwarded from London, his temper grew shorter and his expression darker. It was only Loesby, however, who had the courage to berate him. "Ye needn't bark at everyone like a 'ound wi' distemper," he scolded. "Ye made yer own bed, Cap'n, so it ain't right t' blame the world if the sheets scratch yer backside."

Loesby's homily was not wasted on Lord Kittridge. He made a sincere attempt to hide his unhappiness. He busied himself with the supervision of the renovation work on the farm buildings, forced himself to be a pleasant companion to the women in the evenings and threw himself with such gusto into playing wild games with the girls that Eunice feared he would make tomboys out of them. But in spite of his efforts, Cassie could see the unhappiness deep in his eyes. She found herself wishing, for his sake, that some letters would be delivered soon. If the letters could ease his suffering, she wanted them for him.

One night, about a fortnight after her father's departure, Cassie woke up in the wee hours with a feeling that something was dreadfully amiss. A flickering light from behind the drawn draperies caught her eye. When she opened them, she discovered, to her horror, a strange, frightening red glow in the sky. Something not very far away was burning! Through the trees she could even catch a glimpse of flames!

Alarmed, she threw on her robe and ran out of her room. The halls were dark and silent. Evidently no one else in the house had noticed anything. She ran to Robert's door and hammered on it. "Robert! Robert! Wake up!"

It seemed an eternity before he opened the door. "Cassie?" he mumbled sleepily. "What's amiss? Have you heard another ghost?"

"Look out the window!" she said, trying not to sound terror-stricken. "Something seems to be on fire."

His eyes came instantly awake. Leaving the door open, he ran across the room and flung the drapes aside. "Oh, God!" he gasped. "The new barns!"

"Oh, Robert, *no*!" Cassie cried, her hands reaching out to him in sympathy.

But he took no note of her gesture. He was already pulling on his boots. "If you don't mind, Cassie," he said, "go and wake Loesby. Whitlock, too. And that fool of a butler. We're going to need all the men we can find."

Cassie ran to do his bidding. Before long, everyone was up, dressed and running down across the south lawn, past the outbuildings to the site of the new structure. They all, men and women, struggled through the remainder of the night, passing buckets of water up from the nearest pond. But their efforts were unavailing. By morning the entire structure was a blackened heap of ashes.

The destruction of the new barns was a blow to Kittridge. All his efforts of the past months had burned up in the flames of that new structure. Cassie and Eunice tried to console him with the usual platitudes: that one must be grateful the work was still uncompleted and thus the barns were empty; that there'd been no loss of human or animal life; that the structure could be rebuilt. But Kittridge knew that the cost in time and money meant a major restructuring of his plans. What was worse, he didn't understand how the fire had started or what steps he could or should have taken to protect against such a calamity. Even though Griswold assured him that there was nothing they could have done, either before or during the fire, to prevent what was either an act of God or the carelessness or spitefulness of a trespasser, Kittridge's confidence in his ability to succeed in the task he'd set himself was badly shaken.

Cassie's heart ached for him during the week that followed. He seemed to have been sapped of energy, and all vestiges of joie de vivre were gone from his face. Every circumstance of his life seemed to have combined to defeat him, and she, loving him as she did, grieved that she was unable to ease his lonely lot. She watched from a distance as he stood staring out the sitting room window for hours at a time, his face rigid and his eyes seeing nothing but a bleak future. He did not deserve what fate had done to him, and she, who had married him because she believed she could make him happy, had failed him, too. It was not his fault that he couldn't love her. It was not his fault that she loved him too much. She would have liked to let him know that if he came to her bedroom now, as he'd done those few weeks earlier, she would not refuse to give him whatever solace he required. But he was true to his word and did not come. And she had not the courage to alter what she'd wrought.

After a week of glum passivity, however, Kittridge roused himself to action. He joined the workers in cleaning up the debris, often taking a shovel in hand and laboring with them until he was ready to drop. And he immersed himself in planning the rebuilding. His vigorous activity proved a tonic for everyone else, and soon the household was restored to normalcy.

But an event that was more likely than any other to change normalcy to cheeriness occurred on a bright afternoon in April when Cassie, Eunice and the two little girls were taking tea in the sitting room. A carriage trundled up the drive, stopped at their door and disgorged a handsome, well-dressed, top-of-the-trees dandy. Eunice, glancing out the window, gave a little shriek. "It's *Sandy*!" she cried. "He's *back*!"

"Sandy! Sandy!" the little girls squealed delightedly.

But Eunice's brilliant smile faded at once. "Oh, my heavens, look at me!'' she gasped, jumping from her seat. ''I've got to go up and do something with my hair!''

''Goodness, Eunice, its only Sandy. He won't mind your hair,'' Cassie said, following the hurrying Eunice from the room, the girls trailing excitedly behind.

'' 'Only Sandy,' indeed,'' Eunice retorted, starting up the stairs.

''I thought you were so full of doubts about him,'' Cassie taunted.

Eunice paused and grinned down at her friend. ''I may have doubts about my feelings for him,'' she laughed, ''but I don't intend to give him any reason to doubt his feelings for me.''

While Dickle brought in Sandy's baggage, Cassie and the girls surrounded the new arrival in the doorway, Cassie throwing her arms around his neck in welcome, and the little girls jumping up and down in glee. The commotion had barely subsided when Eunice, resplendent in her prettiest afternoon dress and sporting a jeweled clip in her hastily brushed hair, glided down the stairs. ''Sandy, dear boy,'' she said with complete aplomb, throwing Cassie a twinkling glance while offering Sandy her hand, ''you're back, I see.''

If Sandy was disappointed by Eunice's restrained greeting, he did not show it. They held a merry reunion over the teacups. Sandy, in a bantering tone, berated Eunice for failing to keep their ''appointment'' in London, but, optimist that he was, he didn't seem to be crushed by it. However, he announced firmly that this time he did not intend to leave Lincolnshire until Eunice agreed to return home. ''I promised your mother I would not come back without you,'' he declared.

Cassie, at the mention of her mother-in-law, leaned forward tensely. ''Did her ladyship send any other messages?'' she asked, hoping to learn if he'd brought any letters from Elinor. If ever there was an appropriate moment for Robert to receive love letters, this was that time.

''Messages?'' Sandy echoed, too busy filling his eyes with his ladylove to notice Cassie's intensity. ''She sent affectionate greetings to you all, of course.''

''Did Lady Kittridge . . . send along any letters?''

That question drew his attention. His smile faded. "A few," he said, biting his underlip.

Cassie didn't feel courageous enough to pry any further. But there was something about his response that troubled her.

She was glad when Robert finally joined them. He'd spent the day at the site of the new barn, but when he returned and learned from Dickle that Sir Phillip had arrived from London, he rushed into the sitting room to greet his friend without even pausing to change from his splattered riding boots and breeches.

The gentlemen exchanged warm greetings. But Robert, after ascertaining that Sandy was in good health and intended to make a long stay, did not take many moments before he asked, "I say, Sandy, did my mother forward my letters?"

"Yes," Sandy said, "she did." He seemed uneasy as he removed a small packet of letters from his coat pocket. "I have them here."

Kittridge took the packet and, breaking the string at once, rifled through the letters hastily. There were fewer than half a dozen pieces, not one of which, Cassie noted with despair, was square and buff-colored.

Kittridge, his face unreadable, immediately begged to be excused. "I must not stay in my wife's charming sitting room in all my dirt," he said. "I'll join you all at dinner." He took himself promptly to the door. "It's good to have you back, Sandy," he added, shutting the door behind him so quickly that no one had a chance to protest his abrupt departure.

Eunice, noting Cassie's stricken face, herded her daughters to the door. "Miss Roffey will be wondering where her charges are keeping," she said. "If you both will excuse me, I'll take the girls up to her."

As soon as the door closed behind her, Cassie jumped to her feet. "Goodness, Sandy, what has happened?" she demanded, twisting her fingers together nervously. "Why were there no letters from Elinor?"

"You sound disappointed that there were none," Sandy said in surprise. "One would have thought you'd be glad."

"Then one would have been mistaken," Cassie said shortly.

"You didn't do something mischievous, did you, Sandy, like getting rid of them for my sake?"

"No, of course not," Sandy said, offended. "What do you take me for? A man's letters are sacrosanct, like confessions to a priest."

Cassie's eyes fell. "Yes, of course." She got up and paced about the room, wringing her hands. "Then how do you explain it, Sandy? Elinor wrote every week for two months. Why have the letters suddenly stopped?"

Sandy shrugged. "I'm not certain, but I've heard rumors. The Langstons are staying in Italy now. They say Elinor's been seen in the company of a Venetian count."

Cassie gaped at him. "Good God! Are you suggesting she's fallen in love with *someone else*?"

"How can I tell? But the rumors and the absence of letters do seem to suggest that it's a logical assumption."

"But she *can't*!" Cassie exclaimed, stamping her foot in irritation. "The little wretch can't *do* that to Robert now!"

"But, Cassie, how can you say that? It will be good for your marriage, won't it, if Elinor and Robert forget each other?"

Cassie waved away his words with an impatient flick of her hand. "No, it won't, dash it all! Not now! He hasn't forgotten her, don't you see that? Her letters are all he has left of the life he dreamed he'd have." Tears began to stream down her cheeks unchecked. "When things go b-badly for him, he locks himself in his little study and *rereads* those d-deuced letters for consolation!"

"I say, Cassie, how can you know that?" Sandy demanded suspiciously.

"Never mind. I know. You may take my word." She dashed the tears angrily from her cheeks. "And after all the dreadful things that he's been through, to be so coldly dropped by his precious ladylove is bound to be the last straw! I won't *have* him hurt like that! I *won't*!"

Sandy stared at her in astonishment. He'd never seen Cassie so wrought up. "But I don't see what you can do about it, my dear," he mumbled helplessly, getting up and handing her his handkerchief.

"N-Neither do I," she moaned, dabbing at her eyes. "Neither do I."

He put a consoling arm about her and let her head rest on his shoulder. "Don't cry, Cassie. Tears don't do anything but redden one's—"

The door burst open. "Confound it, Cassie, did you tell that deuced butler to—?" Kittridge, taking belated note of Cassie standing in Sandy's arms, stopped stock still in the doorway, his mouth agape.

Cassie broke from Sandy's hold abruptly. She felt a stab of guilt, not for standing in Sandy's embrace (for, in truth, she'd barely noticed his arm about her), but for the tears she'd been shedding over her husband's disappointment. The last thing in the world she wanted was for him to discover her interest in his private love letters! She turned away so that Robert would not see her face. "*What* did I tell the butler, Robert?" she asked.

"Nothing, nothing," Robert mumbled in embarrassed chagrin. "It's not important. I interrupted. Excuse me." And he backed out of the doorway and shut the door.

"Good God!" Sandy exclaimed, blinking at the door through which Kittridge had just disappeared. "I think the gudgeon suspects me of . . . of fondling his wife!"

"Don't be silly. He must have seen that I was crying. I only hope he didn't suspect that I was crying over him."

"I would much prefer *that* than to have him think you were crying over *me*," Sandy muttered. "He might very well call me out!"

"Call you *out*? Why on earth would he do that?"

Sandy made a gesture of impatience. "Out of jealousy, of course."

"*Jealousy*?" Even in her misery, Cassie had to giggle. "It's you who's the gudgeon, Sandy. Robert wouldn't be jealous over me."

"Why wouldn't he? You're his wife."

"Yes, but you know as well as I that he doesn't love me. What do you suppose I've been agonizing about for the last quarter-hour?"

"Oh, yes. Elinor's letters . . . or rather the lack of them.

I'd forgotten that for a moment.'' He sank down on the hearth
and wrinkled his brow. ''As to that, Cassie,'' he said thoughtfully, ''I think you are needlessly overwrought. Robbie may
suffer a few pangs for a time, but he's bound to get over it.
Elinor's finding a new love will be the best thing for everyone
in the long run. You'll see.''

''Oh, Sandy,'' she chided, both amused and impatient,
''you are truly wonderful. Always the optimist. Has there
ever been a situation so dark that you couldn't find a ray of
light to pin your hopes on?''

''Only when the situation involves me,'' Sandy admitted,
grinning up at her sheepishly. ''Like Eunice not coming down
to London all this time. I was not very optimistic about that,
I'm afraid. Tell me, Cassie, doesn't she care for me at all?''

''I'm not the one to ask, Sandy. Ask her.''

Sandy's full cheeks seemed to sag. ''I think I'm like you,
my dear. Too shy to tell my love.''

''Do you think my problem is shyness, Sandy?'' She dropped
down beside him on the hearth. ''Am I like the girl in *Twelfth
Night*, who 'never told her love, but let concealment, like a
worm in the bud, feed on her damask cheek'?''

''Exactly like her,'' he said, shaking his head admiringly.
''Couldn't have put it better myself.''

''Shakespeare would be flattered,'' she laughed. But soon
her worried frown returned. ''Dash it all, Sandy, I wish my
situation were as simple as that. One can overcome shyness.
What one can't overcome is a love that's placed elsewhere.''

''I wish I could think of some way to help,'' he said.

She got up and crossed thoughtfully to the door. ''Perhaps I
can help myself. Only promise me two things, Sandy, my
dear.''

''Anything. Anything at all.''

''Then first, try not to be shy with Eunice.''

He shrugged dubiously. ''I'll try, but—''

''It won't be hard,'' she assured him. ''Faint heart never
won fair maid, as they say. But the second promise will be
harder to keep. You must promise me that, no matter what,
you won't say a word to Robert about the rumors about
Elinor. Not a single word.''

"But Cassie, what good would it do to keep him in the dark? After all, if no letters come—"

"Perhaps they will," she said mysteriously. "Meanwhile, you must take my word that it will be best for him not to know anything about it."

Chapter Twenty-Eight

When Sandy, on his way to his room to change for dinner, rounded the bend of the stairway, he was startled out of countenance by the sudden appearance of his host, who lunged out of the shadows at him and grabbed him by the lapels of his fashionable riding coat. "What did you think you were *doing*, you damnable bounder?" Kittridge demanded furiously.

"I knew it," Sandy sighed, rolling his eyes heavenward. "I *told* Cassie you'd call me out."

"And so I will," Kittridge snapped, although he was somewhat taken aback by his friend's complacency. "What else can a man do when he finds his best friend trying to seduce his wife?"

"You can loosen your hold on my best coat, for one thing," Sandy said in disgust. "I was *not* trying to seduce your wife. I was letting her cry on my shoulder. Like a friend."

"Like a *friend*?"

"Exactly."

Kittridge released his hold. "It didn't look like a friend's embrace to me," he grumbled sullenly.

Sandy smoothed his crushed lapels calmly. "I don't care how it looked to you. You're out in your reckoning, old fellow. You should think shame on yourself! If you've become so deranged that you believe Philip Sanford would seduce his best friend's wife, your vision is surely askew."

"Am I acting deranged?" Kittridge asked, feeling foolish.

"As the proverbial loon," his friend retorted flatly. "In the first place, any sane man would be able to tell that Cassie isn't the sort to play a husband false. And in the second place, I happen to be in love with your *sister*.''

Kittridge ran a confused hand through his hair. "Then, hang it, why was *my* wife crying on *your* shoulder?''

"That, old fellow," Sandy said, proceeding up the stairs, "is something you'll have to ask her."

"I suppose," Kittridge muttered sheepishly, "I ought to apologize to you."

Sandy turned round and grinned down at his glum-looking friend. "No need for that, Robbie. No offense taken. I know how love can make a man loony."

"Love?" Kittridge gazed up at his friend in genuine astonishment. "Are you suggesting that I'm in love with Cassie?"

"It certainly appears so to me."

"Don't be daft!"

Sandy shrugged. "Have it your way. When it comes to these matters, I'm far from expert." He turned and continued up the stairs. "If I can't determine if Eunice feels the slightest *tendre* for me, how can I be sure about you?"

Kittridge considered the question as he walked slowly to his little study. Could Sandy possibly be right, he asked himself? Was it possible that he'd fallen in love with Cassie without realizing it? His feelings were certainly muddled enough to be the stirrings of love. Ever since the night she'd so adamantly rejected him, he'd become more and more aware of how much he wanted her. But that yearning might only be the automatic response one felt for something one couldn't have. It was certainly not comparable to the adoration he'd felt for Elinor.

He locked himself into his office and, seating himself at his desk, stared at the letters Sandy had brought him today. There was not one from Elinor among them. He'd expected to be devastated by the absence of word from her, but the truth was that he hadn't felt the expected disappointment. In fact, the only feeling he was aware of was relief. He couldn't understand it, but that word "relief" seemed to be the only one that accurately described his emotion.

He took out her letters from their cubicle and opened a few of them. His eyes roamed over the familiar words without bringing him the familiar pain. Was this another sign that he'd fallen in love with Cassie? He shook his head in self-disgust. Was he such a loose screw that he could forget his allegiance to the one great love of his life and attach himself to another in only a few months? The thought sickened him.

On the other hand, rereading Elinor's letters reminded him of the weight of guilt her outpourings of love had pressed upon him all these months. No wonder the absence of a letter brought relief. If Elinor's affection had weakened with time, or if she'd herself fallen in love with someone else, he would no longer need to feel responsible for her unhappiness! As sad as the end of their love might be, it was good to feel the weight of guilt lifted from his shoulders.

He let out a long breath and, leaning back in his chair, tried to stretch his legs out in front of him. But there was not enough room under his narrow desktop. He must, he thought, ask Cassie to find him a larger table. She had a knack for making a room comfortable. Perhaps she would agree to set her talents to work on this place.

Cassie. Even the name had a comfortable resonance. Loesby and Sandy had both been telling him for months how lucky he was to have found her. They were quite right, of course; he could see that now. But that didn't mean he loved her. Even his ridiculous attack of jealousy didn't necessarily mean he loved her, although he had to admit that, when he'd seen her in Sandy's arms, he'd felt a wild, insanely furious desire to wring his best friend's blasted neck!

He had no answer to the mystery of his muddled feelings, but one thought brought a rueful smile to his lips. *Wouldn't it be a delightful surprise*, he asked himself, *if I found myself in love with my own wife*?

Chapter Twenty-Nine

Eunice and her daughters were packing to leave. Cassie would have been heartbroken, except that her sister-in-law's reason for departure was such a happy one. Eunice was going to marry Sandy!

The decision had been made so quickly that it astounded everyone, even Sandy himself. He had followed Cassie's advice and, throwing caution to the winds, made a declaration of love that was not at all shy. "Eunice," he'd declared, pulling her into his arms, "I've been wanting to do this for ten years." And he'd kissed her squarely on the mouth.

"Sandy!" Eunice had gasped. "What does this *mean*?"

"If you don't know," he'd retorted, "I must not be doing it well." And he kissed her again, with even more fervor. It took several more of such demonstrations before she admitted, laughing breathlessly, that he'd made his intentions clear enough. By that time she knew she was his. Her doubts about her feelings for him had entirely disappeared. "I had no idea," she confided giddily to Cassie later, "that he was so . . . so *talented*!"

The day of their departure was a confused amalgam of merriment and tears. The two little girls, while very happy at the prospect of having the cheerful, moon-faced Sandy as their new father, nevertheless stood weeping among the boxes and bags piled up in the Great Hall just before their departure. They'd loved their months at Highlands, and they were thrown into despondency at having to say good-bye to their Uncle Robert and Aunt Cassie. Only the promise that their uncle and aunt would be coming soon to London for the wedding stopped their wails.

Eunice, too, was weeping at the thought of parting from Cassie. Dizzily light-headed as she was at finding herself in love after so many years, she was nevertheless heartbroken at separating from the woman who'd become her best friend. Her ambivalent feelings were clearly visible as she directed the servants in the stowing of the luggage with one hand while dabbing a handkerchief at her eyes with the other.

When the protracted good-byes were under way, and Eunice and the girls were weeping in earnest, Cassie drew Eunice away from the others and asked for a moment of private conversation with her. Eunice, surprised, of course agreed. Cassie led her to the sitting room. "Eunice," she said tensely, carefully closing the door, "I have a very great favor to ask you."

"Anything, Cassie, my love, anything," Eunice assured her, blowing her nose into an already soaking handkerchief.

Cassie put a hand into the bosom of her dress and withdrew some folded sheets of paper. "I've written some letters. Three of them. I want you to . . . to take care of them for me."

"Take care of them?" Eunice's eyebrows rose. "Keep them safe, you mean?"

"No. I mean *send* them."

"I don't understand, Cassie." She cocked her head suspiciously. "Are you up to some mischief?"

"Yes, I'm sure you will think so. They are . . . forgeries."

"*Forgeries*? What on earth—?" Her eyes narrowed. "Has this something to do with Elinor?"

"Yes. Please, Eunice, don't scold. I know what I'm doing is very dreadful, but I can't bear to see Robert so unhappy. If he learned that Elinor no longer cares, it would break his heart. So I've written these in her name. Written them *for* her, so to speak."

Eunice couldn't believe her ears. "You've written letters for *Elinor*?"

Cassie nodded. "All you need do is find the proper note-paper, copy these letters exactly as I've written them, seal and frank them, and have your mother send a messenger back here to deliver them to Robert.''

''You, my love, have taken leave of your *senses*! The whole scheme is impossible. It will never work! Even with the proper notepaper, can you really believe that Robbie won't see at once that the letters are false? Why, the hand-writing alone—''

''I've taken care of that. The first letter explains that she burned her hand badly with candlewax, which is why she couldn't write at all for several weeks. She is now better, but her fingers are still bandaged, so she must write with her left hand. If you use *your* left hand when you write, I'm certain we can be convincing.''

''Even so, Cassie, this is *wrong*. Why should you feel compelled to indulge in so elaborate a pretense? Let him forget her. It will be better for all concerned.''

Cassie shook her head sadly. ''He won't forget her, any more than I would forget *him* if we were separated. Try to understand, Eunice. You and Sandy and the children will be gone. Robert will have no one left but me, and—''

''Good!'' Eunice cut in firmly. ''Perhaps then he will learn to appreciate you properly.''

Desperate to make her friend understand, Cassie grasped her by the shoulders. ''Listen to me, Eunice! Ever since he left the cavalry, Robert has had to make sacrifices. When he married me, he sold his *future*, don't you see that? And it wasn't for his own benefit. It was for the family—for *you*! It isn't fair! Can't we give him this one little gift? Doesn't he deserve to have this one bit of secret happiness?''

Eunice stared at her sister-in-law in awe. ''I don't under-stand you, Cassie. You love him, yet you are willing to give him 'this one bit of secret happiness' with *another* woman. Why?''

''I can't bear it when his eyes get that faraway, yearning look. It makes me miserable. In a way, you know, I am the one who killed his dreams. It can't be right, can it, for a man to have no dreams? We can't change the *reality* of his life, but perhaps we can keep his dreams alive. In the dimness of his future, shouldn't we try to give him one small ray of light that he can look forward to?''

"Oh, Cassie," Eunice moaned in surrender, throwing her arms about her sister-in-law's neck, "when you speak so, you give me no choice but to do your bidding. I'll write your blasted letters for you."

They held each other tightly for a long moment. Then Eunice took the folded papers and stuffed them in her reticule. Cassie, in relief, gave her one last, fervent embrace. "Thank you, Eunice," she murmured in Eunice's ear. "I shall be forever in your debt."

"I don't want you in my debt," Eunice retorted gruffly as she went to the door, "but if truth comes out, and this whole, preposterous scheme explodes in your face, I shall refuse to take even a *speck* of blame!"

Chapter Thirty

The messenger delivered the packet of letters in midafternoon of a rainy day a week later. Kittridge was out at the building site when Dickle accepted the packet. Cassie, who'd waited on tenterhooks all week for this moment to arrive, hid behind the curve of the stairway to await his return. She wanted to see Robert's face when he first glimpsed the letters.

It was teatime when he came home. Dickle, pompous as always, admitted him into the Great Hall and held the packet out to him. "These came from London, my lord," he announced. "A messenger delivered them at three this afternoon."

Robert, in the act of brushing the raindrops from his shoulders, froze. He stared at the buff-colored envelopes for a long moment, quite stony-faced, and then, snatching them from Dickle's hand, strode off to his study without a word. If Cassie had hoped to see a sign of gladness or excitement in his face as a reward for her endeavors, she was doomed to disappointment.

Robert, for his part, was filled with ambivalence. He hadn't thought about Elinor for days. He'd been thinking, instead, about Cassie. She, not Elinor, was his life's companion, and he'd been trying to think of ways to overcome her stubborn resistance to his advances. Now the letters brought his memories of Elinor flooding back to confuse him, and he wasn't sure he welcomed them. The past, he was beginning to realize, could sometimes become a burden. His own past was suddenly appearing so to him. It seemed to be a barricade in his advance to the future, and he had enough barricades to climb already.

Nevertheless, his feelings for Elinor were of such long standing that, almost without thinking, his old reactions swept over him. Staring at her letters, he tried to bring her lovely face to mind, as he had done hundreds of times before. But the vision he conjured up was indistinct, and he wondered guiltily if he was even forgetting what she looked like. Sighing, he broke the seal of the first letter. The awkward handwriting disconcerted him for a moment, but soon the warmth of her words riveted his attention. The mood of the letter was different from the earlier ones. It was more gentle, and sadly reminiscent. And the last paragraph brought a clench to his heart. *"I like to imagine,"* she wrote, *"that sometimes you can feel what I feel, despite the miles between us. When my hand burned, I convinced myself that at the same moment you must have experienced a sting. One day, when I felt an unexplained tingle on my cheek, I let myself believe that you were rubbing yours and sending the touch through the ether right to me. I suppose such thoughts are foolish, but it comforts me to believe that love like ours is capable of creating small miracles. Please, my beloved, when you read this, rub your cheek and think of me!"*

Her continuing devotion, so obvious in her words, made him wince. How was it possible, he wondered, that so lovely a girl—who, with the crook of a finger, could summon a dozen suitors to her side—would keep her affection for him alive so long without the hope of any response? While he, cad that he was, was already growing attached to someone else.

The next letter made him feel worse. *"It was warm today,"* she wrote, *"and I sat on a garden bench looking up at the sky. The cloud formations irritated me, for none of them took your shape. There was one cloud like a man's head, but the nose was not yours. I began to have the silliest thoughts. I wished that I could find a brush long enough to paint on the sky. I could not paint your face, of course—even in dreams I know I am no artist—but I had this ridiculous urge to paint your name—Robert, Robert, Robert!—over and over in an arching line until, like a rainbow, it would stretch from horizon to horizon. I am growing quite demented.''*

But it was something in the last letter that undid him. *''I like to remember your quirks,''* she wrote. *''They keep you real for me. I remember how you rub the underside of your nose with your right forefinger when you're about to say something you're afraid you shouldn't. Or the way a muscle right above your jaw twitches with tension when you're angry. Or the way you run your fingers through your hair when you feel bewildered. Just writing these words is enough to conjure up your face for me, and I can see you in such detail that you become palpable . . . as real as if you were standing here. It's only when I try to touch you that the vision dissolves into nothingness, and I am left bereft.''*

The words made Robert groan in agony. His fingers tightened into fists, crushing the last letter into a crumpled ball. Poor, lovely Elinor! She could conjure him up in every detail, while he cauld scarcely remember her face. She offered him her love with such openhearted generosity that the very words with which she expressed it made his throat burn, while he lusted every day, with an ache in his loins that drove him to distraction, for someone else entirely! He was not worthy of Elinor! Or of Cassie, either, for that matter. The letters made him see himself for the loathsome toad he was. They made him hate himself.

But what sin had he committed to cause this shambles, this triangular trap that had distorted three lives? Had he sold his soul to the devil when he'd made his bargain with Chivers? But that bargain had not been the cause of Elinor's pain. His father, and hers, had done the damage long before he'd signed his devil's pact with Chivers. But even if he took the blame upon himself, it made no difference, for there was no way out of the trap no matter who was to blame. *It's as if I were cursed,* he thought as he tenderly smoothed out the paper he'd crushed, folded it and put it with the others into the cubicle. He was living under some witch's curse for which there was no antidote. Why couldn't he find a magic amulet, a wand, a wizard's potion, a virgin's kiss that would break the spell under which he was doomed to live? But no, not in this life. Only in fairy stories did the toad turn into a prince after a maiden's kiss.

Cassie, meanwhile, having no idea of the turmoil the letters had aroused in her husband's breast, basked in self-satisfaction over the success of her forgery. She'd done it! Robert had been closeted for hours in his study. If he'd found anything wrong with the letters, there would surely have been some sign of it by this time. As the minutes passed, she became more and more convinced that her letters had been a success. Robert was surely finding in them the solace he needed. Just as she wished, the letters were balm to his wounded soul. The feelings they generated would probably nourish him for weeks.

For weeks. The two words seemed suddenly to reverberate in her head. *After a few weeks, what then?* she asked herself with a start. How soon would it be before he began to look for more? What could she do then? She could write more letters, of course, but Eunice would probably refuse to commit her hand to any more forgeries. And even if she did, how could Cassie get the letters to her without being discovered? Why hadn't she thought of that before? The letters, to be effective, had to keep coming, but she had no way of accomplishing that. Yet, if they stopped coming, Robert would be in a worse case than before. What had she done?

She prowled round the sitting room, searching her mind for an answer. And right before dinner time, it came to her. She simply had to get to London, to give Eunice a new supply of letters and convince her to keep up the pretense a while longer. It could be done, if only Robert would agree to take her to town.

At the table that evening, she looked across at him speculatively. He seemed abstracted and somewhat dazed. It gave her a feeling of rueful pride that her words—her own love feelings—had had so strong an effect on him. But the apparent success of the letters made it all the more necessary to solve the problem at hand. She hesitated to raise the subject that was on her mind, but sooner or later it had to be done. After almost an hour of complete silence, she cleared her throat. "Robert?" she began timidly.

"Yes," he said absently.

"Do you remember, that night before we were married, when we talked about settling in the country?"

"Yes, of course." He pushed his plate away from him. "What about it?"

"Do you remember saying that you would take me back to town for a month or so in season?"

He lifted his head abruptly. This was the request he'd expected from the first—her admission of her desire to mingle with the *ton*, to play the role of Viscountess Kittridge on the town! It was the purpose for which he assumed she'd married him. All thoughts of Elinor evaporated as his eyes focused on the woman across the table, his whole body tensing. "Yes, I remember," he said, watching her carefully.

"The season has already begun, you know. Do you think we might go, at least for a fortnight?"

"Well, we shall be going, you know, for Eunice's wedding."

"But that's in June. Two months away. Couldn't we . . . would it be asking too much to go now, and then again in June?"

He leaned back in his chair. "It would be too much for me, I'm afraid. The ground is to be broken for the tenants' housing strip next week. I don't see how I can spare the time."

"Oh . . . I see."

He could hear the disappointment in her voice. He clenched his teeth, trying to bring his own disappointment under control. She'd seemed so satisfied to be in the country all these months that he'd forgotten his original estimate of her motivation for marriage. But now it was clear—she *was* a parvenu after all. Well, if it was a life in society that she wanted, she could have it. She'd certainly paid for it. "You could go without me, I suppose," he offered, testing her.

"Could I, Robert? I do so wish to go. I would only stay a week or so."

"You can stay as long as you like," he said, a wave of disgust toward her sweeping over him. "Until the wedding is over in June, if you like."

His words struck her like a slap. She didn't understand why

he'd said that. She wanted to go to town only to make the arrangements about the letters. The week away from home would seem like an eternity to her. Yet he was willing to part with her until the end of June! "Oh, no," she murmured, her voice choking up with tears. "A w-week will be quite enough."

With his mouth twisted into a sneer, he pushed back his chair and rose. *A week, indeed*, he said to himself in revulsion. Was this the creature he thought he might care for more than Elinor? What a fool he was! She wouldn't come back in a week, or even a month. Not as long as she enjoyed queening it in town! *I'll lay odds she postpones her return indefinitely*, he told himself. But aloud he only said, "Suit yourself, Cassie. It makes no difference to me." And, cold as ice, he strode across the room and out the door.

Chapter Thirty-One

Cassie was utterly confused. As she sat over her embroidery frame in her lonely sitting room, she found herself dripping silent tears on the stitches. What had gone wrong? she asked herself miserably. She'd hoped to make her husband happy by her subterfuge, but if the letters had been, as she'd hoped, a balm to his wounded soul, she saw no sign of it. The two of them were barely speaking. Yet her portmanteau and two bandboxes stood packed and ready in the Great Hall for removal the next morning to the carriage that was to take her to London. Robert had instructed Loesby to arrange for the coachman to be at the door at seven. She was leaving. And without him.

Cassie had no real wish to go, for the terrible coldness that had sprung up between them pained her more than anything else that had happened to her. She had no understanding of the cause, but she feared that her absence would only make matters worse. But her dishonest forgery scheme, now launched, had to be continued. She saw no way around it. And to continue it, she had to go to London to see Eunice.

She wiped her eyes, wondering if Robert would join her for tea this last day before she went away. Taking tea with her was an observance he'd been avoiding for the past few days, but perhaps today he would take the trouble to join her. It would be an act of kindness that would ease her mind a little. When, just at teatime, a knock sounded at the sitting room door, her heart leaped up to her throat. But it was only Dickle. ''A message from London, my lady,'' he said. "The messenger said that no answer was required.''

"A message for his lordship?'' Cassie inquired in surprise. "How strange! His mother forwarded some letters only two days ago.''

"It's addressed to *you*, my lady,'' Dickle said in a tone that was unmistakably disapproving. "Marked 'Private and Personal' in large letters, as you can see.''

"Private and personal?'' Cassie snatched the missive from him and waved him out. The pompous fellow evidently assumed that any letter marked 'private and personal' must contain a wicked message. Did the idiotic fellow think she was carrying on some sort of indiscretion? Cassie herself, however, while amused at her butler, was almost as uneasy about the contents as he was. In fact, her hands were shaking. She'd never received a letter marked "private and personal" in all her life.

It was from Eunice. *"Dearest Cassie,''* Eunice had written in a hurried scrawl, *"I hope you are reading this in Complete Privacy. And I think, when you have Finished, you should Burn this in the Fire. I've taken the Risk of writing because something has Occurred that you should know. E.L. is back in London! I'm sure you can Guess whom I mean. She is Betrothed to her Italian Conte, and I hear she has been Parading him about Town as Proudly as a Peacock. She has not yet Called on me, undoubtedly in Embarrassment over Robbie, but I expect I shall have to Face her soon. I intend to tell her that Robbie is Divinely Happy and in transports over his Wonderful Wife. What Worries me about this matter is, as you've probably guessed, the Danger to You. If Robbie doesn't hear about her before June, he's Bound to learn Everything then, of course, because you will Both be coming to Town for my Wedding! She will Have to be Invited, worse Luck, and then, in addition to Learning about her Betrothal, he might discover that She never wrote the Letters! The Fat will be in the Fire then! I only pray that Robbie may not Murder you! How you are to get yourself out of this Fix I have no Idea, but You, my Love, are Endlessly Resourceful, and I am certain you will think of Something. In the meantime, you may rest*

*assured I am Praying for a Happy Outcome. I Remain Your
Loving and Terror-stricken Eunice.''*

By the time she'd finished reading, Cassie was deathly
pale. She sat where she was, utterly immobilized. Eunice
might believe that she was "Endlessly Resourceful," but she
couldn't even think of where or how to begin to extricate
herself from this nightmare. Of course, the first thing she had
to do was to burn Eunice's letter, but the day was very warm
and no fires had been lit in any of the rooms. With trembling
knees, she marched herself down to the kitchen and, ignoring
the wide-eyed stares of the astounded kitchen staff, lifted one
of the stovelids and dropped the letter in. She waited until she
was sure it was burned to a cinder and then marched out again
with her head high. The staff might think she'd lost her mind,
but if there was one thing in the world she did *not* have to
worry about, it was the opinion of the kitchen staff.

Dinner that night was another silent meal. Cassie did not
know how to tell her husband that she was not going to
London after all. It was, on the face of it, a simple enough
thing to do, but the prospect embarrassed her, especially
because he'd seemed almost eager to see her go. He'd even
encouraged her to stay until June! And, worse, she'd been so
insistent about wanting to go! What would he make of her
sudden change of heart? What excuse could she give? She
was not up to telling him the truth just yet, but she could not
countenance another lie. Perhaps the best thing to do would
be to give no excuse at all.

She tried ten times to tell Robert that she'd changed her
mind, and ten times her courage failed her. It was only when
the meal was almost over that she managed it, and even then
it was because Robert brought the subject up. "If I miss you
in the morning, Cassie," he said in a tone of stiff politeness,
"I hope you have a pleasant journey and an enjoyable stay in
town."

"I'm not going," she blurted out.

"What did you say?" Robert asked in disbelief.

"I said I'm not going."

"You can't be serious!" He peered at her through the
candlelight. "The plans have all been made!"

"I know," she said nervously, getting up and edging toward the door, "but p-plans can b-be unmade. I'm not going."

"But, *why*?" he demanded, pushing his chair back as if to rise.

His movement made her jump. "I changed my m-mind, that's all. I j-just changed my mind." And with that she fled from the room.

Feeling quite like a criminal, she scurried upstairs to her bedroom and shut the door. For the next hour she paced about the room, for she knew her troubles were not over. Not nearly. Elinor was back in London with a new betrothed, and Robert was bound to find out. And he was bound to find out, too, that Elinor had not written the last three letters. Cassie knew that she would have to confess to Robert what she'd done. But the admission would involve informing him about Elinor, and she didn't see how she could do that without causing him pain. Furthermore, he would be furious with her for playing so dastardly a trick on him, and she couldn't even guess what terrible form that fury would take. Even Eunice said he might murder her! She remembered, when she'd invaded his privacy and read Elinor's letters, she'd imagined herself as Bluebeard's wife—one of the six who'd been hacked to death for invading the forbidden room. When she'd first thought of the Bluebeard legend, the prospect of murder had been a sort of joke. It did not seem so funny now. She had done worse than invade a forbidden room! If her Robert became Bluebeard and dismembered her poor body, she'd deserve it!

Her wild thoughts were interrupted by a knock at the door. "Cassie, open the door," Robert ordered. "I have to talk to you."

"I'm already abed," she lied, jumping into it and pulling the covers over her to make it true.

"Dash it, Cassie, one would think I intended to *beat* you! I just want to know why you're not going to London."

"I've already told you," she insisted, not moving from the bed. "I changed my mind. It's a woman's privilege, isn't it?"

"Yes, of course. I have no objection to your staying home," he said reasonably. "I only want to know *why*."

"I'm tired," she said. "Can't we talk about it tomorrow?"

"Oh, very well," came his voice, thick with disgust. "But I must say, Cassie, that your behavior this evening has been very, very peculiar. Well, if you're sure you won't say any more, I'll bid you good night."

"Good night, Robert," she answered in relief.

Once he'd gone, she got up and undressed, but as she crawled back into bed she knew she would not sleep. How could she, knowing that the very next day she would have to tell Robert everything? There was no way out.

Of course, she could postpone it, she supposed. He was unlikely to learn about Elinor before June. Perhaps her best course of action would be to ignore everything and let him discover the truth for himself at the wedding. She shut her eyes and tried to imagine how his discovery might take place. Robert, at the wedding, would come upon Elinor at the buffet table. "Elinor!" he'd gasp. "You are as lovely as ever."

"*Dear* Robert," she'd smile, blushing prettily, "you mustn't say such things to me. Haven't you heard that I'm betrothed?"

"Betrothed?" He would undoubtedly turn white. "You *can't* be betrothed!"

"But, my dear, I am! Since last March, when I was in Italy. There is my betrothed, over there near the window. The Italian, with the *mustachios*."

"Since *March*?" Robert would gape at her in confusion. "How can that be? You wrote me in *April* that you still loved me! You said you wanted to paint my name across the sky!"

"I?" She would laugh a trilling laugh. "I would never have written anything so silly. In fact, I haven't written to you at all since . . . oh, since February."

Robert would stare at his beloved, wide-eyed with horror. "But who," he would wonder aloud, "would have played so dastardly a trick on me?" His eyes would suddenly narrow in comprehension. *"Cassie!"* he would exclaim, tight-lipped with fury. "Who else would be capable of such revolting underhandedness?"

And then, eyes blazing, he would confront her in front of

all the wedding guests. A sword would flash in the air. There would be screams and confusion. Cassie would have to fall to her knees. "Robert, spare me!" she would beseech. "I didn't think—!"

But the sword would whizz swiftly through the air and down! The sounds of women shrieking and men shouting would drown out Cassie's last scream . . .

She sat up in bed with a start. Had she screamed aloud? She really had to get hold of herself. These imaginings were becoming too lurid for words.

She slid back onto her pillows and pulled the bedclothes up to her neck. She had to try to get some sleep, for tomorrow would be a difficult day. Since her imagined scene had made it clear that she could not subject her husband to such a humiliating scene at his sister's wedding, she would have to tell him everything herself. Tomorrow would have to be the day.

She shuddered and burrowed deeper into her pillows. *Yes*, she thought as sleep slowly overtook her, *tomorrow will be my punishment*.

Chapter Thirty-Two

Whenever Loesby suspected that Lord Kittridge and his lady had had a quarrel, he expressed his disapproval by clucking his tongue, shaking his head and behaving as if his lordship had affronted him personally. "I s'pose, m' lord, ye'll be wantin' yer boots removed?" he asked icily after Kittridge had stormed into his bedroom following the exchange with his wife in the corridor.

"Since I'd rather not go to bed wearing them," Kittridge retorted, sitting on his bed and extending a foot, "yes, I'd like them removed, if you wouldn't mind."

"Much ye'd care if I *did* mind," Loesby muttered, dragging off a boot. "Some people don't seem to care about *anyone's* feelin's these days."

Kittridge glared at him. "You were eavesdropping again, I take it?"

Loesby pulled off the other boot. "Didn't 'ave to. Everyone fer miles about could 'ear ye. An' 'ow a man wot calls 'isself a gen'leman cin tell 'is lady that she's actin' *peculiar* is beyond me!"

Kittridge pulled off his coat and threw it at his valet. "Mind your own business for a change, will you, Loesby? You don't know anything about the matter."

"I know enough. She decided not t' take off fer town. Wut's so damn peculiar about that? If I wuz a lady, an' me better 'alf wouldn't go along wi' me, I wouldn't go neither."

Kittridge paused in the act of unbuttoning his shirt and

stared at the fellow speculatively. "Do you think *that's* her reason? That I wasn't going along with her?"

Loesby shrugged. "Wut else?"

"There are any number of other possibilities. But I don't intend to stand here and argue the matter with you. You always defend her, anyway, no matter what I have to say. So you can just take yourself off, you bobbing-block. I've seen enough of you for one day."

"Don't ye want 'elp wi' yer breeches?"

"I can undress myself, thank you. Good night!"

But after the valet departed, Kittridge didn't bother to finish undressing. He threw himself upon his bed in his stockinged feet, still wearing his half-unbuttoned shirt and his breeches, and, with his hands tucked under his head, stared up at the ceiling. He had to think. This undeclared war with Cassie was getting on his nerves. Every time he believed he was beginning to understand her, something would occur to overset him. He'd believed, at first, that she was a conniving parvenu. Then, after the early months here at Highlands, he'd begun to believe she was sincere in her expressed desire to live a modest country life. She seemed to take to it so well. He'd even begun to think of her as rather a jewel—a "wonder" as Loesby liked to call her. But the other day, her request to run off to town, just when the work on the estate was getting into full swing, returned him to his original suspicions. Then this evening, as if on purpose to upset him again, she boldly announced that she didn't want to go to London after all. What on earth was he expected to make of *that*?

To make matters more confused, he still suspected that he'd fallen in love with her. Nothing she did, no matter how annoying or reprehensible, had the power to loosen her growing hold on him. Even Elinor's recent and quite wonderful letters hadn't managed to free him from the subtle, inexplicable allure that Cassie seemed to exert on him. What was wrong with him? How could he have permitted this devious and manipulative female to lure him from his pledged loyalty to his first love?

It surprised him that even the recent letters had not brought him back to his earlier state of mind. None of the letters Elinor had written before had moved him as much as these. They made Elinor seem more gentle and touching, and a good deal less sorry for herself. She seemed, somehow, to have matured. Why, then, hadn't they made a difference? Why hadn't they weakened the growing hold that Cassie had on his emotions?

Perhaps it was because the change in Elinor's style of writing made her seem, suddenly, a bit unrecognizable. He couldn't hear her voice in the words any more. And the strange handwriting added to the confusion. It almost seemed as if someone else had written those letters. Even the way Elinor had said his name sounded unfamiliar. What was it she'd written? *I had this ridiculous urge to paint your name across the sky—Robert, Robert, Robert!* She'd never called him Robert before. From early childhood she'd always called him Robbie. Everyone called him Robbie except . . .

He sat up with a start, a shocking idea flashing across his brain like a lightning bolt. Everyone called him Robbie except *Cassie!*

The idea, once it burst upon him, took over his mind with the crystal clarity of truth. *Elinor hadn't written those letters at all! Cassie had!* He could even hear Cassie's voice saying the words! He didn't know how, and he certainly didn't know *why*, but he was as sure as his name was Robert Rossiter that Cassie had done it. And as the conviction grew that he'd stumbled on the truth, a knot formed in the pit of his stomach, and, slowly, a fury such as he'd never known burst out and spread like a poison to every part of his body. He wanted to take a chair and heave it through a window. He wanted to smash the walls with his fists. He wanted to feel Cassie's throat in his two hands and squeeze it until she went limp and lifeless in his hold. Yes, that was it! He wanted to *murder* her!

Maddened with rage, he lit a candle with shaking hands. Then he plunged down the stairs to his study, pulled out the three letters and stormed up again, the candle in one fist and the letters clenched in the other. Using his shoulder to batter his way in, he crashed through Cassie's door.

Cassie, curled into a ball under her bedclothes, had just dozed off when the crash woke her. She sat up, shuddering in terror as Robert, eyes glittering with rage in the eerie light of his single candle, strode to the side of her bed. "What, ma'am, was the meaning of *this*?" he snarled, holding up the letters before her.

"R-Robert?" she stammered, not sure whether the threatening apparition standing over her was a vision from a nightmare or Bluebeard in the flesh.

"Yes, it's 'Robert.'" He shook the letters in her face. "Well, ma'am? Explain, if you can, why you wrote these damned letters!"

"Oh, heavens," she gasped, turning ashen, "how—?"

"Never mind how! I am a dozen ways a fool, but did you think me such a dupe that I could be humbugged by these . . . these inept imitations?"

"Robert, *please*!" she begged, sitting up and edging along the headboard away from him in sheer terror of his white-lipped rage. "Don't go on! I didn't intend—"

"Didn't intend what? To humbug me?"

"Well, no . . . yes . . . I m-mean . . . not exactly . . ."

He slammed down the candle on her bedside table. "What sort of craven evasion is *that*?" he demanded. "*Of course* you intended it! When someone signs a letter with a name that is not one's own, the intention *must* be to deceive, isn't that so?"

"Yes, but—"

"And you *did* write these, did you not? And you did sign Elinor's name to your fraudulent creations?"

"Yes," she answered in a hoarse, shamed whisper. "Yes."

He stared at her, her admission of guilt killing the last hope, hidden somewhere deep within him, that he'd accused her wrongly. "How could you?" he asked with unmistakable loathing, dropping the letters from his hold as if releasing something noxious. "What have I ever done to you to make you wish to make a mockery of my private sorrows?"

"Robert!" she cried out, agonized. "You *can't* believe that I meant to mock you!"

"What else am I to believe? The more I think about it, the

more repugnant the act becomes. I never intended for you to know anything of Elinor's existence, since it was not a matter that had anything to do with you. But you learned of it somehow—Eunice's glib tongue, I have no doubt. And having learned of it, you couldn't just let it be. You had to interfere, is that it? You somehow discovered that she wrote to me, although I don't know how—" Just then, another hideous awareness broke upon him like a blow to the jaw. "Good God!" He glared down at her with increased revulsion. "You must have stolen into my study, opened my desk and *read her letters*!"

Cassie shut her eyes in utter humiliation, unable to face the burning hostility in his. "Oh, Robert, I'm s-so . . . *sorry*," she mumbled helplessly, dropping her face in her hands.

"Sorry!" He spat out the word with utter disdain. He pulled her hands from her face, grasped both her shoulders and lifted her up until her eyes were on a level with his. "Never mind your 'sorry'! What I want to know is *why*!"

Tears welled up in her eyes. "I thought . . . I only w-wanted . . . for you to be h-happy."

"Happy!" He gave a mirthless, disbelieving snort. "I'd like to wring your blasted neck!" he ranted. "If you're going to keep on *lying*, you surely can do better than that!"

Her eyes looked pleadingly into his. "It's the truth, I swear. What other reason—?"

He shook his head. "I wish I knew." He dropped his hold on her and let her fall back upon the pillows. Their eyes met, hers wide with acute, tormented remorse and his narrowed with such bewildered antipathy that she had to turn away and bury her face in the pillows.

"All these months I've wondered what sort of woman it was I've married," he said after a long silence, his voice now quieter but infused with scorn. "I've never been able to understand you. It didn't seem possible that you, with your oh-so-gentle manner and oh-so-modest demeanor, would agree to shackle yourself to a stranger merely for the sake of calling yourself a viscountess. But I could think of no other motive. Yet you came to live here, far away from any society among whom you could preen yourself with your new title. And you won everyone over, even Sandy, who'd once described you—before you put him in your spell—as a 'manipulative *intrigante*.' You even had *me* believing I was falling in love with you. What a damn fool I was! You *are* a manipulative *intrigante* after all! You first wrested control of the household from Eunice—and so cleverly, too, that you now have her eating out of your hand. And now, I suppose, it is *I* whom you want to control, although how you intended to manage it with forged letters from Elinor is beyond my puny understanding. As to the why of it, it is all too subtly devious for me. But all at once I find I don't care any more. I don't *want* to understand. I just want to take myself out of here, before I choke on my disgust of you!'' And with those cutting words, he slammed out of the room and left her to her shame.

Chapter Thirty-Three

Robert drank all of an almost full bottle of brandy before falling on his bed. He hoped that getting himself soused would help him forget the devious little schemer to whom he was leg-shackled. He fell asleep hugging the empty bottle to his chest. Several hours later, deep in a dream in which he was holding Cassie tightly against him and trying desperately to make out the words she was murmuring softly into his chest, he felt someone tugging at what he was holding in his arms. He opened his eyes to find Loesby trying to take away the empty bottle while glaring down at him with a pinched-mouth expression of disgust. "So ye're awake, are ye?" the valet sneered, removing the bottle from his lordship's suddenly unresistant grasp.

Robert shut his eyes again. "Someone's hammering inside my head," he mumbled miserably.

"Serves ye right," Loesby retorted unsympathetically, stalking to the windows and pulling back the draperies with such loud force that his lordship groaned. "Do ye wish to wear wut ye slept in, me lord," he asked, his nose wrinkled in revulsion, "or do ye wish to change?"

Robert put a hand to his aching forehead. When his valet called him "me lord," it always meant trouble, but his head pained him too much to exert himself to find out why. Besides, he had troubles enough. His last words to Cassie were still reverberating in his brain and making him feel like a bounder. In his sleep his brain had been actively recalling to his consciousness the many occasions when she'd seemed so completely sweet and charming that it was hard to believe that she could be the devious schemer she had seemed last night. She'd committed a serious transgression, true, but he hadn't given her sufficient opportunity to explain. He'd said many unkind things that he was now sorry for; the hammer blows in his head were not the only things making him feel sick. Somehow he knew that he would not feel better until he spoke to her again. All he wanted now was to go to her room and talk things over calmly.

He lifted himself up from his pillow, groaning with the effort. "I'll change later," he told the valet. "Just hand me my boots."

"Wut fer?" Loesby asked scornfully as he took a clean shirt from the chest of drawers. "Do ye think ye're goin' somewheres?"

"Yes. I'm going to see my wife, if you don't mind," his lordship retorted, pulling himself erect by hanging on the bedpost.

"Ye'll 'ave to run pretty quick," Loesby said. "She's miles away by now."

Robert felt his chest clench. "Miles away?"

Loesby nodded. "Sent fer the carriage at seven this mornin'. Said she'd changed 'er mind again and was off to town. She looked mighty red-eyed about it, too, if ye ask me."

A feeling of desolate emptiness swept over him. "Did she leave a message? A note?"

Loesby shook his head. "No, but I found these in 'er room, tossed in the grate." He gave Kittridge a sly look as he handed him the three crushed, buff-colored envelopes. "Fished 'em out just before the maid set about lightin' the fire."

"I suppose you think you've earned my undying gratitude for that," Robert growled, stuffing the letters into his pocket. "Well, you haven't. Don't think I'm not aware that you read them. I have as much privacy in my life as a damned fish in a jar!"

Crestfallen and angry, he ordered Loesby out of the room and lowered himself slowly back down on the bed. Cassie was gone. His wife had left him. Was her departure supposed to be a punishment? And if so, was it meant for him or for herself? Well, at least he knew the answer to that. *She* might have been red-eyed, but *he*, he acknowledged as he put a shaking hand to his hammering head, was sick unto death.

A few days later, however, he'd recovered not only his health but his rage. He'd spent the time of his recovery dwelling on his injuries. His wife had injured him by her inexplicable invasion of his privacy. His sister had injured him by supporting his wife against him, for he'd soon deduced that it was Eunice who'd been enlisted to post the fraudulent letters. Sandy and Loesby had injured him, too, by siding with Cassie all the time. He'd been wounded to the heart by all of them!

By the time three days had passed, his rage was full-blown. He was furious that Cassie had left without a word. He was furious that he'd even *considered* making it up with her. He was furious that he was unable to put his mind to anything else. Something had to be done to release all the fury pent up inside him. "Send for the phaeton, Loesby," he ordered suddenly. "I'm going to settle things once and for all. We're going to London!"

Loesby, who'd been glowering at his lordship for three whole days, broke into a smile. "Well, well," he chortled, rubbing his hands together in approval, "*now* ye're talkin'!"

Chapter Thirty-Four

The first person who greeted Lord Kittridge on his arrival at the Rossiter House in Portman Square was his brother Gavin. "So, Robbie, you've finally come back to town, have you?" the lad asked, not even pausing on his way out the door. "That's splendid."

"Just a moment, Gavin," his elder brother said, catching his arm. "Why aren't you at school?"

"I've been sent down. But I'm too busy to go into details now, old fellow. I'm off to Tattersall's to look at a roan. See you at dinner."

Kittridge looked after his brother with a troubled frown. The boy was wasting his life, and no one seemed to be in the least concerned about it. He was about to call after him when his mother suddenly appeared, descending the stairs with her delicate grace. "Darling!" she exclaimed in delight. "We weren't expecting you until the nuptials. What a lovely surprise!"

He kissed her cheek. "You look thriving, Mama," he said. "Planning a wedding must agree with you."

"I wish I could say the same for you, my dear," his mother said, peering at him keenly as she took his arm and strolled with him to the sitting room. "You've shadows under your eyes, and you're looking too thin. I knew that your marriage to that *bourgeoise* would undo you, no matter what encomiums Eunice heaps on her."

"See here, Mama," Robert chided while he handed her over the threshold and into an easy chair, "I won't have you casting aspersions on my wife. If I look worn, you may blame it on the fourteen-hour drive from Lincoln—''

"Robbie!" The scream came from the doorway, and in flew Eunice in a flurry of ruffles and flounces. She threw her arms round his neck ecstatically. "What are you doing here? We weren't expecting you for weeks! How lovely that you came so soon! Where's—?"

He removed her arms from about him with icy formality. "Never mind the effusions, ma'am. I'm sure you'll understand that, under the circumstances, I don't care to speak to you. Please be good enough to inform Lady Kittridge that I'm here."

Eunice blinked at him in stupefaction. "Do you mean Mama? She sitting right behind you."

"Of course I don't mean Mama. I mean my wife, as you very well know."

"Your wife? *Cassie?* Isn't she with you?"

It was now Robert's turn to look stupefied. "She left Lincolnshire several days ago. Do you mean she isn't here?"

"I knew it," his mother said with some satisfaction. "You've quarreled. I knew the marriage was a mistake. I said so from the first."

"Oh, Mama, do be still," Eunice snapped, glaring down at her. "Your baseless judgments do you no credit. Cassie is too good for your idiot son, if you ask me. Now be a dear, mama, and do go away. Why don't you see to Robbie's baggage or make sure his room is ready? I want to talk to Robbie alone."

"Eunice, really!" her mother exclaimed, rising in offense. "I have as much right to hear what the new Lady Kittridge has been up to as you do. More, in fact."

"It might be best, Mama, to do as Eunice asks," Robert said. "I have a few words to say to your idiot *daughter* that are not fit for a mother's ears."

The dowager Lady Kittridge looked from one to the other of her offspring with raised brows, poised to debate them both. But then, capitulating with a shrug, she turned on her heel and sailed proudly from the room, muttering under her breath that it was a mistake ever to have bred them.

Eunice rounded on her brother as soon as their mother was gone. "What do you mean, a few words not meant for a mother's ears? Have I done something to offend you?"

"Don't play the innocent with me, ma'am. I know about the letters."

"Oh!" Eunice's eyes fell. "I *told* Cassie it was a terrible idea. But how on earth did you find out?"

"I'm not such a fool as you both seem to think. I can tell the difference between Elinor's style and Cassie's."

"Yes, I thought you might. Cassie has so much more . . . sincerity." She looked up at her brother with a troubled crease in her forehead. "I suppose you and Cassie had a dreadful row over it."

"You suppose correctly."

"And she's run off? You must have been horrid to her."

"Wouldn't you have been, in my place?" he snapped. "It's a bit degrading, to say the least, to have one's privacy invaded and one's inner feelings mocked by one's own wife . . . and one's own sister."

"Mocked?" Eunice gaped at him. "What are you talking about?"

"Isn't that what motivated you both? I admit that I find the whole incident too confusing to comprehend. But you, Eunice, have too strong a character to let Cassie manipulate you into doing something you believe is wrong. So I don't know what else could have convinced you to agree to such a despicable deception. What else could your purpose have been but to have a vulgar laugh at my expense?"

"You *are* a fool, Robbie. Do you know Cassie so little that you can believe she did this just to laugh at you? And do you know me so little, too?"

He stared at his sister in confusion. "Then why on earth—?"

"To make you happy, confound it! What else?"

"To make me *happy*?" He ran his fingers through his hair in frustration, feeling as though she were speaking gibberish. "That's the same nonsense I got from Cassie. What would possibly make you believe that forged letters could make me happy?"

Eunice shrugged. "I don't know any more," she admitted,

sinking down on the sofa as she tried to reconstruct the logic of Cassie's little scheme. "Cassie was very convincing at the time. Elinor had stopped writing, you see, and you were glooming about the place looking as if you'd lost all chance of salvation. Cassie said you'd sacrificed your future for us, and it wasn't fair that you had no sunshine in your life, or some such nonsense. She was almost poetic about it. I suppose I was carried off on the tide of her emotion."

"Are you saying that you both believed that letters from Elinor would bring *sunshine* into my life?" Robert asked in disbelief.

"Well, *didn't* they?"

He gave a snorting laugh. "All they brought was a sense of guilt. It seemed to me that while Elinor was remaining loyally attached to me, I was disloyally building a life without her."

"*Really*, Robbie?" Eunice smiled broadly and drew a deep, relieved breath. "Then may I conclude that the latest news of Elinor won't pain you?"

"How can I say until I know? What news?"

"Your lost love has gotten herself betrothed to an Italian count."

His eyebrows rose. "Has she, indeed? Is that why she stopped writing?"

"Is that your reaction?" Eunice shook her head in amusement. "And to think we were so afraid of breaking the news to you!"

"Well, you needn't be so deucedly gleeful," Robert said sourly. "The news doesn't have me dancing in the streets. It doesn't puff up a man's pride to learn that he's been superseded in a female's affections."

Eunice laughed. "My dear brother, you are as inconsistent as a child. I needn't remind you, need I, that you can't have your cake, etcetera? Isn't the loss of a bit of masculine pride worth the loss of the guilt?"

He sighed. "I suppose so. But all this talk of Elinor has distracted us from the more important question. Where on earth has Cassie gone?"

"Back to her father's, I assume."

Robert jumped to his feet. "Yes, of course! I should have

thought of that myself. Somehow I always assumed that she'd come here, so that she could play the grand lady and go running about with you and Mama to all the balls and routs and galas.''

"*Cassie*?'' Eunice gave her brother a look of disgust. "She doesn't give a fig for such things. I think, Robbie, that you have much to learn about your wife.''

"So it seems,'' he said thoughtfully as he headed for the door.

"Do you intend to go to King's Cross to find her?''

"Yes. Right now.'' But he paused in the doorway. "Eunice,'' he said, his brow wrinkled in bewilderment, "I still don't understand. Why would my wife wish to make me happy by giving me love letters from, supposedly, another woman? It doesn't make sense.''

Eunice threw him a strange, almost pitying smile. "Doesn't it, my dear? Think about it. Think about it hard. And if I were you, I wouldn't go seeking Cassie until the answer was absolutely clear.''

Chapter Thirty-Five

Robert did not take his sister's advice but rode over at once to King's Cross and hammered with the knob of his cane on the Chivers' doorknocker. Eames, the butler, answered the door and was about to admit him when Miss Penicuick loomed up in the doorway and barred his way. "Her ladyship is not at home," she said firmly.

"Come, come, Miss Penny," Robert cajoled. "You and I both know she is. Eames as much as admitted it."

Miss Penicuick glared at the butler. "Then he exceeded his authority, my lord. Her ladyship told us all, quite distinctly, that if Lord Kittridge called, she was not at home."

"Oh, she did, did she? Then, Miss Penny, will you please go up and tell her ladyship that I have come to apologize? Perhaps that will convince her to admit she's at home."

Miss Penicuick looked dubious. "I'll tell her, my lord, but you know Cassie. She doesn't change her mind easily once it's made up."

"Yes, I've noticed that. But do try."

The attempt was not successful. Miss Penicuick repeated that her mistress was "still not at home," and closed the door before he could say another word.

Robert tried again an hour later. This time Miss Penicuick opened the door only a crack. "Perhaps her ladyship has returned by now," he suggested, smiling charmingly at the eye that peeped out at him.

"No. Still out," Miss Penicuick insisted.

"Tell her I must see her . . . on a matter of immense

importance. Enormous importance. Please, Miss Penny. It's a matter of . . . of life and death.''

"I'll try again," Miss Penicuick said with a sigh, unable to resist him.

Lord Kittridge cooled his heels on the doorstep for fully fifteen minutes. But when the housekeeper returned, the answer was the same. Not at home.

Kittridge went back to Portman Square in a rage. "If she doesn't want to see me," he snarled at his sister whom he passed on the stairs on his way up to his room, "then the devil take her! I'm going back to Lincolnshire tomorrow. I have more important things to do than to hang about on her damn doorstep!"

"I told you not to call on her until you understood her better," Eunice said. "Did you think about the answer to your question?"

"I've given the whole business too much thought as it is!" Robert declared. "*I'm* not the one who pried into matters that don't concern me. *I'm* not the one who forged letters! How have I suddenly become the penitent, standing about with my hat in my hand waiting for absolution?"

Eunice shrugged. "I have no idea," she said callously, proceeding down the stairs. "Go back to Lincolnshire, then. No one here will stop you."

Robert shut his bedroom door and threw himself down on the bed. What was his sister trying to tell him in that annoyingly enigmatic way? That he loved Cassie? He'd discovered that already. That fact had become clearer with each passing day. But that didn't explain why Cassie had forged the letters. That was the enigma the answer to which seemed to be the crux of his confusion. Why had Cassie done it? Why had she peeped into his private letters? Why had she written him love notes from another woman? What had she hoped to gain by it?

Before he'd left Lincolnshire, he'd crammed Cassie's three letters into an inside pocket of his coat. He got up from the bed, pulled them out of their storage place, removed them from their envelopes and laid them, side by side, on his bedside table. He read them over, and then over again, but if they held an answer, he could not see it.

They were, however, an interesting puzzle in themselves. Cassie had composed them by pretending to be Elinor—putting herself in Elinor's place, so to speak. But she'd never even met Elinor and didn't know anything about her. So where had the ideas in the letters come from? They had to have come from Cassie herself, of course. But where had she learned about those feelings she'd expressed? Had she been in love before? Were these memories she'd stored away from an earlier experience? Had she herself once tried to touch her lover from a distance, "through the ether," as she'd put it in her letter? Had she sat on a garden bench and yearned to paint her lover's name across the sky? Had she conjured up his face, that face with the muscle twitching in the jaw? But, wait! That face described in the last letter—wasn't that *his*? All those "quirks" she'd so carefully detailed, weren't they his quirks? And hadn't she described them just as a lover would?

"Good God!" he exclaimed aloud, staring at the letters in front of him with wide eyes. Could *that* be it? His heart began to hammer in his chest as it occurred to him for the first time that Cassie might have been expressing her own feeling toward *him*! Could she really love him, even though she'd kept him at arm's length, even though their marriage had been a business arrangement, even though he'd kept himself distant from her for Elinor's sake?

Not trusting himself to answer, he ran out of his room and down the hall to Eunice's room. "Eunice, may I talk to you?" he asked, banging on her door.

"Of course, you gudgeon," she answered. "Stop that hammering and come in."

She was sitting at her dressing table rubbing a strange, greenish liquid on her face. "It's called Balm of Mecca," she explained, laughing at his shocked expression. "It is made up of all sorts of magical ingredients, like lemon oil, crushed cucumbers and tincture of turpentine. It is guaranteed to make my complexion as youthful as a schoolgirl's if I use it every day for a month. I intend to be a glowing bride a month from now."

"You'll be a glowing bride whether or not you use that

stuff," he said, perching on her bed. "But I didn't come here to talk about complexions. Tell me, Eunice, were you hinting this afternoon that you believe Cassie *cares* for me?"

"Any fool could tell that in a moment," Eunice said in her blunt way.

"Oh, God!" Robert breathed, feeling a glow of joy in his chest.

Eunice beamed at him. "Fool!" she said affectionately.

He eyed her askance. "But I still don't see why, if she really loves me, she would want me to receive letters from *Elinor*."

"For some people, Robbie, love is more a matter of giving than taking. I think that Cassie would hand Elinor over to you on a silver platter if she could . . . and if she thought it would make you happy."

He expelled a long breath. "Damnation, Loesby was right. I *don't* deserve her."

"But she deserves you, so you'd better win her back."

"How am I supposed to do that," he asked, turning glum, "if she won't even see me?"

"Oh, you'll find a way," Eunice said airily. "Now, get out of here and let me get on with making myself ugly so that I can be beautiful. Good night, my dear."

Yes, he told himself before he fell sleep that night, *I'll find a way.* Life had suddenly opened up for him this unexpected new chance for happiness, and he'd be more of a fool than he even thought he was if he failed to grasp it.

The next morning he was on Cassie's doorstep early. "Miss Penny," he said to the housekeeper confidently, "just give her this note. She'll see me then."

He'd spent half the night writing it. Love letters were not in his line, so every word had come hard for him. In the end, he'd had to plagiarize some of hers. *Dearest Cassie*, he'd written, *it has slowly dawned on my sluggish brain that I am one of those lucky husbands who truly loves his wife. I have wanted to tell you so for a long time, but many foolish and quite imaginary impediments seem to have gotten in the way. I am not skilled at expressing my feelings, so I can only say that I've been trying since you left me to conjure up your face, but when I try to touch it, the vision dissolves into nothingness. Do not, I beg you, leave me so bereft.*

He hummed under his breath as he waited for Miss Penicuick to return. His pulse raced at the prospect of their imminent reunion. He would take her in his arms in so passionate an embrace that—

"Sorry, my lord," Miss Penicuick said, handing him back his note unopened. "Her ladyship is still not in."

Robert reddened in anger. "She would not even *read* it?"

"No, my lord. She said that any written communications could reach her through her father."

"Oh, she did, did she?" he muttered furiously, ripping the note in half and then in half again and throwing the pieces on the ground. "You may tell her for me that the note was for her eyes or for no one's!" And he stalked off to his curricle and drove furiously away down the drive.

When he'd put a couple of miles between him and her father's house, he grew calmer. Perhaps it might be a good idea at that, he thought. He would pay her father a visit at his office. Mr. Chivers would be on his side. Perhaps he might be able to help.

But Chivers' greeting was not warm. "I can't 'elp ye, Kittridge," he said flatly. "The girl is too cut up. She doesn't wish to live with ye any more."

"But dash it all, Chivers, we're *married*! And what dreadful thing did I do to her, after all? Fell into a rage because she read some private letters, that's all. Many a man, finding himself in my place, would have done much worse."

Chivers shrugged. "I don't say ye're at fault, Kittridge. In my eyes ye seem a perfectly amiable fellow. But I'll admit to ye that I don't understand these newfangled notions about love and romance and all. Cassie's got it in 'er 'head that marriage doesn't work without love, and per'aps she's right." He looked up at his son-in-law in embarrassment. "She's confessed to me that yer marriage isn't . . . wasn't . . . er . . . consummated."

"Has she?" Kittridge asked carefully, wondering what his father-in-law was getting at.

"So I've an appointment to see a solicitor. To ask about the possibility of annullin' the marriage, ye see."

"Indeed?" Kittridge managed to keep his expression impassive.

"Ye needn't poker up that way," Chivers said. "I won't ask fer the return of the settlement. Ye tried to keep yer part of the bargain, so the money's yours."

"Hang the money!" Kittridge's mind suddenly began to race. A scheme to win his wife back came rushing into his mind. It was shocking in its vulgarity, but it might work. "I'm not concerned about the money," he repeated. "But you're wasting your time with solicitors, Chivers. No one will believe you. Your daughter didn't tell the truth. The marriage *was* consummated."

Chivers blinked up at him in surprise. "What's that ye say?" he jumped angrily to his feet. "I'll 'ave ye know, Kittridge, that my Cassie doesn't lie!"

His lordship smiled coolly and picked up his hat. "I am also known for telling the truth. Your daughter and I lived in the same house for five months. Who do you think is more likely to be believed?"

He sauntered out of the office and down to the street. It was a lovely day. He smiled to himself as he saw Cassie's face in his imagination. He pictured her reddening in indignation as her father recounted the conversation he'd had with her husband. Robert didn't know what action her indignation would lead her to take, but he hoped it would bring her rushing to Rossiter House to confront him. That confrontation was what he hoped for. It would be all he'd need.

He was still smiling to himself as he approached Bond Street. The street was busy with shoppers, but Kittridge took no notice of them. His head was so full of plans that he didn't hear his name called until someone hissed in his ear, "Robbie! Wake up! It's I!"

He turned and found himself face to face with Elinor. She was a vision in a high feathered hat and a green and white striped walking dress. She seemed taller than he remembered, but her red-gold hair and translucent skin were as remarkable as ever. "Elinor!" he gasped. Recovering quickly, he bowed over her hand. "I'd heard that you'd returned from the continent. And that you are receiving best wishes on your betrothal."

She blushed. "Yes, I am. As a matter of fact, Mama has stopped in at the stationer's just behind you to order the cards for the wedding. I escaped from her because I caught a glimpse of you and wished to . . . to speak to you. Who knows when, if ever, we shall get such a chance as this to be private."

He smiled at her gently. "There's not much need to be private, is there? I think that what we have to say to each other has already been said."

Her eyes misted. "Oh, Robbie, I . . . I suppose so. Have you missed me, my dear? I've missed you dreadfully, especially at first. Mama was right, though. One does get over things after a time."

"Yes," he said.

She looked at him tenderly. "Have you gotten over me, Robbie?"

He hesitated, wondering how to answer her. He couldn't help studying her, trying to remember how she'd felt in his arms the night they'd said good-bye. It had seemed to him then that her tall, shapely form was a perfect fit for him and that there would never be another who would feel quite so thrilling in his arms. But that hadn't turned out to be true. He'd found another girl, of a very different size, who was even more thrilling. But Elinor was looking at him now, half coquettishly and half earnestly, waiting for an answer to her question, and he had no wish to give her an unkind one. "I've thought of you more often than you can imagine," he said with perfect truth.

She smiled tremulously, pleased with his answer. "I used to think of you all the time. Until Paolo. He swept me quite off my feet, as they say."

"You're happy, then. I'm glad for you, Elinor."

"Thank you, Robbie. I'm glad, too. Everything has turned out well after all, although for a while I didn't believe that it would. After all, we'd loved each other for so long."

"Yes," he said, wondering how she would feel if he admitted that matters were turning out well for him, too.

"By the way," Elinor continued excitedly, "did Eunice tell you that Paolo and I shall live in Florence in the winters? I think I shall like that. It's so lovely there. But we plan, every year, to be in London for the season. Shall you be glad to see me, if we meet sometime this way?"

"Of course," he said politely, suddenly wishing for this stilted conversation to end. Elinor had become too self-absorbed to be interesting, he realized with surprise. She'd twice queried him about his feelings for her, to make certain she still held a string on his heart, but she'd not asked once about his wife or if he was happy. Now that their feelings for each other had died, they had little else to say to each other. Elinor now seemed a distant acquaintance, someone with whom conversation was a strain. He was glad when her mother emerged from the stationer's, forcing Elinor to whisper a hurried good-bye and bustle off.

By evening he'd already forgotten the encounter. He had other things on his mind. He'd calculated that Chivers would have returned to his home by six and would certainly have told Cassie about his conversation with her odious husband by seven. It was now eight, and Robert was sitting at the dinner table with his mother, Gavin, Eunice and Sandy. He was waiting tensely for Cassie to come bursting in on them, wondering if he'd miscalculated her reactions. She might be too shy, even now, to take the action he hoped she'd take.

But just as the possibility that she would not come was becoming a real fear, the dining room doors were thrown open and Cassie, heedless of the butler who came scurrying up behind her, stalked over to Robert and slapped his face.

One of the footmen dropped the roast. Eunice gasped. The dowager Lady Kittridge screamed. Gavin exclaimed, "I *say*!" And Sandy cried out, "Cassie! What on earth—?"

Robert, grinning broadly while holding his tingling cheek, got to his feet. "Good evening, my dear. What has impelled the shy Lady Kittridge to break in on us and create such a dreadful scene?"

"You know very well, you . . . you blackguard!" she said, coloring to her ears but going on with her prepared accusation anyway. "How dared you tell Papa that you . . . that I . . . that we . . . ?"

"That we *what*?" he taunted.

"That we consummated the marriage!" she finished, her fury making her daring.

"My dear young woman," the older Lady Kittridge reprimanded, "how can you speak of such things now? We are at *dinner*!"

"Your son," the enraged Cassie snapped, wheeling on her mother-in-law, "is a blasted *liar*!"

"Who, *me*?" Gavin asked, bewildered.

"No, you nodcock," Robert corrected. "Me."

"He is not!" Eunice declared loyally. "You know how much I adore you, Cassie, but I won't have you calling Robbie names."

"He's never lied to me," his mother said with finality.

"Good God!" Sandy said, his belief in Cassie's sincerity causing him to eye his friend with suspicion. "You wouldn't lie about a thing like that, would you, Robbie?"

Robert laughed aloud. "Yes, I would. I did. And I will again."

Everyone stared at him. Cassie was completely taken aback. "You admit it?" she asked in disbelief.

"Yes," Robert said, taking her hand and grinning down at her, "I admit it openly. Before all these witnesses. But I will not admit it outside this room, I intend to keep on lying . . . to your father, to his solicitors and to anyone else who tries to nullify our marriage."

"Robert!" Cassie gasped, wrenching her hand from his grasp. "*Why*?"

"*Why*? How can you ask? I love you! I shall declare to my dying day that we are well and truly wed, in the sight of God and all this company. So you may as well give up, my love, and come home."

"I will n-not come home!" Cassie declared, bursting into angry tears. "I will never g-go home with a man who l-lies about such things. You d-don't love me! I don't know why you're saying that you do, but you don't."

"But he *does*," Eunice cried. "He *told* me. Why won't you believe him?"

"How can you say that, Eunice," Cassie asked, dashing

the tears from her cheeks, "when you know as well as anyone that it isn't true?"

"But—" Eunice began.

"Confound it, Cassie," Robert said, grasping her shoulders in desperation as his confidence in his ability to sweep her off her feet rapidly dissipated, "can't you unmake your stubborn mind for once and *listen* to me? I love you!"

"You needn't pretend any more," Cassie said, pushing him away. "Papa will not renege on his business agreement with you, so you don't need me. Your money is safe."

Robert's face whitened. "This has nothing to *do* with the blasted money!"

"Hasn't it?" Cassie turned and faced him, erect and defiant in spite of her trembling lips and tear-streaked cheeks. "I heard you speak the t-truth to me that last night in Lincolnshire. You said I d-disgust you."

"Cassie!" He stared at her in agony. "I never meant it. I was crazy with anger and confusion. You can't believe that I—!"

She held up her hand. "No more, please, Robert! I can't b-bear it. Let us go our separate ways. It will be better so." And she went quickly out the door.

"*Cassie!*" Eunice ran forward as if to catch her. "Wait!"

"Let her go," Robert said in despair, sinking down on his chair and dropping his head in his hands. "It's no use. I married her for her money. As long as that damnable forty thousand pounds stands between us, she'll never believe me. Never."

Chapter Thirty-Six

Robert disappeared from the house in Portman Square for several days, and when he returned he had a long conference with Sandy. Then, the next morning, he called his family together in the sitting room. "I have some things of importance to announce," he said quietly. "They may not be pleasing to you, but there will be no argument. All the decisions I've made have already been implemented, and they are final. I've decided, you see, that I cannot keep the forty thousand pounds that Mr. Chivers gave me. So I've made some difficult financial decisions that will enable me to return the money to him. First, I've sold the Suffolk properties. Since I'd already paid off the debts on them, I realized a goodly sum. Second, I sold this house to Sandy. Hush, Mama, there is no need for you to fall into hysterics. He and Eunice will be happy to have you remain in residence here with them for as long as you wish, provided, of course, that you don't let your penchant for reckless expenditure get out of hand. Sandy is generous, but he's not a mogul. If you become extravagant, I've instructed him to ship you out to me in Lincolnshire where, you can be sure, the opportunities for extravagance are extremely limited. You, Gavin, since you obviously have no love for school, will come to live in Lincolnshire with me. There is no point in protesting, for my mind is made up. We cannot expect Sandy to take charge of you when he has Eunice's two girls to raise, to say nothing of whatever offspring he and Eunice may have in the future. Besides, I intend to set you to work learning farming and estate management. With your instinct for horseflesh and love of animals, I think country life may suit you better than you think. For the rest, I've been given a generous loan by the Duke of Bedford, who is interested in my plans for my herds. This will enable me to keep Highlands, at least as long as I can make it a paying enterprise. Since that won't be easy, and I will be hard pressed for years to pay him back, I am counting on your help, your encouragement, and your good wishes.''

At the same time that Robert was making this announcement to his family, Chivers was making an unaccustomed trip home from his office in midmorning to bring some bewildering news to his daughter. "I don't know what to make of it," he said to Cassie, perching on the sitting room sofa and drawing her down beside him, "but Kittridge came to see me early today and returned all the money."

Cassie paled. "*Returned* it? How could he?"

"I'm not certain of all the details. For one thing, 'e sold the town 'ouse to Sir Philip Sanford, 'is brother-in-law-to-be. And, for another, 'e sold the Suffolk properties."

"But *why*?" Cassie jumped up in agitation and began to pace about, the flounce of her morning gown swishing about her ankles. "The Suffolk lands would not have brought enough to pay you and the debts on Highlands as well."

Chivers gaped at his daughter in astonishment. He hadn't been able to interest her in financial matters in twenty years of trying, but Kittridge had done it in five months. "How do you know that?" he demanded.

"Robert explained it to me. Don't tell me he sold Highlands, too! It would break his heart!"

"No. It seems 'e procured a loan from some other source. A duke, I think."

"It must be Bedford," Cassie surmised, sighing in relief. "The Duke of Bedford likes Robert's ideas about raising sheep. But why is Robert doing all this, Papa? He can't be thinking that the return of the money will free him to marry again. Doesn't he know that the solicitors told you that nullifying our marriage would be impossible?"

Chivers shrugged. "I don't know what 'e knows. I don't

know what 'is motive is. All I know is that the fellow appeared at my door and plunked down a bank note for the entire amount. *'Tell Cassie,'* was all 'e said.''

"Tell C-Cassie?" She stared at her father openmouthed. "He said *that*?"

"That's what I'm tellin' ye. What do ye think 'e meant by it?"

"I don't know," she said, but her eyes widened and her cheeks turned bright red.

"If ye don't know," her father snapped, "then why're ye blushin'?"

"I don't know," she insisted, suddenly turning and crossing quickly to the door. "All I know is that you shouldn't have taken the bank note. You made an agreement, and the money is rightfully his."

"Is it my fault the cod's 'ead wouldn't take it back?" he asked in irritation, following her out of the room just in time to see her flounce disappearing round the turning of the stair. "What was I to do? Tear the damned note up?" he shouted up the stairs. "And where are ye runnin' off to?"

"Nowhere, Papa." Her voice floated down to him from the upper floor, sounding cheerier than it had since she'd come home. "I just thought I'd better change my dress."

Less than an hour later, Lord Kittridge appeared on the Chivers' doorstep. Eames, as soon as he saw who it was, signalled for Miss Penicuick to come to his aid. She stepped up to the doorway. "Here again, are you, my lord?" she asked, blocking the door.

"Yes, here I am," his lordship said to the housekeeper pleasantly. "May I ask if Mr. Chivers has come home from the city this morning?"

Miss Penicuick looked surprised by the question. "Yes, he has, but he's gone back to his office."

"Good. Now, Miss Penny, one more question. Are your instructions to inform me that her ladyship is not at home still in effect?"

"Yes, my lord. Still in effect."

"Then I'm sorry to have to take liberties, ma'am," Kittridge said, "but it's a matter of necessity." He placed his two hands on her waist and lifted her bodily out of his way.

"Now see here, my lord," Eames said, stepping into the breach, "you can't shoulder your way in like—"

"Yes, I can," Kittridge said, fixing a threatening eye on the butler. "I'm very handy with my fives. Would you like a taste of them?"

"No, my lord," the butler mumbled, stepping away hastily and holding Miss Penicuick back, too.

Kittridge crossed the hallway in three strides. "Where is she?" he asked over his shoulder.

"In her room," Miss Penicuick said in tearful surrender.

"And her room is—?"

"Upstairs," the butler admitted, giving Miss Penicuick a helpless shrug. "Second door on the left."

Kittridge mounted the stairs two at a time. When he found the door, he didn't bother to knock. He merely burst in, startling his bride into emitting a small scream. "Robert!" she gasped, turning red.

She was sitting at a small writing table near the window, looking utterly delicious in a light blue gown with a deep lace ruffle at the neck. Her unruly hair was tied back with a blue ribbon, and the sun behind her head lit her curls with such delightful glimmers of gold that he almost didn't notice her attempt to cover something on her table with her hand. "Well, my dear, I'm here," he said, crossing the room to her. "If your father gave you my message, I imagine you were expecting me."

"I was not expecting you at all," she lied.

"Really? And I thought that pretty blue ribbon was for my benefit. What a disappointment. But tell me, my love, what is that paper you're trying so hard to hide from me."

"Nothing," she said, shifting nervously in her chair. "It's nothing."

He made an abrupt dive for it and snatched it from her hand. When he saw what it was, his face lit with a broad grin. "My love letter!" he exclaimed. "However did you find it?"

"Miss Penny picked up the pieces," she admitted, "and I . . . pasted them together."

He pulled her to her feet and into his arms. "But I thought you didn't believe my declarations of love."

She hid her face in his chest. "I wanted to b-believe them," she said in a small voice. "And I believe them now."

"Of course you do," he laughed, lifting her chin. "Any girl would believe a man's declaration if he backed his word with forty thousand pounds."

"It was a grand, but much too expensive gesture, Robert," she said softly. "Let Papa tear up the note."

"Not on your life. We shall do very well without it. Without that blasted dowry, we can embark on a proper marriage, based on those 'newfangled ideas of love and romance' that your father says you so adamantly believe in. The truth is that I believe in them, too."

"But . . . do you truly love me, Robert? In spite of having to give up Elinor because of me?"

"Elinor?" he asked. "I don't remember any Elinor. I haven't really remembered her since the night you and I went hunting for the Rossiter ghost. And if you doubt me, I have some irrefutable proof to offer." And he lifted her high on his chest and kissed her so soundly that she grew dizzy in his arms.

She wound her arms tightly round his neck and surrendered to the long-postponed joy of indulging in a completely unreserved embrace. No longer did she have to hold back. The result was so breathtaking for them both that they had to pause and recover themselves before indulging in a second, and then a third. By the time he let her go, all they could do was gaze at each other besotted with joy. "When did you first know you loved me?" he asked, smoothing back the wild curls from her forehead tenderly. "Was it when I stood up for you against Eunice?"

"Oh, no," she confessed shyly. "It was long, long before. Before you even knew my name."

He held her off and stared down at her with eyes narrowed. "How can that be?" he asked dubiously.

She wrapped her arms about his chest and hid her face in his shoulder. "It was when you stood up for me at the linendraper's, remember?" she whispered. "I've loved you ever since."

He expelled a long breath. So *that* was why she'd married him! It had nothing to do with being a.viscountess or making her way in society. He tightened his hold on her and pressed his lips to her hair. "I *don't* deserve you," he murmured. "But I promise you, my love, that I will never again make you sorry you married me."

It was a long while before Robert remembered the main purpose of this invasion of her room. "Get your wrap, my love, and let's be off. We're going back to Highlands right now."

"Oh, but I can't!" she exclaimed. "Not so soon. I must prepare Papa, and make arrangements, and pack my things, and order some furnishings for the drawing room, and have a fitting for my gown for Eunice's wedding, and—"

"That's just what I expected," he said in disgust. "Do you realize, Lady Kittridge, that we've been married five months and have not yet had a honeymoon? Any sane person would agree that five months is the outside of enough. That's why I took an oath that I would not go back to Lincolnshire without you. So will you or nill you, you are coming home with me *now*!" And without giving her a moment to object, he lifted her off her feet and threw her over his shoulder.

She gasped for breath as he clambered down the stairs. "Robert, have you gone mad?" she cried. "Put me down!"

"I will, my love," he promised, "as soon as you're safely locked inside the carriage."

But Miss Penicuick, who'd been standing at the bottom of the stairs wringing her hands ever since his lordship had burst in, began to scream. "What are you *doing*?" she cried. "Someone, *help*! My Cassie is being *abducted*!"

"Out of my way!" Kittridge ordered, brushing by the hysterical housekeeper.

"Cassie, my dearest!" Miss Penicuick shrieked. "What shall I *do*?"

Cassie gave her a cheery wave as Kittridge carried her out

the door. "Nothing, Miss Penny. Everything's fine, really. Lovely, in fact."

Miss Penicuick, breast heaving in dismay, followed them to the door. "But where are you *going*? And *what* shall I say to your *father*?"

Kittridge, having arrived at the carriage door, set Cassie on her feet. "Tell him that we've gone to consummate our bargain," he said, grinning down at his bride.

"Oh, Robert, hush!" the blushing Cassie ordered, putting a hand over his mouth. She looked up at Miss Penicuick and waved again. "Good-bye, Miss Penny. Just tell Papa that I've gone back to Lincolnshire. That message will be quite enough."